Priscilla Hughes

Man with a Squirrel

ALSO BY NICHOLAS KILMER

Harmony in Flesh and Black

Man
with a
Squirrel

Nicholas Kilmer

Henry Holt and Company
New York

Henry Holt and Company, Inc.
Publishers since 1866
115 West 18th Street
New York, New York 10011

Henry Holt® is a registered trademark
of Henry Holt and Company, Inc.

Published in Canada by Fitzhenry & Whiteside Ltd.,
195 Allstate Parkway, Markham, Ontario L3R 4T8.

Library of Congress Cataloging-in-Publication Data
Kilmer, Nicholas.
Man with a squirrel / Nicholas Kilmer.—1st ed.
        p.   cm.
            I. Title.
PS3561.I39M36   1996   96-10181
813'.54—dc20   CIP

ISBN 0-8050-3666-0

Henry Holt books are available for special
promotions and premiums. For details contact:
Director, Special Markets.

First Edition—1996

Designed by Michelle McMillian

Printed in the United States of America

All first editions are printed on acid-free paper. ∞

1   3   5   7   9   10   8   6   4   2

FOR JULIA,
whom I dearly love

Man
with a
Squirrel

1

"There's a man coming into my library who scares me," Molly said.

They were watching wasps gutting a pear one of the kids had dropped in the dust under Molly's big maple in the backyard, during a hot evening with the shadows lying horizontal and cicadas somewhere in the wilderness of Arlington, Massachusetts, grinding their warning: there won't be much more of this, folks.

Fred shifted carefully in his aluminum folding chair. He'd broken one already this fall. ("They're too flimsy," Fred said. "You're too large," Molly said.)

"Scares you how?" Fred asked her. He was paying attention to the wasps. If they were ants, you'd say it was industry; but the wasps were having fun doing what they were doing. They treated the pear as if it were an elephant they had killed.

"It's the books he wants to read," Molly said. "And even without that, he's the kind of person that if he's in the elevator when the doors open, you take the stairs; if you're in it when he gets on, you suddenly want to get off."

Molly was drinking cheap red wine, and the wasps were interested in that too, so she had to keep an eye on her glass and shoo them away. She was pink and pretty, with short brown curls that caught the glancing evening light. Molly Riley did not look like the mother of two children: a twelve-year-old boy, Sam, and his younger sister, Terry. Molly was still wearing her work clothes, a blue linen dress today.

"He really scares you," Fred said.

Molly stood up, threw her face into a goonish, vacant stare, and gulped, almost slavered, while she moved her feet up and down in place, as if uncomfortable on the earth.

"God, Molly," Fred said.

"It's what he does," Molly said.

"What does this guy want in the Cambridge Public Library?"

"He only reads there," Molly said. "I can't find out who he is. If he took books out, I'd have his library card and he'd be on the computer, his name and address and the rest of it."

Molly worked at the reference desk. She knew everything, usually; or she could find out.

"Ask him his name," Fred said. "Unless—is he one of the homeless that gather around there? A lot of them are vets. Maybe I . . ."

Molly sat down again, shooed wasps out of her wineglass, and took a sip. They had finished supper late, and Molly had sent the kids to start their homework at the kitchen table.

"He scares me, and I'd rather not talk to him," Molly said. "Though I have to answer questions. I don't want him to think I'm eager to converse, you know?"

"What does he ask about?"

"Serial killers," Molly said. "Mass murderers, ax murderers, poisoners, Bluebeards, and such."

Fred put his cup on the sparse gravel next to his chair, catching the flavor of her alarm.

2

"He wants to talk about these things with you?"

"He wants me to find him material," Molly said. She batted a wasp and sipped at her wine. "It's all he reads about, and it feels like an obsession; it seems—he seems—unbalanced."

Her heavy brows were drawn together.

"It's like having a pornographer around, except the prurience fixes on death, not sex."

"I'll follow him," Fred said. "I'll talk to him or see where he goes. At least I can find out who he is."

Molly stood, poured the remains of her wine onto the grass next to the bristling pear, and turned toward the stairs to the kitchen.

"I'm making conversation, Fred. Don't feel you have to move into the active mode just because the little woman voices a concern. Drink your coffee, why don't you?"

It had been like that for a couple of weeks, ever since construction started on the new bathroom upstairs, off Molly's bedroom. Fred would say something and Molly would go after him.

As Fred put it to himself, a family is an act of nature that consists of a female and her young. The adult male is an odd thing looming into it. This was especially true in Molly's house, because in this case the children were not Fred's.

It was as if this new bathroom he was giving her—gorgeous and generous, and which he had meant to be a testament and promise to her, an extension of the turf carved out by their mutual intimacy—as if that were an assault.

He'd had a windfall, and had dropped it immediately into Molly's house—with her eager cooperation. Now the mess and havoc of this promise, which for the time being condemned Molly's bedroom and forced them to camp downstairs on her foldout sofa, was making Fred feel like the Mongol hordes arriving in Isfahan.

"You can't own anything, can you?" Molly had spluttered at him one night while the two of them were not sleeping on her sofa.

3

That was true. Fred's bargain with the world included an unspoken vow of poverty. It was the only way he knew to keep wanting to live.

"I work for a man who wants things," Fred said. "Let Clayton Reed collect art, as if art is in the things we find and buy. I want their life; their beauty and their history and their wild spirit. I won't keep a fucking zoo." He sat up, trembling. He did not own pajamas. Here, in Molly's living room, where the kids might stumble through, he slept in his shorts and T-shirt. "What am I supposed to buy? A butterfly? And nail it to the wall?"

Molly, almost asleep in one of his white shirts, mumbled, "I'm glad to have the bathroom. You know that. Thank you. But maybe you need a new car, Fred. For yourself. One that isn't brown?"

She slipped into sleep in the blue dusk of her frilly living room, leaving Fred wide awake, confused, and mortified—a talent she had.

He looked now around her garden, with the darkness of late summer closing over it, and unnecessary clatter coming from the kitchen, and picked up his cup. The coffee left in it held no interest for the wasps.

Fred dropped the subject Molly had raised and then warned him off: the man who scared her. He and Clayton Reed were concentrating on a project that would take Fred to Paris. Clay was looking at a couple of fifteenth-century miniatures coming up for auction there, and Fred had to work to understand the paintings' history and their proper value. This let him root contentedly in libraries and museums, persuading live information from inanimate objects.

Then, in October, Fred was out of the country on the business of the miniatures. When he returned, the bathroom was finished, in purple tile of Molly's choosing, and they moved back into her bedroom, now a "master bedroom," Molly said.

The first snow fell—unusually early—late in November, and Fred went out the morning after to stretch his legs. He stopped dead at the foot of the short walk from Molly's house to the sidewalk, where two footprints splayed out side by side into large obsessive man-tracks that faced the front door. It was six-thirty. There was not much light; barely enough to see the tracks. They were blurred, as if they had been made over some time.

The tracks brought back immediately to Fred's mind Molly doing that shuffle of discomfort, acting the part of the man who made her nervous. Fred went inside and woke Molly.

Molly sat up when he touched her shoulder. He'd gotten covered with cold air and she was warm in bed. "You remember the man you told me about?" Fred asked. "The one you said comes into your library, and scared you? What happened to him?"

"I haven't seen him again," Molly said. She wasn't wearing clothes and she was slightly creased from the sheets. She shivered, got up, and put a red terry-cloth robe on. "He stopped coming. Just stopped. I never did find out who he was. Did you make coffee?"

"I put it on before I left the house." Fred's instincts were rippling with alarm. Those tracks proved this house, like any other, a trap.

"What's the matter?" Molly asked, catching Fred's concern.

"Nothing, maybe," Fred said. "Footprints outside in the snow reminded me of what you said that evening in the yard, with the wasps."

They went downstairs and sat in the kitchen. Molly hadn't seen the old man since September, before Fred had gone to Europe. Fred made her describe him. He was sixty-five or seventy, she said. Maybe older. He was thin. He bent when he stood. No, he looked vigorous; the only thing about him that was sick was the way he acted. He looked frayed, but he wasn't a derelict. It was more as if he had no one to care about him, to tell him he'd left a big patch of shaving soap on his face.

"Snow!" Terry yelled, coming into the kitchen in her Red Sox pajamas, top and bottoms worn backward, with her thin brown hair in a tangle. "No school, right?"

"Wrong, Monster," Molly told her. "Dream on."

"It could snow more," she protested, looking out the window

5

at a sky rapidly clearing to a blue that would melt the snow within the hour.

Molly sent her to get dressed, and to bounce on her older brother Sam until he acknowledged the new day.

"Don't get me worried," Molly said. "OK?"

"The tracks looked as if a man was there for a while, watching the house," Fred said. "During the night or very early morning." He didn't add, And this is the first time I could know about it, on account of the snow.

They got the kids off to their buses, and Molly left for the library. Her shift had gone to a regular nine-to-five, weekdays, which was better for everyone. Molly was touched by Fred's concern, but not interested. She'd had a look at the marks in the snow, but really, Fred, there are plenty of marks in the snow.

Fred called Clayton Reed's place, on Mountjoy Street on Beacon Hill, and told him, "Don't expect me." They didn't have anything special stirring right now, and what there was could wait. The two of them, in fact, were getting on each other's nerves, because they hadn't a current project to work on, and idle hands, as Molly's mother frequently remarked, are the devil's toothpick.

Fred waited until midmorning, then drove into Cambridge and parked on Broadway, in a spot from which he could see the library's front entrance. He walked past the desk into the bright and almost vacant reading room and found Molly at her post at the reference desk.

"Is he here today?"

"Who? Oh, him. I told you, not for months," Molly said, touched and irritated with him. "And, Fred, don't circle the wagons around me, all right? I can't see the landscape. Or the enemy."

Fred went outside and sat in the car, waiting, watching the entrance. The snow ran away into the gutters. The sun shone.

In the evening, and until they went to bed, Fred looked out the front windows from time to time. After that it was harder, because Molly's bedroom was in the back of the house, overlooking the backyard, with its now-dormant wasps and lilacs hunkered down waiting for spring. The kids had their bedrooms in the front and he would disturb Terry or Sam by going in after they were supposed to be asleep.

Fred made himself wake up at three-thirty, roamed through the dark house, and looked out the windows of the living room. The street was dark and empty. He went out to the sidewalk and looked up and down the quiet, mildly prosperous street of single-family houses with small yards showing black grass and shaped bushes.

2

Fred didn't tell Molly, but he began looking out the front windows every morning at around three; and in a week or so it paid off: he saw the man watching from across the street, bent over, moving from one foot to the other, stepping down toe-first, as if both the earth and loss of contact with it gave equal torment. It was as if his feet had been skinned, or the earth burned, or both. The man wore a long dark coat, and a cloth cap with a brim. He was a dark shape under the pine tree that decorated the front of the house across the way, and he would have been hard to see in the shadow there except that he wouldn't keep still.

Fred had slipped on a pair of khakis when he got up, and he ran barefoot out the kitchen door, through the yard and the side gate.

The man made no attempt to run, or even to dodge, when he saw Fred coming. Fred, filled with anxiety for Molly, and with the wrath that accompanies sudden action, had to stop short before he ran the old man down. He stood there moving his feet in place.

Fred took hold of the sleeve of his coat. It was a herringbone, threadbare, through which he could perceive the thinness of the old man's arm.

"What do you want?" Fred asked.

The old man looked at him with a vacant, watery stare. He gulped as if there were speech somewhere in his past, which he hoped to find again. "Taxi waiting," he said.

Fred looked up and down the quiet suburban street, seeing nothing of the kind. "You were here last week. Why?"

"I don't sleep," the old man said. "Are you arresting me?"

Fred still held the man's arm. He let go of it, embarrassed. When the man turned and started walking toward the corner Fred stayed beside him. The sidewalk was cold on his feet.

"You are not Jeff," the old man said.

"My name is Fred," Fred said

"I thought my daughter lived in that house," the man said. His voice was thin and discouraged. It had very little of the tremble or modulation of a living voice. It was a voice on its last legs.

They turned the corner. A Cambridge taxi idled under a naked maple tree, its meter on, its radio quietly feeding an all-night talk show to the dozing driver. The inside of the glass was fogged with his breath.

"The woman who lives here, her father passed away years ago," Fred said. The old man was deluded. He had seen Molly in the library, saw a resemblance to his daughter, got her address from the library—they shouldn't give it to anyone—and, driven by a senile hope, came out to find her.

"You are the person who reads so much about murders," Fred said. "Yes?"

The old man's face was narrow, rather horselike, with large bones in the nose and chin, and a notable upper lip. He had, coming from under the cap, weak strands of long gray hair. He ventured, "She talks about me?"

"She is not your daughter," Fred said gently. "She mentioned you had been in the library. What's your name?"

"Martin."

"And you live?"

"For now," the old man said. Then he hesitated and fumbled, realizing that Fred was wondering not if, but where, he lived.

"In Cambridge. Cambridge," the man said. "Cambridge is where I am living."

The taxi driver, wakened by the mumble of conversation, had rolled the window down and was listening. He was a man in his mid-forties, with a cherubic face, wearing a brown leather jacket and a Miami Heat cap. He nodded his large, square head and gave Fred an intelligent look, summing up the situation. "He's going back to Harvard Square," the driver said, the heavy lilt of his speech showing him to be not long out of Haiti. "He say wait, I take him back to Harvard Square there. You ready, Mister?"

"You made a mistake," Fred told the old man, putting him into the backseat. "She's not your daughter. Don't come back now, Mr. Martin."

"She's someone else."

"Right," Fred agreed.

Warm air rushed out of the backseat of the taxi. The sidewalk under Fred's feet was about forty degrees. "You'll be all right?" Fred asked the driver, who nodded once, accepting Fred's money. "Make sure he gets back into his house." Fred watched the taxi drive off. Depending on how long the taxi had been waiting, the old man had invested about fifty dollars on the fare from Cambridge.

Molly was in the kitchen, looking worried, standing by the table, her hands clasped. "What's going on, Fred?"

Both suspicion and accusation were in her voice, mixed with a mother's proprietary fear.

"It was your mass murderer," Fred said. "Out in the street, looking at the house. The one from the library. His name is Martin and he lives in Cambridge. He seems inoffensive."

"He came to my house?" Molly exclaimed. "To my house? What does he want? What is he?"

"Something deluded him into thinking you are his daughter. I told the cabbie to see he got back home, and gave him twenty bucks."

Molly said, "The poor old guy is senile. No mass murderer, then. It gives me the willies he was on my street."

It was almost four o'clock. They sat in the kitchen, debating whether to condemn sleep and make coffee. Fred said, "The normal mass murderer is pretty well groomed; has nice clothes and a new haircut and lovely manners. Mr. Martin presents himself more like the underneath of a yard-sale sofa. I don't think you have to be afraid of him."

"You were the one upset," Molly said. "You should have brought him inside, so we could call his family."

Fred, having already classified the guy as a potential menace, and knowing Molly was afraid of him, wasn't going to bring the old boy into Molly's house.

Molly said, "Poor fellow. I'll see tomorrow if I can locate anyone in his family: the daughter he's lost, or a wife, son—something." Fred had looked in the Cambridge phone book and found too many listings under Martin. "I'll check our cardholders to see if we have somebody in his family. Common name, though."

Fred shouldn't have let him go. He didn't like to leave such things unexplained. "Rats," Fred said, and they went back to bed.

Next day Molly spent some time on the telephone, but failed to find a Martin that fit their visitor. Molly had a wide acquaintance in Cambridge, which stretched even into the police force. No one could place him.

"Could be his first name," Molly said. "That would broaden the field."

3

"Look at this," Fred said to Molly, pointing at the front page of the *Globe*.

"I've seen them before," Molly said. "I believe you'll find those are lighter than air." Molly was barely sitting at the kitchen table, where Fred was drinking coffee. She dunked a piece of dry toast in her coffee, and looked at it with displeasure. Her idea of a healthy breakfast conflicted with anyone's idea of a good breakfast.

"I don't mean the picture," Fred said. The *Globe* had gotten Blanche Maybelle Stardust to re-create her acrobatic start of alarm, on the bank of the Charles River, beneath the cherry trees still looking like winter, showing how she had responded to the realization that her dogs had struck a corpse, which was described as dead and white and male.

Blanche Maybelle Stardust's start of alarm had a flavor of well-rehearsed rah-rah to it. But it showed energy and goodwill, and the eagerness to please that encourages photographers.

On this rainy March morning, her dogs had ruined the run for Blanche Maybelle Stardust, who was seeking to maintain a figure that left little to be imagined in the way of unrealized perfection. It ruined the morning's run, but it got her in the paper, wearing a jogging outfit that also left little to the imagination.

According to the article, her matched set of golden retrievers had discovered the corpse, naked and wearing a cinder-block necklace, on the bank of the Charles River, on the Cambridge side, where he'd been washed up by the passage of the spring's first pleasure boats. The body's former occupant had not yet been identified. But the *Globe* appeared more than satisfied to discover Blanche Maybelle Stardust, who was as alive as she was photogenic. The John Doe, in the water for several months, was presumed to be a derelict.

Blanche Maybelle Stardust, it was revealed, had come from Arkansas a couple of years ago, semiattached to a test pilot stationed at the Hanscom Air Force Base. Her real name was not Stardust, she told everyone. She had recently become detached from the pilot in the interest of furthering a career in entertainment, the same reason her morning run regularly took her in front of WBZ-TV's offices.

"My idea," she told the reporter, "is that the weather could use a Vanna White. Which could be me."

"Even stark naked and chewed by bottom feeders," Fred said, "the old boy can't compete with youth and beauty. But that isn't what I was pointing out, Molly."

"If it isn't Blanche Maybelle's matched dogs or breasts, what are you showing me?"

"This doctor. Eunice Cover-Hoover is in the news. Isn't she the woman who's been leaving messages on the machine?"

Molly jerked the paper out of Fred's hands to see the paragraph pointing toward an article inside: "Cover-Hoover To Give Talk Outside Boston." Molly dropped her toast onto the white Formica and slipped the Metro section out of the paper.

"I've heard the name, but wasn't paying attention. What's this woman's game?" Fred asked.

Molly looked up. "Division and destruction," she said, "in the name of healing. Ophelia wants me to talk with her, get the inside dope on what she's like: the person behind the science. According to what I've picked up, Cover-Hoover's coming out of feminism, and wants to change the patriarchal foundation of our thinking about the human mind and social institutions."

"That's fair."

"Except what was theory once has turned into a goddamn crusade," Molly said. "Therefore it can't be either fair or right, much less reasonable or intelligent. Also, in the new book she adds religion to the mix. She's a practicing shrink, going for tenure at Holmes College, and has two books out, both based on the simple, catchy theme that civilization is designed to prey upon women and/or children, but mostly women, and her proof is, 'Just look at civilization!' "

Fred said, "*Power of Darkness*. That's her new book, yes? I saw the *Times* review a couple weeks back, but failed to take it seriously enough to read."

"*Power of Darkness*, but don't forget the subtitle: *The Myth of Satan in Twentieth-Century America*. She looks academic and scientific and balanced," Molly said. "The first book, *Culture of Abuse*, gathered five years' worth of serious discussion from professional journals. In every one of them you find the line—I don't care whether the article is pro or con—'No one denies that this abuse is widespread and common.' "

Molly dropped the paper on the table and stood up, about to charge into her routine of waking and dressing the kids. She and Fred had risen early in order to have time together. "The new book says that the revived myth of Satan is a flagrant gesture by the culture of the male, designed to offset feminism's gains by asserting male dominance of the female psyche."

"*Is* there a revival of interest in Satan?" Fred asked.

"Better to call it the power of darkness," Molly said. "It's more acceptable in PC terms, and leaves room for the discussion of the age-old struggle between the powers of darkness and of light. Cover-Hoover's interested in power. She's ambitious enough to

14

be looking for popular support now that she's got establishment backing. If she's willing to move toward the talk-show circuit, the theme of satanic cults would come in handy. Cover-Hoover is building a movement to go with her reputation. That's where Ophelia comes in, because Ophelia knows the medium, and Cover-Hoover is thinking in terms of a TV presence. Ophelia's stuck out west for the time being, but she's talked to the Doctor on the phone. 'Just see what she's like,' Ophelia says, 'before we start talking ways and means.' I'm leery of the whole business, so I've been dodging the Doctor's calls. Whenever my sister asks my opinion she has some hidden agenda."

Molly went upstairs to get the day moving.

Fred left his car at the Alewife subway station and took the Red Line toward Boston. He got off at Kendall, across the river. There was a sting in the air as he came up from underground, surrounded by the new wilderness of tall office buildings. He stepped out onto the ratty old bridge called the Pepper Pot. The slouched low skyline of the "real," old Boston on its hill, complete with gilded State House dome, stood out in silhouette against the new Boston.

The river was broad and dirty above the dam. The body had been discovered several miles farther upstream, not far from Harvard University, probably not that far from where it had taken its last dive. It would be a nasty body of water for the dead white male to lie down in. The Charles is a small river. Fred, if asked, would have advised a person wishing to dispose of a corpse to choose another place.

Fred watched the river, where a few intrepid sailors strove to keep their little boats erect. Red Line trains clattered behind him. He wasn't in the mood for Clayton's nervous puttering, which became more trying the less there was to do. This was a good morning, therefore, to check Charles Street. For about four blocks, Charles Street, running parallel to the river on the Boston side, supported a sequence of antique shops where paintings occasionally arrived. Works of obvious quality tended to surface

15

first on Newbury Street, at which point Clayton Reed normally lost interest in them; but occasionally something of not-obvious quality turned up on Charles Street, mixed in with the Bavarian glass, armchairs made of horn, and stereopticon photographs of dead families.

Fred's job with Clayton Reed had never been defined. It was quite well paid and subject to endless redefinition, according to what was happening. Basically, Clay was as much a collector as Fred was a noncollector, and Clay didn't pick things up; so Fred did a good deal of lifting and kept his eyes open for paintings that might appeal to Clayton.

It was standard practice that if Fred saw something he thought interesting and that might otherwise escape, he should grab it for Clayton's account, as long as it wasn't too expensive. If Clay didn't think much of it, they'd ditch it later.

Clay had disposed of a few things Fred still regretted; but Clay had never once faulted Fred's choice. Clay's tastes in painting were so broad, and his personal foibles so particular, that Fred had a twenty percent chance of choosing something that actually stayed in the collection when he did haul in a painting on his own.

In general, especially when a large expenditure was involved, they had plenty of time to confer before a commitment was made. Clayton loved the period of deliberation, because it allowed him to perfect his foibles.

Once over the Pepper Pot, Fred crisscrossed the street, finding nothing to hold him until he came to Oona's. Oona was sitting in the back of the shop behind her big table, which was cluttered as always with breakable objects.

"Come on back, and watch your feet, Fred Taylor," Oona called. She was busy gluing price tags to a row of unmatched cut-glass liqueur goblets.

Oona was in her mid-sixties, a comfortably fat woman who boasted that she had kept a shop on Charles Street since shortly after Noah's Flood. She knew everything there was to know about any human artifact made between A.D. 1700 and 1940. After 1940 she lost interest and proclaimed, It's all junk. She was as honest as

16

she was ruthless. Fred had never found anything he wanted to buy for Clayton from her shop. If he bought jewelry for Molly, though—which must not be expensive or Molly would refuse it— he would get it from Oona.

Oona today was wearing a dark green dress that looked like a surplus tent, with many silver pins attached to it. Her hands fluttered around the crystal, seeming to hypnotize it so that it moved from place to place without her actually touching it.

"Something I want you to see, Mr. Fred Taylor," Oona said, groaning as she rose to her full five feet, and started for the back room. It wouldn't be unusual for her to have the best things out of sight, reserved for preferred customers or being kept from the light of common day.

Fred followed Oona between cases where china and glass swayed; against these were stacked portfolios of prints and drawings that he could go through later.

"A painting just came in," Oona said, opening the door to the room in back, which looked like a small version of the one they had just left, packed with furniture, glass, china, books, and portfolios. A square canvas leaned against the legs of a small desk, representing a man's feet, in shoes with buckles, shrouded in greasy dirt. The man was wearing stockings, and all around the feet was a smooth darkness. The thing was nailed clumsily into a frame, and Fred winced, seeing how the heads of the nails had scratched the canvas. Slowly he realized that this was the back of something, the back of a framed picture. Oona turned it around.

"The frame is Woolworth's," Fred said. "Or the next class down."

Oona puffed slightly, holding the painting. "You take it, Fred Taylor," Oona said. "What do you think?"

The thing was almost two feet square and, behind the dirt, quite interesting. The bell on the shop door clanged and Oona stood in the back room's doorway, to keep her eye on the newly entered client.

The picture that the frame displayed represented a squirrel, half life-size; a common gray squirrel sitting in a patch of sunlight

17

on a floor, with a little collar from which a chain—gold, and done with great care (if one could read correctly behind the dirt)—extended upward through the gloom to the top of the canvas. The chain seemed to come out of the frame, one of those Mexican things, real wood carved to look poured, like plastic. Beside the squirrel, on the floor, was an acorn. The floor was laid out in a pattern—either marble or wood painted to resemble marble. Most of the floor was in shadow, like the background of the feet on the other side.

"Tell me your story," Fred said.

4

"I'm crazy," Oona said. "I bought it from some people this morning. I just like it, crazy as I am. I know nothing of paintings."

"It's interesting," Fred said.

"I know, but what is it?"

"A squirrel," Fred said. Oona was asking, What is the painting? but Fred wouldn't bite. If she was selling and he was buying, why should he tell her what she had?

"Why don't I take it out of the frame?" Fred suggested.

"Be my guest. Tools in the top drawer." Oona went into the shop to wait on a customer, closing Fred into the back room. Fred cleared a space on the desk and laid the frame on its face, to examine those shoes with the buckles. Almost dissolved in shadow behind them appeared the legs of a piece of furniture, round, curving feet in back of the human feet and legs, and a central shaft of wood that should support a round tabletop. The vandal who had nailed the picture into the frame had scarred the canvas in back with the hammer and scored it with the heads of the nails.

Fred found diagonal pliers and slipped an index card behind the nails as he removed them so as not to cause more damage. Then he lifted out the canvas. It had been cut out of something larger. This length was bent around a cheap new stretcher and stapled, so that the squirrel was made the subject of an exclusive portrait, the legs and feet of its human companion folded away. Staples had been fired through the painted surface around the stretcher's top and sides. Only the bottom edge was where the artist had intended. Even more of the painting had been bent over at the top, cut off brutally just below the man's knees. That cut was fresh. This was a living fragment of a thing recently destroyed.

Fred took the staples out carefully. It was a job more properly done by a conservator, but in an emergency the brave bystander must attempt the appendectomy. The canvas, when he had gotten the whole thing off, was heavy and quite dark with dirt and age. It looked to be from the eighteenth century.

It was the relic of incredible vandalism.

Fred laid the fragment across the desk. The paint, for all the dirt and the abuse it had suffered, was in reasonable shape. The artist had not used bitumen, and so the darks were not severely crackled. What appeared on Oona's desk, once the fragment was freed of its stretcher, was about two by three and a half feet: an image, stitched up and down with the holes the staples had made, in which the gentleman's buckled shoes were on the left, and pointing off left, and his squirrel was on the right and facing to the right. The top edge of the fragment had been cut, with a knife or a razor blade. Hesitation marks were hacked at the edge and where the blade had run off-square and done extra cutting across the man's shin.

When Oona came in, Fred said again, "It's very nice. It was. What a mess. What a crime. It's ruined. Still, at least they folded it instead of chopping out the squirrel and gluing it on a board, which they could have done."

20

The marks on the top looked so fresh that if it had been a human body cut that recently, the blood would still be oozing, wet, not yet settled to scab.

"Oona, what can I say?" Fred said. "Except I like it. It's been destroyed. Wrecked. It's a disaster. I'll buy it."

"I paid a lot for it," Oona said. "Because I'm crazy, Fred Taylor. I like the squirrel more than the feet. It's better without the feet. Overcome by the squirrel, I paid them too much money. It had cardboard over the back. I didn't understand it was cut from a bigger picture. The rest was damaged maybe?"

"How much?" Fred asked.

"It's not for sale. I paid too much," Oona said. "So I have to charge you too much."

"Tell me what you want," Fred said. "I'm in your hands. If you paid too much, you'll want too much, and I'll pass."

Oona thought for a minute. They stood on either side of the dismounted canvas. Fred studied the stretcher. It had a paper inventory sticker from Bob Slate on it, as well as the Fredrix brand name burned in. The vandals were local talent. Fred knew of three Bob Slate locations in Cambridge. Slate himself, recently dead, was a legend of Cambridge entrepreneurial success and stability. The size of the stretcher bars was stamped on them too: twenty by twenty inches.

"How does five thousand dollars sound?" Oona asked.

"Jesus!" Fred said.

"Hmm," said Oona.

"Can I see the cardboard that you took off it?" Fred asked.

"Nothing on it," Oona said, shaking her head. "Just cardboard from a box."

The door's bell clanged, with the mailman entering, and again, departing. Fred strolled toward the front of the store and looked at the portfolios of prints, indicating that his interest in the transaction was dwindling. Oona went back to her table and sat there, writing prices and fluttering them onto the crystal, indicating that if Fred didn't want to bite, plenty of other people in the world would.

"The thing is, Fred Taylor," Oona said, "they may come again, with something better, as long as I buy the first time, for which reason I pay too much. In case they have something good next time."

"Have you seen them before?" Fred asked.

Oona shook her head and kept shaking it, falling into a different key, adding, "I always lose money."

Fred said, "How about a thousand?"

It was not possible that Oona had paid more than five hundred, tops, to someone coming in off the street with this vandalized object in its ludicrous frame. But she knew quality when she saw it—and her own opinion could only be reinforced by Fred's interest.

They went back and forth until they settled on a figure slightly over two thousand dollars. It was a lot of money to pay for a fragment, but Fred wrote a check on Clayton's account.

"You want the frame?" Oona asked him, starting to fold the picture around the stretcher again until Fred held her back.

"The frame's yours, Oona." Fred rolled the fragment carefully, with the paint side out, laying newsprint down as he rolled so the paint was protected. He wrapped the package in newsprint. He took the stretcher also. "If you want, call me when they come in again," Fred said.

"In case they have the rest of it," Oona hinted.

Fred said, "Likely the rest was destroyed, but you never know—maybe it was torn and they didn't know it could be saved. If I can see the rest before it goes into the rubbish, we'd make sure you were included. But go easy, you know, Oona, in case . . ."

"I was in this business, and making a living at it, before you peed your first long pants, Fred Taylor," Oona said. "But give me your number there on Beacon Hill."

Fred wrote the number of his office at Clayton's Mountjoy Street brownstone and spent a little more time looking at this and that before making Oona's bell ching as he stepped into the street again.

Clay heard Fred come into the office in the basement of the

22

building on Mountjoy Street that Clay called his flat. He came downstairs, a gangly figure with a shock of white hair that no one, in earshot, would accuse him of having filched from Andy Warhol. He was dressed in reserved opulence, as always; today in a deep blue suit and a crimson tie with miniature green paisleys running in choreographed riot upon it.

"Ah, Fred," Clayton said. "You found something." Clay could see that Fred was excited as he cleared a table so as to lay the fragment out. They weren't bothering with good-mornings. Fred had a blood trail. "What have you got?" Clay asked, even before Fred started unrolling it.

If Fred had asked Clay such a question, there would have been a pregnant pause in reply, which could continue for the full nine months. But Fred didn't waste time on games when he could help it.

"The bottom third of a Copley," Fred said, unrolling it slowly. "Unless I miss my guess, and if the Lord is kind."

"The former being more likely than the latter," Clayton said, coming to watch.

When Fred had the thing rolled out, Clay asked, "Where did you pick it up?" Not, How much?

"Oona's," Fred told him.

"Oona's?"

Clayton had never heard of the place. It was six blocks from his house.

5

"You say Copley on account of the squirrel," Clayton Reed said, turning his full attention to the fragment of the painting. Clay's lean face was eager, inquisitive. Fred's office space, as always, was crowded: with books, periodicals, paintings they were thinking about buying, and the racks in which paintings were kept while they were not hanging upstairs.

Fred had a good look at the fragment himself, now that he could do it without Oona around. The manner was right; the age, the subject, the feel of it was right for Copley. If it was Copley, even just a fragment, it was a major find. This was a gray squirrel. Sometimes you'd get a flying squirrel instead, with that scalloped frill down the side.

"Because of the squirrel," Clay repeated, flipping the fragment over carefully and looking at the back, his excellent eyes needing no glasses. "But as far as squirrels are concerned—and clearly, Fred, you have in mind Copley's 1765 *Henry Pelham (Boy with a Squirrel)* in the Boston Museum of Fine Arts—the squirrel wasn't an unusual subject in the mid-eighteenth century. As you know, there are other Copleys with squirrels in them. The portrait of Daniel Verplanck in the Metropolitan's collection; the portrait of Mrs. Theodore Atkinson from 1765, I forget where it is, but the husband is at the Rhode Island School of Design. No doubt there are others.

"My point, Fred, is that there was plenty of contemporaneous precedent. Copley's sitters were not the only portrait subjects who wanted to be immortalized in the intimate company of squirrels. Why should this fragment not be by William Williams? You recall Williams's portrait of Deborah Hall, or Hill, with a squirrel and roses, at the Brooklyn Museum? Williams was English, but he was active in these colonies between 1746 and 1776 when he, like Copley, inferred that there was personal and professional risk to remaining here."

Clayton Reed turned the painting over so as to look at its face again.

"I see no immediate reason to think this is either American or even done over here. I could show you a Joseph Highmore from the same period, as English as Westminster Bridge: *Portrait of a Boy with a Pet Squirrel*, which was sold out of New York within the past few years. That picture, which was entire, incidentally, brought about five thousand dollars."

Clay was on a roll, as if he'd had a premonition Fred would give him the chance, and he'd been studying the subject of the arboreal rodent in eighteenth-century portraiture in England and her colonies— and Fred had walked into his trap.

The squirrel as subject caught his interest, not the money expended. In fact, a cavalier disregard for the reputed financial value of paintings they cared about was one of the things Fred and Clayton held in common. Fred cared about the thing: the wrenching violence, held in suspension, that makes up a work of art. And Clayton—well, Clayton cared about whatever it was he cared about, which Fred respected though he could not divine it. But both of them liked a puzzle.

Fred took the cut fragment and pinned it by its original

25

tacking edges to an empty place on the wall where he could see it from his desk. It felt like Copley. It had that naive juice and bounce and hope of the young Copley when he was striving to educate himself. "I'm going to work on it," Fred said. "It takes my fancy. It may never be more than what we're looking at." If Clayton did not want to associate himself with this project, he had only to say so. That wouldn't stop Fred.

"It does have a certain Colonial charm," Clay admitted. He went upstairs and Fred got started.

By noon Fred was surrounded by books from Clayton's library. He called Molly at her reference desk. "Why don't we do lunch?" Fred asked. When Molly welcomed the idea, he suggested she hop on the subway and come into town, but she wanted to meet in Harvard Square.

"I won't eat," she said. "But I'll ingest tea and watch you."

Fred was sitting in a booth, drinking thin yellow tea, when Molly came into the Japanese place they'd decided on. It was horribly cold for March, and Molly wore Sam's red down jacket with the hood, which Fred watched her take off beside the door. Sam wouldn't wear the jacket because it wasn't the right style for this year. Under the jacket Molly had on her black wool cardigan and a violet silk blouse that made her green eyes show across the room. Her dark brown corduroy pants matched her hair.

"You found me," Fred said, as she came to his table.

"You stand out. Not making comparisons, but I recall the cinder-block restrooms for tourists at Versailles," Molly said. "They are easy to see, and people who are looking for something of the kind are grateful for rude comfort." Fred poured tea into a cup for her. Fred had already ordered sushi, and when it came he offered Molly some, which she refused, although she was normally a dedicated carnivore.

"Kids coming in from the high school next door," Molly said, "from a teacher who wants them to research their family trees. They ask me for help, and for most of them there's not much to say. They're trying to find their roots; meanwhile, a few blocks

26

away, Cover-Hoover's encouraging her patients to sever theirs. Most of us can't find them beyond a couple generations. Suppose I wanted to press the search for my own disreputable roots, which are as Black Irish as Madonna's—or is she Italian?" Molly fumbled in the large bag she carried and found a set of Xeroxed pages. "Look what I pulled out this morning. It's an advertisement, from the *Boston Statesman* of September 13, 1714 . . ."

Either could get the other started, in research matters.

" 'To be disposed of,' " she read, " 'by Mr. Samuel Sewall, Merchant, at his warehouse near the Swing Bridge in Merchant's Row'—that's down near Faneuil Hall—'several Irish Maid Servants, time most of them for Five years; one Irish Man Servant, a good Barber and Wiggmaker, also Four or Five likely Negro Boys . . .' "

"Very multicultural slavery," Fred observed.

"My ancestors could be in any Irish job lot—not one Irish person ever gets a name. Why can't I have the Wiggmaker?" Molly said. "Not that the indentured servant and the slave were equally deprived of human rights, but I do note a lack of interest in reporting names where both are concerned. The bonded illiterate and the captive owned no identities worthy of record. The likely Negro boys would be as easy to identify as the so-called Irish Maid Servants, for any of their descendants."

"Let me tell you about a picture I bought," Fred said. "At least part of it."

"You're changing the subject," Molly said.

"I am, but not exactly, in that I am searching for an identity to apply to a pair of eighteenth-century feet," Fred said.

He described the fragment he had purchased, and Molly spoke at length about the difficulty of establishing the family lines of any but the most fortunate among the citizens of Boston, or anywhere else. After he'd eaten, Fred was eager to look at Copleys. But the urgency of the March wind suggested a joint amble along the river before they returned to their respective labors.

They walked upriver, stood in the raw wind, and sniffed at the water. Cars rushed along the parkways on either side of the slow

27

gray water. The cherry trees were far from starting to fill their buds. They came to a place where the dirt of the bank was scuffed and tire tracks crossed the sad-looking mat of grass. They were way above 1010 Memorial Drive, where a wealth of residential condominiums dwarfed the view.

"It must be where they pulled the old boy out," Fred said. "Blanche Maybelle's dancing ground."

Molly shuddered at the reminder of the dead white male of this morning's newspaper. "She must make a loop, taking in both sides of the river so she can be seen at WBZ on the Boston side, trot over one of the bridges, and give the early academics a treat on this side. Strange," Molly said. "I'm looking for the cinder blocks from around his neck. Of course, they take those with the body, since they're part of the package."

Fred looked speculatively up the river, maybe a half-mile, to where a bridge crossed connecting Soldier's Field Road, on the Boston side, to Cambridge and civilization and the road to Concord. The body could have been dropped off there and come downriver.

"You think he jumped in there?" Molly asked, following the direction of Fred's glance.

"If he went in from the bridge, he could have washed down this far," Fred said, "although in winter a person might not stand naked on the parapet of a bridge with twenty pounds or more of cinder blocks around his neck."

They turned back to Harvard Square and parted company. Fred went into Boston, to the Museum of Fine Arts, to look at Copleys.

There was a time after the Revolution when the first pirates of Boston got civic religion and established a temple for it in the form of the Athenaeum, into which only they were permitted to venture. Here they hoarded books and paintings, privacy and male courtesy. When their civic religion became tainted by democracy, certain of the pirates established a second temple, put art into it, called it the Museum of Fine Arts, and decreed that it should be available to edify the common citizenry. The idea was for people to enter and gaze at the portraits of the pirates hanging in the museum (rather than on the yardarms they had merited), and they, the common citizens, would be encouraged. It was a subtle form of terrorism.

A century later, the trustees noted that citizens were not coming to the temple to be edified, and so they undertook to make the museum more attractive by raising the admission price, building a couple of new wings, flushing through blockbuster exhibitions of French pictures, selling souvenirs, gifts, and fancy luncheons, taking their cue, Molly said, from 2 John:13–16.

A number of the founding pirates, in the good old days, had themselves painted by John Singleton Copley, and these were among the portraits that later formed the basis for the museum's collection. Copley was a local boy who managed to paint almost as if he had seen European pictures, and certainly something more couth than the flat, mean renditions done by his only rivals, the part-time barn painters called limners, who rendered folks as if they were no more complex than turnips.

Fred found in the early Copley a native intelligence and inquiry. Whatever the subjects assigned to him, he had his own interests, and played with space. He was most aware of the places you thought of looking last—under the table, for instance, or in the shadow of a hand or foot—until he went to England and lost it. Copley had no choice but to leave the Colonies, because his marriage, a move up socially, allied him with the Tories, and the country's impending first election (in the form of the Revolution) was not going to go the Tories' way.

So just before the Revolution, Boston's best native painter escaped to England and, since he'd been moving upward socially anyway, continued in a parallel aesthetic direction that took him into pious and/or history painting and worse, until he traveled to the Continent, became mortally infected by an Italian stylistic venereal disease, and lost his honest character entirely in a pompous riot of gilded frippery.

The Museum of Fine Arts had enough Copleys to cover the subject. Fred studied them, more convinced every moment that he had, tacked to the wall of his office, the earnest amputated stockinged feet, in their buckled shoes, of a Boston worthy who, in about 1765, was sitting with his pet squirrel on a leash and thinking furiously about either the injustice of the motherland's tax on tea, or of how to go about getting a piece of that selfsame tax for himself.

At some point down the line, if they were going to establish this fragment as a certifiable Copley, Fred would have to get an official vetting from the Copley fellow; still, he was feeling reasonably smug when he called Molly at four to check in. If this was Thursday, Fred was supposed to go to a teacher's meeting at Sam's school, because Sam was messing up and Fred thought he could help. But it was Wednesday, he assured himself; he told Molly he might be a while and don't keep supper, except maybe save him something to warm up later if she wanted to, and if there was enough, and if the kids didn't finish it.

It was a tricky thing about Sam, because the children were Molly's, not Fred's. Sam had a father somewhere, who didn't give a shit about his children. Sam could use a friendly man leaning on him sometimes; but whenever Fred tried it, he feared the both of them felt it was Fred trying to push Sam away from his mother, and Sam quite properly resisting, while Molly observed, ready to blast at Fred with both barrels if he leaned too hard.

But Sam just wasn't doing his work in school.

Fred and Molly argued about it. Molly wanted to throw the TV away, but Fred pointed out that sports are an important part of the adult world and a boy has to know about them. If the kid was having trouble working up interest in what he had to do, maybe you shouldn't take away the only thing he was interested in, at which point he could lose interest in everything. "I don't know anything about boys," Fred said. "But that's what I think."

Molly was not convinced. It was a problem, since she didn't know how to punish Sam anymore and wouldn't want Fred to try. "He's not your child, and he's not your friend. You're not his big brother, either. He's the son of the woman you are living with. And he cares for you."

"I'll come back early," Fred said.

"I don't need you," Molly said, distracted. "I mean, not till I see you."

Fred had errands to do, and had as well to check with the men at the place in Charlestown, where he kept a room in case he found himself needing a room again. It was eight o'clock when he stepped into the Boston wind.

6

When Fred got back to the house, Molly was on the kitchen phone, apparently talking to her sister, Ophelia. Ophelia Finger, whose success in popular showbiz, mostly daytime TV, was limited only by her attention span, was presently contributing her energy to a think-tank seminar in Colorado, which Molly and Fred characterized as plotting ways to Cash in on Others' Unfortunate Body Images and Bad Habits. Terry was at the kitchen table doing her math homework. Sam was crouched in the living room, watching the Celtics mortify the Pacers while pretending to refer to his social studies book.

Fred looked over Terry's shoulder and pointed out a place where a 6 might get on better if it resembled an 8 more closely. Presently Terry's most earnest interest was the impending start of the Little League season, in which her pitching, on her on days, could prove crucial to the chances of her team. She did not live and die for math.

"What did you have for supper?" Fred asked her.

"*Ugh. Ugh*plant," Terry told him. "Most of it's in the fridge." Molly made a mean eggplant parmigiana.

Molly, overhearing, told Ophelia, "I don't have the time or the interest for this, Pheely. I don't like the woman's politics, and I don't like her cause. If you want to get involved with her . . ." She hauled open the refrigerator door and made a gesture. Fred put a chunk of the eggplant into the oven to warm and went to loom over Sam.

They talked about important things for a bit, as determined by the screen before them, and then, during a time-out, Fred reminded Sam, "We're talking to your teachers tomorrow night, Sam." Sam tried to grin, then tried to look insulted, and neither succeeded. "Why don't we look at your geography after the game," Fred suggested. "I've been to some of these places."

Sam said, "I can do it, Fred." He closed the book so Fred could not see what he was working on.

"In my opinion there's no room left on your bandwagon," Molly said into the telephone the next morning. "And I don't like where it's been going since everybody and their mother started climbing on it back in 1965. I'll walk." She hung up. "I don't know why Ophelia won't let me be," she said. "I want to be part of this as much as I want to join the Moral Majority."

They'd seen to the kids' last-minute departure for their school buses and were drinking a final coffee, standing at the kitchen sink, looking out at the yard. Red birds, a brand of finch, on their way north, were congregated around Molly's feeder for the flax seeds.

"What worthy cause calls for money at eight A.M.?" Fred asked.

"Not money. It's that Cover-Hoover woman, finally making contact by surprising me at breakfast. She says all she wants is to get acquainted." Molly rinsed her cup and put it beside the sink. She'd leave before Fred did. Fred could wash up. "Fred,

33

nothing's going to steer that woman's wagon now that she's opened it up to the cult theme. The crazies are going to be shouting directions and meanwhile there's no place to go.

"It used to be you had the oppressors and the oppressed, and everyone understood. Now everyone wants to be a minority. It provides self-justification and identity. So the rich kids push the poor out of their slums and take their clothes and music, and white kids become black, since black kids became cool, and everyone pretends to be a brutalized Indian or gay person, though you can't say 'Indian,' or at long last you can be a benighted female or an oppressed cross-dresser or the invisible victim of suppressed invisible child molesting. Done by a perpetrating parent victim. You should hear them talking at the PTA. With the power of darkness thing, Cover-Hoover opens the field as wide as the universe, since there's no boundary to the imagination, is there?

"You can't find the victim because everyone with clout and money and happy expectations in life is pretending they are it."

"You should join Cover-Hoover's campaign," Fred said. "She needs you."

Molly was in her red wrapper, and on the point of starting the spinning rush that would clothe her and take her out the door in one continuous, sinuous movement. The phone rang and Molly motioned Fred to pick it up.

"I didn't give you my number," said a smooth female voice on the other end.

"That's fair," Fred told it.

"I was speaking to someone at this number," the voice said. "Mrs. Riley."

Fred made a sign to Molly that meant, It's the same person calling back. Molly shrugged and headed for the stairs, making a sign to Fred that meant, You handle it, OK?

The pause on Fred's end continued.

"Hello?" said the voice.

"Hello," said Fred.

"I thought you were bringing Molly Riley to the telephone."

34

"She's not available."

"I was talking to her," the voice said.

"Even so." Fred took a sip from his coffee in the mug Molly had inscribed for him with her idea of a morning wake-up motto: DEATH BEFORE DISMEMBERMENT.

"Will you take a message?" the voice asked.

"If it will bring this to a conclusion."

"This is Eunice Cover-Hoover," the voice said. "Please take my number."

Fred made the sounds of looking for a pencil and something to write on. Molly spun through the kitchen, wearing a red corduroy jumper with her purple cardigan, brushing at her tight brown curls as she flew and waving a kiss at Fred that didn't reach him until after the back door had banged shut.

"Are you there?" Doctor Cover-Hoover asked. The voice was sweet.

"I am," Fred said.

Cover-Hoover said, "My telephone number is unlisted. Directory assistance will not reveal it." She gave the number. "What is your name?" she continued. "Mr. Riley? May I rely on you to permit this information to reach Molly Riley?"

"What may I rely on?" Fred asked. The doctor gave up.

Fred parked in Harvard Square and walked over to Harvard's Fine Arts Library, glancing around him at the continually changing display in the streets. What had come over the world, this teeny piece of it at least? There was a poster ad depicting Picasso's satyr at work, a pirated reproduction without attribution, inviting attendance to an evening's exposition of short films and discussion entitled Call It Rape. Beside that, a green flyer attached with masking tape to a light pole invited one and all to an evening of "sharing" with a Dr. Goldmirth, under the banner Circumcision: Breaking the Silence; the fine print suggested that your present male-female or male-male relationships might have been harmed by the suppressed trauma caused by "this particularly violent form of genital mutilation." Another flyer, fringed with detachable telephone numbers, began, "We are three non-smoking caring vegetarian women seeking . . ." A Xeroxed scrawl from Somerville announced a "men's group forming" in somebody's garage, so "bring your drum."

Fred went into the library's big reading room to think.

He was distracted. The painting fragment he had purchased clamored for his attention, but he could not focus for the intervening image of a dead man taken from the river. The body he imagined was old and gray and bloated but still gaunt. So few bottom feeders could survive the cold river that the features were well preserved, although Fred could not see them.

7

Each of us encompasses our own corpse. He'd seen so many in his day; that didn't bother Fred. What caused the rising of objection in his gorge was the old man's isolation and anonymity. It is a bleak thing to finish life with a cinder-block necklace as your dog tag of identity. As an unpleasant but naked young woman had put it once to Fred, "Everyone's an island, you know?"

Fred riffled through glossy art periodicals in the library's reading room, using them as a mental screen between his interest in Copley and the phantasm of the dead man. It's an old blind alley in your own bad habit, Fred, he told himself. The man without responsibility is a derelict, as far as your inner wisdom is concerned. Let it go.

Living with Molly and the children, he'd begun to cultivate a layer of respectability to insulate him from his native horror of having no one to depend on him, or notice how he died.

The new library wing at Harvard's Fogg Museum was quiet.

You could count the patrons and figure to yourself, That's 750,000 bucks per person they spent on the construction.

Harvard's policy is to make its library facilities available to all alumni—and, nudged by its worldly-wise development office, it extends alumnus status to include those like Fred whose Harvard careers were brief and catastrophic, who may use the library for a premium reduced to the level of near charity.

Fred indulged a nonexistent taste for German art photography, putting off the moment when he might face incontrovertible evidence that *Squirrel with Attendant Feet* was no more than a daring flight of fancy by such a drudge as Reuben Moulthrop. The periodical room Fred sat in still smelled new, as if someone sprayed canned newness into it every Wednesday morning: new shelving, new glossy magazines. Even the few students, entering or reading, wafted strains of shampoo and designer coffee freshly brewed.

The thing about the fragment he had purchased, that had attracted him as much as the quality of the painting's workmanship, was the contrast between the old canvas—dirty and honest—and the new slash of separation from its matrix: the presence of staples where tacks should have been, and the cut-rate inadequacy of both the stretcher bars and frame. The contrast shrieked, Something is wrong here—like a man otherwise in business dress wearing sneakers and no pants, or the feral pig carrying a child's head, trotting through dappled woods.

It was the juxtaposition that grated. In Fred's experience, you wanted either to follow the money and see where it flowed, eddied, and guttered, or to watch carefully the points where juxtapositions were awry.

Fred realized he was staring at a particularly Mapplethorpean German exercise in black and white involving, it appeared, twinned melons and a flamethrower in dirty weather. He rose, tossed the magazine, stretched, and went down the new but brightly dismal staircase to poke in the stacks and think about Copley. The desks around the stacks had a feeling of panic:

Christmas on death row. The intellective energy seemed caused more by anticipation than by thanksgiving. To begin with, the place smelled like a hamper. Homemade paper signs warned users away from certain of the carrels, reminding clients of persistent drips from plumbing overhead. One empty desk was covered with pleas scrawled in Magic Marker on the backs of 8½-by-11-inch flyers: "Help! I am studying for my generals. I need these books. Please!!! If you must use them, put them back." Not a volume remained. The user had already, Christmas morning, been led to execution. Fred pulled an armload of books on Copley out of the stacks and sat at the victim's desk.

Perhaps people existed somewhere who could look at the stockings on the man's legs in Fred's painting and announce, That's prime Worcester worsted, woven in 1763 by Dame Hannah Trimble and dyed by her in an iron cauldron using buckthorn and oak bark. Perhaps the shoes or their buckles, to a seasoned eye, would divulge age and place of origin—the shoes no doubt of local manufacture, and the buckles either imported or inherited (they would pass from one pair of shoes to another, being silver and precious), or made by Paul Revere.

Fred started looking at the accessories in the reproductions of early Copley portraits, as if the dull, flat effigies of three-dimensional paintings were advertisements from old Sears catalogs, showing the satisfied users of the gateleg table (cat. #1763-a) or the china import plate (cat. #567-c) heaped with overstuffed clingstone peaches (see Garden section).

The gold chain on the squirrel might have considerably more market value than a Negro Man, being offered for sale below the reproduced fragment from a newspaper advertisement announcing the removal of Copley's widowed mother, together with her tobacco store, from Boston's Long Wharf to Lindel's Row, against the Quaker's meetinghouse . . .

"If I'd ever finished college," Fred told Molly later, over a selection of books he was carrying with him to study at home, "or gotten a Ph.D. in art history, or found myself teaching a Copley seminar to a passel of grad students, I'd make them take all the portraits he did between 1760 and 1774 and compute the fair replacement values of the accessories shown—not the architectural motifs, which are wish-fulfillment fantasies on the part of the sitters, but the necklaces, tables, chairs, pots, books, rugs, clothes—and figure Copley's social rise in terms of purely crass materialism.

"It's how the human killed the painter in him," Fred said. "Success leads to gilding, which is no more than fat with sunlight on it."

"Did you say gilding or gelding?" Molly asked. Fred had stopped in at the public library and was failing to persuade Molly to come out in the rain for lunch. "And if you are trying to trick me into eating with you," Molly said, "it would be tactful not to mention fat. I am working for lean and mean."

The reading room at the public library looked like death row after a long-postponed general amnesty has been proclaimed: the few inmates left seem bemused by a sudden relief that might, in time, lead to their generating a purpose in life.

"You're not forgetting the thing at Sam's school?" Molly asked.

"Seven-thirty," Fred said. "I'll eat lunch for us both."

"Meanwhile I was going to have a look at Cover-Hoover's book, the first one, *Culture of Abuse*," Molly said. "But it's always out, and there's a waiting list. Can you get me a copy out of Harvard's Widener?"

"You can't call Cover-Hoover and ask her for a copy," Fred said. "I failed to record her secret number. Come have lunch."

"Can't. I have work to do. There's a student coming in at three looking for ancestors."

"Send him to the New England Historic Genealogical Society," Fred suggested.

"I don't think she's got those kind of ancestors," Molly said, "any more than I do. As far as yours go . . ."

"Mine went as far as they could," Fred said. "To Iowa, where people don't write books. Too busy stamping on grasshoppers."

Fred wandered toward the T stop. As long as he was in the vicinity, he'd stick his nose into Bob Slate's. That was the warmest trail he had to follow concerning the squirrel—except for maybe the cheesy Mexican frame. He paused at the first pay phone he encountered and telephoned Oona. "Hold that frame for me, would you? I've decided I can use it."

Whoever had stapled the old canvas to the stretcher bars had gone into Bob Slate's—one of the two in Harvard Square, or the one at Porter Square. Fred came first to the Mass. Ave. branch, across from the forbidding entrance to Harvard Yard at Widener Library. He located the bins where stretcher bars were offered—the twenties in between the eighteens and the twenty-twos—and became no wiser.

Fred found his way to a desk in back where he waylaid an individual wise in the ways of the world, with special knowledge of inventory control. "Suppose I found a Fredrix stretcher bar with a Bob Slate sticker on it reading TAR 6020? What would the sticker tell me?"

The individual wise in the ways of the world scratched a honey-colored chin, brushed crumbs off a checked shirt, and told Fred, "Not a whole lot. 'The 'TAR' is short for Tara Distributing Inc. The 'sixty' likely means it's for a stretcher bar, which you say you already know, and the 'twenty' means it's a twenty-incher. Why?"

Fred dodged a frantic young man smelling strongly of second-hand smoke who pressed through the aisle carrying stacks of cardboard meant to be folded into boxes so that when you moved, everything you owned would be the same size.

"I wonder if, starting from the label, we can work back to which of the three stores the stretcher bar came from," Fred said. "The particular one I have."

The individual shook a head whose wealth of reddish curls moved in counterpoise. "Everything comes through Porter

41

Square," the individual said. "Before it's here it's there. But that doesn't mean the person who bought it bought it there. They could as easily get it here or in the Church Street store. Do you need one?"

"Not yet," Fred said. He turned to go, and had another thought. "If a person brought in an unstretched canvas, you wouldn't put it on stretchers for them, would you?"

The wise head continued shaking slowly from one side to another. "You want a framer," it told Fred. "We can't help you."

"Thanks anyway," Fred said.

"No problem."

At Mountjoy Street Fred surprised Clay, who was standing pensively next to his cluttered desk, staring at the fragment. Clay never dressed in anything other than a suit, unless, in a state of leisure, he dispensed with the suit jacket and substituted a red satin gown over his shirt and tie. The suit today was what Fred would call, in Copley's honor, Royall blue.

Fred took his battered brown tweed jacket off and hung it over the back of his chair. He leaned the frame against his desk. He'd picked it up from Oona's on his way over. Clay stood rapt, as if he heard the distant voice of someone else's conscience. Fred sat at his desk and popped the cap of the Dunkin' Donuts coffee he'd brought with him. Clay, as he often remarked, did not require stimulants, so there was no point picking up coffee for him.

Clay coughed, ran his fingers along the smooth angles of his cheek and chin, and said, "I believe you are right, Fred."

"Think so?"

"All wisdom points in the direction of its not being by Copley," Clay said. "But under the dirt, the manner, the brushwork, the apparent layering of color in the glazes, the awkward naïveté of the drawing, the clumsy goodwill of the detail if I see it correctly—I have to admit, Fred, it says Copley; and Copley almost at his best, before he fell in with bad companions." Clay meant

42

the English, the French, and the Italians. On the matter of the deleterious effect of the European influences on Copley, Fred and Clayton Reed were in agreement. "It introduces a nice diplomatic problem, Fred."

Clay twisted with discomfort, corkscrewing on his feet, his long legs imitating those of an ostrich overcome by modesty.

"Because I found it and identified it?" Fred asked, touched at Clay's unusual generosity in acknowledging Fred's part in what could prove to be a major discovery. Clay looked blank. "You know I don't want anything," Fred said. "If it turns out to have value we're not going to sell it."

"Sell a Copley? Even a fragment?" Clay exclaimed, aghast. "I don't know what you are thinking, Fred."

"My mistake," Fred said. "I thought you felt uncomfortable because it was my discovery."

Understanding blossomed with a mild blush, beneath Clay's stack of white windblown hair. "No, no," he said. "I would not insult you, Fred. If you wish to purchase something for your own account we have established that as your prerogative. No, what I meant as a nice diplomatic problem is, how can you make that woman tell you where the painting came from?" Clay folded his arms and tapped his foot, blocking the squirrel out of Fred's view.

"You've been to Oona's," Fred concluded.

"It was a beautiful morning and I took the air," Clay said.

"It was raining," Fred reminded him.

"The saturated air led me along Charles Street. I spoke to the woman but said nothing to betray my interest. She struck me, Fred, as one whose family has, for generations, handily withstood what I have heard you refer to as augmented interrogation."

"You understood Oona well," Fred said. "For God's sake, Clay, don't go back. She's no dope, and if she smells she sold us a Copley she will become an enemy immediately. Our adversary. Competition."

"Suppose she were informed I might budget a substantial figure for the rest of it?" Clay suggested.

"She'd know whatever you have in mind is a fraction of the real worth of the thing. And she would mention she has been in this business since you peed your first long pants."

It was not often Fred was able to engineer a look of astonished guilt on Clay's face, and he exulted in this one, which betrayed little Clayton Reed, buttoned into a sailor suit, with an increasingly navy stain spreading down its legs.

"Let me work this out," Fred suggested.

8

Molly had not yet arrived when Fred brought Sam back from the open house, relieving Cindy Baker, who had been roped into sitting for a furious Terry.

"It isn't fair," Terry said.

"What isn't?"

"Everything," Terry shouted, and stamped upstairs to slam her door dramatically, twice.

"Terry's jealous," Sam said, smiling. He had wet and combed his hair for the evening, put on clean jeans and a sweatshirt, and led Fred affably from one teacher to another, not opening his mouth once. The occasion had left Fred feeling like a parole officer.

"As long as we have a minute," Fred suggested, sitting at the kitchen table and gesturing toward a chair, "why don't we review what we learned this evening—some of the recurring themes?"

"It's OK, Fred, I get the message."

Sam was looking more like Molly this year, as if the hormones kicking him mercilessly into adulthood were molding his features toward the nearest available example of his own genes' maturing. Sam was going to be a handsome man. Fred heard Sam yelling through Terry's door, "You didn't miss anything, jerk."

Every one of the teachers had suggested attention to homework would be an appropriate alternative to Sam's present course. At least he's not playing hooky, Fred thought. He's going to school, anyway.

When Molly came in, Fred was sitting on the couch in her living room reading Rothenstein's memoirs. The room was frilly, mostly blue and white, with posters of paintings Molly liked: Watteau, Sheeler, Alma-Tadema, and Kline. Her taste was random.

"Terry said you were out and she didn't know where," Fred told her. Molly shook off the damp chill of the evening and hung up Sam's red down jacket—too large for Sam and about right for her—next to the kitchen door. Fred had gotten up to meet her as she came in. She was wearing a blue corduroy jumper over a white knit something with long sleeves, and looked like a fourth-grader.

"How'd it go at Sam's school?"

Fred told her, "Friendly but inconclusive. There's a general sense that homework would make a difference. Terry, saying everything is not fair, is closeted in her room. I do not feel crowned with success." Fred took the book back to the couch while Molly went upstairs. She was gone for five pages, during which Rothenstein and Wilde exchanged pleasantries. When Molly came in again she observed, "Terry says you and Sam had pizza and didn't bring her any. She smelled it on you."

"Guilty," Fred said. "We got anchovy and olive, which Terry hates, and we ate the whole thing, bonding."

"You got something she hates on purpose and then didn't give her any," Molly said. "That makes you doubly guilty. Triply guilty, since you didn't bring any for me."

Fred offered, laying his book down, "You want to go out for pizza?"

Molly phoned an order in to Arlington's nearest Pizza Haven, and while they were on the way to pick it up, Fred put the question again: "What were you up to this evening?"

Molly drove her car through the rain—it hadn't stopped raining all day—and Fred crouched in the suicide seat. Her car, an old red Colt, was too small for him. Molly pursed her lips and shook her head. "I'd hoped you wouldn't ask again, Fred, because if I get started I don't think I can stop."

"OK," Fred said.

Molly pulled up in front of Pizza Haven and Fred went in for the pie.

Fred called outside Terry's room, "Yo, if I slide your pizza under the door the pepperonis will scrape off."

He waited until Terry, in her Red Sox pajamas, her wan face grinning, her mousy hair falling in fine wisps, opened the door and accepted the pizza, yelling, "Yah, Sam, I got pepperoni."

"It's not fair," Fred heard from behind Sam's door.

"The thing is," Molly said, sitting at her kitchen table with a Sam Adams and the lioness's share of the pizza, "I got interested, with Ophelia hounding me and the damned woman after me on the telephone. So I went tonight and listened to Doctor Eunice Cover-Hoover perform. Fred, she is a pheenom. She is a reassuring snake of righteousness."

Molly took a bite from the leading edge of a slice of pizza and with a look questioned whether Fred wanted a bite, or a swig of her beer. He shook his head.

"She used to teach, but no more," Molly said. "Says she's too busy. Her position's gone more to research and various committee and board activities here and there, and I gather Holmes College is getting grants through her also, though this year she's on sabbatical. Her dog and pony show, her lecture, whatever that was I attended—she's worse than I expected because she's absolutely open, absolutely sincere, and she doesn't come on like a crusader. The bulk of her argument is assumption and innuendo which need not be examined since they are postulated in her first book. But it turns out this gal Cover-Hoover's really serious about the power of darkness thing."

Molly chewed and swallowed. She drank from Sam Adams's neck and looked around the kitchen, shuddering. "Something walking on my grave," she said. "She's into it in a big way. Fred, after you make it past the graphs and footnotes in her talk, and all the political wisdom and quotations and statistics she pulls from the book, anybody can read the real story under the scholarly line. She's talking witchcraft and Satanism, pure and simple."

"Satanism," Fred said. "That would sell. But how is she, given her degrees and training, waving that banner? Can you, in any East Coast institution, get away with teaching supernatural forces in the sciences?"

"Disregarding whether or not sociology is science—and I'd say a lot of it is yellow journalism in a suit—what Cover-Hoover claims she's doing is deprogramming," Molly said. "Her main argument is that this century and this country have seen the growth of organized forms of worship of the power of darkness— call it Satan if you want, she says, offhand—to which children and women—natural-born victims—are victim.

"You should see her, Fred. She's white as a napkin, dresses like a banker, and is built.

"It was a public meeting at a Presbyterian church in Brookline, though she's not tied to any church. Not many people there, maybe a couple dozen, but half of them claimed to be former victims of cults from all over the country. Or they think maybe they are or were, or they know one or some. See, one theory of hers is that once you are a victim you remain so, because the bondage is repressed along with the memory, until you are healed by a conscious and contrary imposition of the power of light. That's the side she's on.

"These people are being guided by Cover-Hoover as they cast off the guilt and shame and dread and shackles of their newly recovered remembered former years. She's very effective, and she'd be especially convincing for people at a crossroads of grief or indecision, who are looking for someone to be." Molly walked to the cabinet over the sink and pulled down coffee mugs. "You want coffee?"

Fred shook his head. "That doesn't sound like your sister Ophelia," he said. "Believing all this? At her age?"

"Nope. But, Fred, these people in the audience were not kids. They're half of them as old as you and me. Some look fifty and older."

Fred said, "Your sister is concerned with the bottom line, and in this case I don't see where it is. I mean, what soap or mouthwash or kitty litter wants to sponsor a Satanism TV show? How does the profit motive fit in, and doesn't the shrink lose all credibility if she starts driving a big gold Caddy?"

Molly ran water into a kettle, put it on the stove, and stood over it, fidgeting. "The lecture was free and Cover-Hoover made a point of insisting that she charges nothing for private deprogramming," Molly said. "It looks like reckless volunteerism of a purely eleemosynary nature. Since it must represent a lot of labor with people who are not by nature a barrel of laughs, I am mystified at the moment. I didn't stay through it all. Partly on account of my misspent youth, I hightailed it when they started chanting."

Fred fetched himself a beer out of the fridge. "Chanting," he said. "Right."

"Victim of Darkness, child of Light," Molly chanted softly. The kettle squealed. "It's catchy and persuasive, and meaningless, like much that impels the human race to take decisive action." She put water onto brown crystals and stirred.

Fred poured beer into his coffee mug. "When they say 'Light,' I presume they mean God?"

"The idea is to replace the formulae for repression with new, positive mantras. You are allowed to think in terms of God and Satan if you wish."

"Right," Fred said. "Wash out the brainwashing. God's too male. 'Light' is better, maybe, for the purpose. Did they work it like AA, everyone having a story to tell?"

"Enough to give us all the cold grues," Molly said, "for the next forty months. And the stories told were pretty devil-specific. A lot of victims out there."

Fred said, "As I walked through the highly literate wasteland of Harvard Square earlier, I noticed lots of them go to Harvard."

"I'm calling Ophelia," Molly said, "to try to warn her off. This woman is poison. It'll be nine o'clock in Denver. It's going to take a while, so hit your *Men and Memories* again if you want."

Coming in fifty pages later, Molly said, "The thing about Ophelia is, like Oprah or Roseanne, you understand their intellective processes in the light of the profit motive. But Pheely's sounding as if there's something in it for me as well, which I am not used to. I told her I want no part of whatever she has in mind and she insists: 'Talk to the Doctor is all I'm asking, honey.' "

She looked over Fred's shoulder at the book. "Incidentally, Ophelia found a painter in Denver, she said. Wants you to know, Fred, because of your interest in the arts. She says this guy is going to be the new Leroy Neiman.

"Anyway, 'Just talk to Eunice,' Pheely says. 'Please? For me?' God. She's done so well with the Learning to Love the Body You Have series. I can't imagine Ophelia Finger's really got designs on the mystic realm now, do you?"

"Most everything mystifies me. I spent half my day looking at a captive squirrel and thinking about a dead man's feet."

"Dead feet?"

"The ones in the painting. Since it's over two hundred years old, I figure my guy croaked."

"Good. All this cult talk," Molly said. She kissed the top of Fred's head—the bristle of dark hair he kept short so it needed no brushing. "I started seeing dark woodses and dancing divils. I'm going upstairs. I thought you meant the old person Blanche Maybelle Stardust found by the river."

"No, I was talking art," Fred said. "Nothing but good old art."

"That goddamned Ophelia," Molly said later, curled into Fred in her bed. "I'll tell you what I hate, Fred."

Fred became more awake. Molly's house was far enough from Spy Pond so you couldn't see water, except from the roof peak. Nonetheless, tonight watery darkness lapped against Molly's bedroom windows. There was no star- or moonlight, only a furry dusk that allowed Fred to make out Molly's dresser and the mirror over it; the open door to the new bathroom, which had once been a closet or a borning room; the bedroom walls, papered with cornflowers and pinks in vertical swags. Fred's presence in the house was betrayed only by his bulk in Molly's bed and the clothes he kept in the smaller of Molly's two clothes closets.

Fred put a palm on the warm round of Molly's knee where it pushed against his stomach. She was wearing the white shirt he'd taken off. "What do you hate, Molly?"

"The stories were all about how these grown-ups were betrayed in childhood by their minister or their parents or the head of the PTA "

"There are hideous people in the world," Fred said.

"I gather the new book is full of them—but I'm not so impressed by the stories," Molly said. "Though a tale about how a fifty-year-old woman was almost sacrificed to death on an altar of sin by her father, the respected symphony conductor who's been dead twenty years—and who would have guessed he had that much spare time for a hobby?—it suggests an interesting tide of revisionism."

"And may be hard on the old man," Fred observed. "Except he's deader than my guy's feet."

"No, what I hate," Molly said, stroking a hand absently down Fred's chest and fingering a nipple, "is that all of it sounds like the wisdom of the four-year-old, with heavy guns backing it up."

"Mm," Fred said.

"I remember Sam convinced, at about four, that his mother— that was me—had been replaced by a witch who looked exactly like me. Imagine if at that point he'd had the benefit of a kindly chorus gathering around him wearing capes and chanting, 'You're right, kid.' "

They listened to a spasm of rain attacking the windows and

crossing the roof. "I know it's only March, but if something green doesn't happen out there pretty soon," Molly said, "I'm not going to be responsible." Her questing fingers rested on the scar under Fred's left shoulder. She was getting used to his scars, telling him he was battered like any old tree that doesn't know to stand farther from the driveway. "It feels like another nipple," Molly said.

"A witch's tit," Fred said.

"I was amazed," Molly said. "For all I've railed and raged against organized religion, I have to say it beats the disorganized kind."

"I'll tell you, Molly," Fred said, sliding his hand along Molly's fragrant-feeling back, under the wilted shirt, "I am beset by a sense of duality, because our mutual body language belies the content of our conversation."

"We'll stop talking," Molly suggested.

"Tell you what," Molly said, turning efficient after the expiration of the moral equivalent of twenty-three pages.

"What," Fred said drowsily.

"I keep remembering you running out naked into the snow that night."

"What?" Fred asked, almost sitting up.

"The night you caught the man watching my house."

"I put my pants on," Fred protested.

"That's irrelevant," Molly said. "What I *remember* is my man naked as Adam's off-angel, with knobs on, standing in a scurry of snow in the middle of the dark street—the snow in the streetlight makes a halo of white feathers around you, Fred. That's what I remember. As if it was yesterday."

Fred stared into the room's muddle of darkened forms.

"You were on your way to meet the other witches," Molly said. She went to sleep.

9

Oona, in her front window, beckoned to Fred as she saw him passing, carrying a large container of espresso from Chico's. Jesus, that's fast, Fred thought, pushing the door open and listening to its bell ching. They came in again? It was not yet ten o'clock. Oona shouldn't be open.

"Fred Taylor, I'm in love," Oona said. She blushed. She was in black watered silk, which set off the blush. She clasped her rotund hands, beaming like a farm wife pleased by productivity on the part of her gang of chickens.

"I'm glad for you," Fred said. He dodged a collection of andirons, stepping aside to let Oona get to her street door and lock it.

"No, not like that," Oona said. "My little thing rests on its laurels. But nevertheless, Fred Taylor, this confirmed widow is in love."

Oona had never entrusted anything remotely confidential to him. Fred took a sip of his coffee, black and bitter.

"I have slivovitz to put in that, Fred Taylor," Oona offered.

"Thanks, maybe not," Fred said.

"Mr. Clayton Reed, the man you are working for," Oona whispered, leading Fred toward the back room. "He came in yesterday pretending to be someone else, in order to trick from me my secret of the squirrel, and I am in love. I had not dreamed such a man could exist outside of fiction. He is—he is, I do not know which, the Wooden Prince or the Miraculous Mandarin?"

Fred sat next to the desk while Oona installed herself behind it, where she could see to the street. The desk was covered with china salt-and-pepper shakers in the forms of birds and animals. "It's a collection I bought," Oona said. "Mostly American, mostly 1950s, but people like them." She shrugged.

"How about Wooden Mandarin?" Fred suggested. "As a compromise. For Clayton Reed."

"You are making fun," Oona said. "It was love at first sight. Immediately I knew him, strutting like a stork who has just swallowed a fat frog filled with eggs and does not wish you to guess what pond he fished it in. And he was whistling an air from Szekelyfono, which not everyone can do, Fred Taylor—not on purpose, as he did it, in order to win my heart with a Magyar melody. I wept." Bright tears even now stood in the corners of Oona's eyes, and broadened their normal brilliance. "For Kecskemét is also my hometown."

Oona sighed and gazed past Fred toward distant Hungarian fields just the other side of Charles Street.

"I must tell you I am partially bewildered," Fred said.

"Naturally," Oona said magnanimously. She began marking prices on paper labels and sticking them onto salt-and-pepper shakers, which she coupled with rubber bands.

"Seven-fifty?" Fred exclaimed, looking at one of the labels for a set of lurid post-Impressionist tortoises.

Oona winked. "If you price them what they are worth, people think they are junk," she said. "This reassures them they are not making a mistake. They can trust their eye, which tells them to like this. What can I do?"

Fred had a drink of his coffee. Oona was taking her time.

"And," Oona went on, "not only did we speak together of the great Hungarian composers Jenö Hubay and Ferenc Liszt, Bartók, Kodály, and Dohnányi, but the painters Szinyei-Merse and Béla Iványi-Grünwald, and István Czók . . ."

"Jesus!" Fred said.

"Not just Mihály Munkácsy, who everyone knows because he tried to pass for French." Oona spat into an elephant leg lined with china: an umbrella stand.

"You took to Clay then, did you?" Fred said. He finished his coffee and, with permission from Oona's nod, tossed the cup into the same elephant leg.

"We spoke of Gyula Krúdy, whom Mr. Reed compares favorably to Proust," Oona said, putting a price on the head of a gaping china sparrow with salt holes in its throat. "We became great friends, although he did not care to leave his name. Fred, I am smitten. Whatever I have is his for the taking, as long as he will pay my price."

"Gyula Krúdy, huh?" Fred said to Clayton on the house phone. "Plenty of people have compared me favorably to Marcel Proust, but I don't go on about it."

Clayton made a Hungarian sound—word or expletive. "I suppose I must go to Holland."

"Oona is smitten," Fred continued. "But she can control herself. You don't have to interpose the whole Atlantic between your bodies."

A clinking from Clay's end was his pencil point bouncing on the Wedgwood plate he kept on his upstairs desk for that purpose. "I don't know what you are going on about, Fred," Clay said. "I cannot leap the gap between your synapses."

"Holland?" Fred prompted.

"Unless I ask you to go in my place," Clay said. "But I suppose I should execute this errand myself."

Fred groaned. "You've thought of something Molly's mother would call another wild blue herring, haven't you, Clay?"

"Again, I am not following the zoological references, Fred."

Fred looked across his room at the pinned fragment with the squirrel. Big bright eye on the animal. "You found another excuse to stall on the Vermeer," Fred said. "When all we need to do is easy as taking it to the dentist for an X ray."

"I'll not have people shooting rays through my painting," Clay proclaimed. "It alters cells."

Fred hung up. Indulging in argument on this subject would lead inevitably to fury. The issue of the Vermeer could come between them, as lasting and contentious as a messy divorce. Some time before, Fred and Clay—their paths of investigation crossing—had purchased at auction a nondescript study of salt-marsh haystacks painted, it was generally agreed, by Martin Johnson Heade. Clay's research suggested that a nineteenth-century North Shore widow, careless of posterity's shifting taste, had given Heade a painting by Vermeer, which she disliked, to paint over.

The hope and expectation was that Fred, acting for Clay, had purchased a painting that, if one cared to think of it in such terms, was worth millions when the Vermeer was laid bare. But once he owned the picture, Clay refused to initiate direct examination of the possibilities. The one thing Clay and Fred agreed on was that both canvas and chassis were too old, and of the wrong origin, to be consistent with Heade. Clay wouldn't have it tested and he wouldn't have it looked at. It sat in the racks, uncleaned and unhoused.

"He's like someone who's so excited anticipating the prospect of finding what's below his or her belt," Molly said, "that he won't look to see if he or she is a boy or a girl." Or, as Clay put it, "I prefer, Fred, to rely, in the fullness of time, upon my own connoisseurship." Fred was exhausted with the whole business. He sat to look at the day's mail, saving the auction catalogs for last.

Clay came spiraling down the circular staircase, cordovan shoes first, followed by lime-green socks, a suit designed to make a virgin dove ashamed, and a silk tie of green to echo, and rebuke, the socks while teasing them with orange spots. "Ah, Fred," Clay said, as if surprised to see him. "I shall make a pilgrimage to examine the known Vermeers. I wish to become expert upon their supports, so as to make structural comparisons with my own."

Fred said, "Interesting sale coming up in Detroit. Three studies by Gérôme." He held the flyer out for Clay to see the illustrations. "You want me to telephone for the catalog and transparencies?"

"Gérôme is pornography. Like French chocolates," Clay decreed.

"It's not harems," Fred pointed out. "These are still-life studies of what the decorators call accessories."

"Nonetheless," Clay said, glancing briefly at the photograph of Gérôme's rendition of a large clay pot, "you know what the man is thinking." Clayton tapped his right foot. "What will be their response at the Gardner if I ask to see their file on *The Concert*?"

"Bells and sirens. And a lot of attention you don't want, for a long time," Fred said. "You will wish you were in Holland."

Boston's only known Vermeer had been among the cream of Isabella Stewart Gardner's collection—a choice, Clay loved to point out, not of Berenson but of the painter and socialite Ralph Wormeley Curtis. However that might be, it was among the paintings stolen some years ago, along with Rembrandts, pastels by Degas, and a wonderful Manet. The stolen pictures had not been traced or recovered or heard of again.

"My painting is exactly the same dimensions as the Gardner's," Clay observed.

Fred said, "We've been over that. And fractions of an inch away from Beit's *Lady Writing a Letter* in Blessington, Ireland; and easy spitting distance from London's *Lady and Gentleman at the Virginals*. So what? There may be reasons to go to Dresden and the Hague, Clay, but you are playing games."

"It would be so much easier if I could go straight to Director Hawley," Clay said.

"And put all your cards on the table," Fred reminded him, "as you are wont to do."

"If only I could conceal my identity," Clay mused.

"Clay, everyone always knows you," Fred said. "With the exception of one airplane stewardess who mistook you for George Plimpton. You don't disguise well."

Clay smirked and tutted. "My position would be improved if they had not mislaid the keystone of their collection. As you say, Fred, we want no one to suspect what we might have here. It puts us in a painfully anomalous position. I shall go to Holland. What do they call it now?" Clay went upstairs.

Fred opened his paper. There was trouble in South Africa. Trouble in what had once been known as Yugoslavia. His eye fell on a lavish article, with action photo, in the Metro section, concerning Molly's sphere of activity the previous night.

"Hope for the Devil's Children" was the headline, under the picture of Dr. Eunice Cover-Hoover striding through a crowd that did not show Molly, unless she was behind a hefty young man who was following or flanking the doctor. Cover-Hoover was gorgeous in a *Vogue* way and looked as if she were a black-and-white photograph made dangerous flesh. She seemed tall, almost as tall as her attendant; and the grim, no-nonsense appearance of her cheekbones and jawline belied the lush bulge at her chest.

"She looks like Anjelica Huston trying to pass for Tonya Harding," Fred told Molly on the phone.

"Or like a Puritan Mae West," Molly said. "Listen, Fred, do you know an artist named Pix?"

"Picks? Sounds Dutch. *C-k-s?*"

"*X*," Molly said.

"One *x* or two?" Fred asked. "Sunny-side up or over easy?

"One *x*. Doesn't ring a bell. Lemme look. Here's Théodor Pixis, born Kaiserslautern, July 1, 1831—genre painter, history subjects—painter of such forgotten gems as *Thwarted Departure* and *Doubtful Arrival*; and *Moltke in the Black Forest*. What do you think? Sound right?"

"It's supposed to be just Pix."

"Or a French sidewalk painter from Montmartre?" Fred

offered. "They make all their signatures out of diagonal strokes that look like x's. Why?"

"A patron was asking," Molly said. "It's not my project, it's Billy's, but he mentioned it and I thought I'd ask you. According to Dee, the man's neck was broken."

Dee was a friend who worked for the Cambridge Police Department's department of traffic and parking. She kept her ears open in the canteen and gossiped regularly with Molly. Walter, her husband, was head of Molly's library.

"This artist?"

"I'm changing the subject, Fred. The derelict in the river—his neck was broken."

"You'd think so, with cinder blocks around it."

"No," Molly said. "Before he went in. He didn't drown."

"So it's an unsolved murder," Fred said. "Boston's or Cambridge's?"

"We own it, Dee claims. We being Cambridge. That's where he touched ground. I'll tell Billy to tell his client to check the spelling and try again. I can't talk now, Fred. Got a line of people waiting for help."

Fred had a quick look at the coverage of Cover-Hoover. The reporter, with uncritical straight face, announced the Cover-Hoover view that organized cults sacrificing victims to the powers of darkness were as common as they were widespread. The literature, and the growing treasury of narrative evidence, allowed no doubt. Her work in deprogramming those whose previously repressed memories revealed them to be former victims was similar to replacing a learned but unsuitable dead tongue (such as Phoenician, language of Baal) with a language of light, hope, and loving-caring. Loving and caring were hyphenated, like Cover and Hoover. She was quoted as saying, "It comes down to the question, Shall we be ruled by love or force? The culture of abuse, the power of darkness: all this is force. Light is synonymous with love, which we associate with the nurturing female power."

"Right," Fred said. In his experience the boundary in any human person between what passes for sanity and being completely off the deep end was easily breached, razor thin, and transparent.

Cover-Hoover, according to the article, sponsored a group of "patient-colleagues," victims in the recovering-healing process, who lived in an undisclosed location—they had reason to fear reprisals—where the work of loving-caring progressed under her supervision.

"Right," Fred said again. He looked at the legs and feet in the roughly edited painting he had bought. The squirrel was so well painted, and so satisfying an emblem, his inclination had first been to assume it was the star—that the rest of the picture was cut away because it was damaged, or judged by its owner to be indifferent; if a Copley, maybe one of those in which the head of the subject is twice the size it ought to be.

Fred said to the feet, "People reckon that as soon as it is shared by many, whatever it is, a practice must be sane. A single person chanting by itself, for instance in the elevator, and facing the rear, however, is shied away from."

10

Fred, cross-eyed with crossed legs, drove to New Bedford. He'd been looking at the eighteenth-century portrait-painters' manners in rendering feet until he longed for Copley's John Hancock solution. So he'd called Roberto Smith, in New Bedford's North End, and asked if he could drive down with something.

"Two o'clock," Roberto said.

That would give the people at Gene's in Fairhaven time to fry a mess of clams for Fred's lunch beforehand.

Roberto's studio was a large, bright space on the third floor of a modified mill building whose first floor housed a fish store and a large bakery. The second floor hummed and thumped with people manufacturing factory seconds for a nationally famed brand of jeans.

The drive had been encouraging. Wet fields on either side of the roadway after Fred got past Quincy showed illusory highlights that resembled blossom or leaf. Bare twigs of fruit trees in the scraps of second-growth woods hinted at bloom on account of the tattered remnants of webbing from last year's tent caterpillars.

Fred carried the fragment—rolled again, but inside a heavy cardboard tube—through the corridor separating fish store and bakery and up two flights of stairs, to Roberto's steel-clad door. The stairwell smelled of fish, bread, and cut fabric.

When Fred knocked, Roberto's spy hole flickered before the door swung open. Roberto was tall and broad and bald and stooped. He worked in a suit, which he protected with a butcher's canvas smock—one of a supply he had bought at Building 19. Today's was blazoned at the heart, in red, with the name "Dick." Offering Fred a hand to shake, Roberto caused the white Bismarck soup-strainer mustache he favored to twitch in an indication of a smile. The mustache, and his exuberant eyebrows, were the only hair he had left above the neck.

"Fred, welcome," Roberto said, stepping back.

Roberto's passion was stringed instruments. Violins, mandolins, theorbos, and psalteries of his making hung on stretched strings along the sides of the studio where the sun from his north window would not reach them. Roberto's easel in the window, next to the table with his paints and varnishes, was empty. Whatever he might be working on for a client he would have turned to face the wall. Clay loved Roberto not just for the delicacy of his work, but because Roberto was, if anything, more paranoid and secretive even than Clay. For all that, and though he was more than seventy, Roberto moved with muscular agility to his big worktable.

"It's a crime, what I'm going to show you," Fred warned him. He handed his cardboard tube to the old man. From this moment onward only Roberto would be permitted to touch the painting until it was outside his door.

"It's been cut down," Roberto said, shaking his head and brushing a thin finger along the cut edge as he laid the canvas out. He put a circlet with a miner's lamp and magnifying bar onto his pink head, and studied the cut and its attendant scars and scratches.

"Very recently," Roberto said. "There's no dirt in the scratches. What are these holes down the middle from, staples? Yes, it was folded here and here—around a small stretcher, I understand this, but not for long or the paint and priming would be worse cracked, abraded, lost."

Roberto shook his head, distressed at the condition of the patient—like the medic presented with the twitching lower half of a person.

Fred explained the fragment's condition when he found it.

Roberto sighed and shook his head. He spread his arms. "What can I do? I want no part of this, this crime."

"I wanted your opinion first," Fred said. "Not to play games, but knowing you worked on practically everything in Cleveland before you retired to the Wailing City, what does this look like to you?"

Roberto's mustache made wings as he pursed his lips. "Do you know?"

"What I think may be guided by what I want," Fred said. "What you think would be guided by what you know."

"Flattery," Roberto said. "I like that." He studied the painting while Fred strolled toward the hanging instruments. As far as he knew, Roberto did not play an instrument.

"I won't be asked to testify in court?" Roberto asked suspiciously.

"In court?"

"About this crime," Roberto said, gesturing toward the chained squirrel.

"No, no," Fred assured him. "The crime I referred to was an aesthetic one."

"Because the monster who did this is without human sense, passion, or reason," Roberto said. "It is as if he took a meat ax to a dulcimer. I would gladly see him jailed for such a crime but I would not wish, myself, to testify."

"I meant, who is the painter?" Fred said.

"Someone like Copley?" Roberto suggested slowly. "Although finally no painter is like any other. Look at the way he has done

63

each individual highlight on the pelt . . ." Roberto took out a jeweler's loupe and lowered his eyebrows and mustache almost to join the animal's fur.

"I'd have to clean it," Roberto said. "And before I clean it I prefer to line and stretch it. There's no point in asking for the other piece? Do you not want them put together again?"

"I wish I knew where it was," Fred said. "Of course I want the rest if I can find it."

"To clean it I'd want to reline it," Roberto said, looking dubious. Once it was relined they'd be committed to this lopsided fragment, a ludicrous composition. On no account would Clay, or Fred, or Roberto, allow only the part of the fragment representing the squirrel to be lined. They wouldn't confirm or abet the crime already committed.

Fred said, "If you can clean it without lining it, I'd as soon we do that, in case I come up with the other part."

"I can't fill the holes," Roberto said, shaking his head. "Not without lining it. There'd be no point doing the inpainting either. It would all have to be done again."

Roberto would normally use a formula based on beeswax to adhere, using a vacuum blanket, a vulnerable old canvas to a new one that would support the old fabric. This procedure was easily reversed with heat, but any filling of cracks and holes, and inpainting to make up for areas of loss, would stand out if and when they should be so fortunate as to discover the missing part and remarry the two fragments.

"Let's wait to line it," Fred said. "If you can stand it, I'd love to see it clean."

"That's going to reveal a lot of crackle," Roberto said. "Which you don't notice now on account of the layers of dirt and the discolored varnish. I can't do the inpainting if it's not lined. I have explained that, Fred."

"What do you think, can we go one step at a time?" Fred said. "As long as that won't damage what's here."

Roberto turned red and stammered, rising almost to his full

height. "If Mr. Reed has qualms or reservations, Fred, about my professional tact . . ."

Fred reassured him. "We do not want our eagerness to see the painting clean to induce you to undertake a procedure that is against your better judgment."

"It would not," Roberto said. "And I would not. First do no harm is my motto." He stood waiting, like an offended secretary of state. A cloud crossing the sun made swooping shadow darken the whole window behind him like a bad memory.

"Maybe I can clean and varnish it so you can appreciate the real nature of the paint," Roberto said finally. "So we can see it. No filling and no inpainting. If you want to leave it I will test it and call you. Sometimes a thing like this has been shellacked, not varnished, and then there's trouble, as you know. I have to use alcohol, which is the mortal enemy of paint, to remove it, and try to remember my prayers while I am doing it."

"I leave it in your good hands," Fred said.

Roberto would not test it while he watched. His solvents, like his methods, were his secrets.

As long as he was in the Old Country, Fred picked up fresh bread and mackerel for Molly and the kids from the shops downstairs from Roberto's. New Bedford's North End was populated by groups who clung to their recent European identities, many of them Portuguese. The cosmopolitan working class, like the city's old character as a fishing center and the low real-estate prices caused by decades of neglect, was among the attractions that had beckoned Roberto here from the Midwest.

Roberto's own Old World orientation did not come naturally to him. It was generally agreed by those who knew him that the final vowel on his first name had been added at whatever point in his life Robert Smith decided to make it impossible for anyone to think of addressing him as Bob, Bobby, Rob, or Bert. He had acquired a retroactive Italian identity at the same time, which complemented his dual careers of conservation and instrument building.

"What I'd love to do or make or imagine," Fred said, standing on the sidewalk with his groceries, next to his car, "is the rest of the damned picture—even if I'm never going to see it."

Shoppers and strollers pushed by him. A café and bar across the street suggested itself as a place to think, but it was after four and if the mackerel were to compete successfully with whatever Molly had in mind for dinner, he'd better get their bodies back to Arlington.

Fred drove up 140, watching the road as best he could while at the same time visualizing, without arriving at a concrete image, a Copley painting that was made up of combined elements of Copleys he could think of (a standard way for the forger to work—a pastiche made by copying fragments of known pictures by the forger's victim-model).

The squirrel and chain he had; and the feet placed in such a way as to indicate a posture like John Irving Junior's (but facing the opposite direction). The head, body, and arms could come from John Hancock (reversed); and the table could be borrowed from Mrs. Ezekiel Goldthwaite, complete with—why not—the plate of stuffed fruit. The painting Fred envisioned, using this method, could not help being two-thirds forgery. He could not see a hint of the truth established by the bit of the room's interior, the floor, on which the shaft of light defied the forger's servile invention.

"Clay's going to have a fit," Fred said, avoiding Taunton by leaving 140 and taking 24 north. "My surrendering the fragment to Roberto without negotiating about it with Clayton for two weeks beforehand. But he's not going to use his delaying tactics on this one. This is my baby."

Terry and Sam, when Fred got back to Arlington, were playing catch in the street in front of Molly's house. Fred eased his car around them and put it in the driveway, leaving room for Molly to get into the garage. Arlington's laws forbade anyone to park all night in the street.

It was six o'clock and still light. Molly was not home. Fred climbed out of his car and watched the children. Sam threw the ball hard, to make it sting his sister through the glove. Terry threw high to make Sam jump and barely miss.

"How about three-corner catch," Fred said, "until your ma gets back. Where is she, shopping?"

"For Froot Loops if she knows what's good for her," Terry said.

The kids were dressed alike by accident, in jeans and red sweatshirts and sneakers. The coincidence had produced a fight at breakfast, but neither wanted to be the one to back down and change.

Fred put the fish in the fridge, the bread on the kitchen table, and came out again, telling Sam, "Throw to me and I'll throw to Terry. But Sam, ease up some since I don't have a glove, and Terry, see if you can get the ball down. It's showing a tendency to ride high."

"How come you don't have a glove, Fred?" Terry asked.

"Too much to keep track of," Fred said.

"Fred travels light," Sam said, "according to Mom."

Fred tossed the ball to Terry. That was a bitter edge in Sam's voice. Was it an off note in Molly's voice Sam had picked up? Terry threw the ball at the center of Sam's chest, forcing him to dodge in order to catch it without being hit. Sam burned one at Fred.

"It's like you don't live here," Terry said. "You really live some other place where you keep your piano and your pet fish and everything, and here it's a hotel where we live."

Fred tossed the ball high, to be fielded as a pop-up. He rubbed his stinging left hand. "Ease up, Sam," he said.

Terry tossed the ball to Sam's left, making him reach and stumble. "Bring your glove," Sam said. He burned one at Fred as Molly pulled her Colt into the driveway. Sam marched into the

67

house while Fred and Terry unloaded groceries. Molly, in Sam's red jacket, took one load in and disappeared upstairs to change into jeans and a red sweatshirt, it turned out.

"The Riley uniform of the day," Fred said, when Molly came in to start supervising the putting away.

"What?" Molly said. She hadn't noticed.

Fred took off his coat and tie to take upstairs later, and set about preparing the fish. "We will have mackerel à la Fred," Fred said.

"What's à la Fred?" Molly asked. "Fried or broiled?"

"The latter," Fred said. "But with the added secret ingredients of salt and pepper."

"And lemon, I hope."

"Each customer will be permitted to apply his own," Fred said. "Ad libitum, ad labias, or al dente. A la table."

Molly said, "Must I change into something more chic?"

Terry escaped to the living room with the Froot Loops.

"Sam's pissed at me," Fred said. "Or else you are and Sam's smarter than I am at seeing it."

Molly started cutting cabbage for slaw. Fred had potatoes boiling already, and the broiler heating. Something about Molly's activity brought Louis XVI to mind. "What did Sam say?" Molly asked.

"Blamed if I understand it. He told me to get a glove," Fred said.

"A glove?"

"Baseball glove."

"Ah," said Molly.

11

From the feel and the heft of it, the wood from which the offending frame had been constructed was a cross between Styrofoam and pine.

The back of it bore a purple stamp, HECHO EN MEXICO / 20 × 20. Fred looked at it in hatred, assigning it primary blame for the violation performed on the painting. He was sitting with it in the subway, riding outbound from Charles Street station after an uneventful Monday. He'd put the puzzle out of his mind during the weekend. On the way in this morning he had confirmed what the Yellow Pages told him, that there was no place in Harvard Square to get a frame for anything other than a poster or photograph. Molly said he'd have better luck at Porter.

So now, with the Procrustean object in his lap, he bounced noisily through Harvard station, swayed, and indulged the moaning complaints of the line of cars. The frame was joined in

Mexico and shipped north, with a cavalier stick-something-in-this approach. And if it doesn't fit, cut off a piece that will.

The frame's face was harder than plastic, and more gold and swirly than the most opulent music box ever imagined. It made Fred recall the ovoid chapel at Versailles—hadn't Molly been talking of Versailles the other day?—which Fred always referred to in his mind as the Eye of the Needle.

Porter gave you a choice between cardiovascular stimulation and one of the lengthier escalator rides on the East Coast. Fred chose the latter and arrived at street level to find bald, cold sunlight glaring midafternoon onto the semimall and complex intersection, presided over by Susomu Shingu's stubbornly stable red mobile, threatening the citizens of Cambridge with politically correct public art as determined by committee.

Fred slid the frame into the shopping bag he'd been carrying it in. Molly was right. Ahead of him was a line of shops—Allrite Liquors, Phast Photo, E-Z Tanning Salon—nestled along a parking lot. Across the street, next to an Indian restaurant, was Kwik-Frame. Fred crossed both parking lot and street and had a look. Walking past bins of backed posters in acetate and shelves of precut kits, he headed for the remainders, against the right wall, in front of the desk separating the showroom area from the broad tables in the workspace.

Kwik-Frame was having a sale to rid itself of its line of Mexican frames. The brothers and sisters of the one in Fred's bag, identical in finish, in various dimensions, were specially priced (on red tags pasted across their former wishful thinking) from $6.95 up to $15.00 for the largest, sofa-sized model.

"You're not going to see a deal like that every day," the woman in back of the counter said. She wore a striped apron of ticking, carried a head of short red curls, and looked at Fred belligerently from a gray face dismayed by most of her forty-some years of living in the world.

"True," Fred said.

No doubt the frame he carried was from here; the stretcher

70

was from the Bob Slate down the road a block, on the other side of the street. Having come this far, it was not clear what his next move should be. He wanted something this place might lead him to, but if he advertised his interest to the potential seller things might get complicated. The key to successful buying is to be visibly not in the market, just as the key to successful selling is to be owner of something that is not for sale. It is why the successful dealer, striving to represent both sides honorably, is properly regarded as a lying snake.

"Can I help you?" the woman asked, tormenting a paper clip that had betrayed her in the past.

Fred said, "A lot of framers carry these Mexican prefabs?"

"We're dropping the line," the woman said. "NAFTA. It's not worth it."

"I wondered, are they widespread and common?" Fred said.

"The frames? Kwik-Frame has three hundred franchise outlets nationwide," she said. The phone rang on her desk. She picked it up. It was pink. She said into it, "I know." She repeated the phrase six times, with pauses in between. Then she called into the workspace behind her, "Manny!" A young man put down the glass he was cutting and picked up the shop extension.

"People think we're making donuts," she told Fred. "They don't understand the art business."

Fred said, "If I brought in a loose canvas, you people could frame it for me?"

"You mean like a piece of fabric? Sure," the woman said. "Bring it."

Fred was watching the young man in back talking into the phone, saying, "I know." Something about the man was off, wrong, or familiar. He was beefy and quick, dressed in a white T-shirt with a Mickey Mouse head grinning on the front and much-worn blue chinos. Something walked along Fred's spine. He'd seen Manny somewhere.

"Thanks," Fred said. He turned for the door. The colors visiting the inside of his skull were those of an unspecific danger.

We're only talking about a picture that's been violated, Fred told himself in the street. Not danger.

He started walking along Mass. Ave. toward Harvard Square, looking to bypass it and get to Molly's library. He'd catch a ride to Arlington with her and leave his car at Alewife until tomorrow.

No, he thought, he'd better keep access to his independent wheels. He took the stairs down into the bowels of the Porter station and rode through Somerville to Alewife and his car.

He had a location to work out from—Porter Square—and could fairly assume, as a starting point, that the person who owned, or found, or stole, or bought, and massacred the painting whose bottom portion was laid out under Roberto's eye had a routine that took him or her through Porter.

Why not ask the discouraged lady in the striped apron, Did you people recently put a frame on a squirrel? Because once he asked he was committed to that approach. He could always ask later, but he couldn't withdraw the question. His vague recollection of the young man in the Disney T-shirt raised a warning he couldn't read but wanted to respect.

From Alewife station he called Molly and asked her to meet him at Porter after work.

"Walk in the place, buy a frame for one of Terry or Sam's school portraits, and look at the guy in the back," Fred said. Molly had found an open meter in front of Bob Slate and crossed the street to meet him. "He wears a Mickey Mouse T-shirt."

Molly was in black pants and Sam's red jacket this cold day. The scarf around her head boasted Eiffel Towers: a present from Ophelia, which one of her admirers had given her.

Fred looked over the menu in the Indian restaurant while Molly did his business.

She came out.

"I know I've seen him," Fred said.

72

"Is it urgent?" Molly asked. "Can it wait till we get home and I confirm it?"

"I'm behind you," Fred said.

"Were at the park til super," read Terry's note, obviously written under duress applied by Sam. The note was stuck to the fridge with a magnetic ladybug.

"They must be freezing," Molly said. "You want to find something for super while I poke through the recycling?"

"How about Spaghetti al Fred?"

"If that means fried or broiled, maybe not."

"The package suggests placing it in hot water."

"Try that way," Molly said, "but first remove it from the box." She went out to the garage, calling back over her shoulder, "Give me a yell when you are about ten minutes from the moment of truth and I'll go get the kids."

Fred heard Molly's exclamation of triumph while he was opening the jar of generic red sauce. "Got it," she called. She came in with a section of newspaper and showed him the photograph he had been looking at a couple of days earlier: Cover-Hoover surrounded by a small crowd of people, from whom she seemed somewhat distanced by a husky male.

"He's the one on the right."

Wearing a white shirt, necktie, and sport jacket instead of Mickey, the man looked different. He sported a crop of light curls—too short for an opponent from the avenging powers of darkness to get a grip on. "He's moonlighting as Cover-Hoover's bodyguard?" Fred asked.

"That's what it looked like. In her talk she claimed death threats are widespread and common against a person doing her kind of rehabilitation and to her present, former, and future clients."

Molly went for the children. Fred watched the red sauce throb in a saucepan. He put plates on the table, stirred the spaghetti in its boiling water, and brought out the remainder of Molly's coleslaw from the previous evening along with the cheese that Molly and the kids called "Protestant." "Small world," Fred muttered. He had a man to think about, or ask about now, in connection to the crime of altering an old canvas. He had a man to ask, Who did you stretch and frame that fragment of a painting for? Where's the rest of it?

It was not amusing that the same road led to Cover-Hoover's operation. That was a can of ugly worms, which he would as soon not think about.

Molly and the children came in, the kids throwing wet sneakers and baseball gloves into the corner near the dryer.

"How come you're following that guy?" Molly asked, after they had eaten.

"It isn't that. I'm looking for the rest of the picture."

"That leads to Cover-Hoover?"

"To Kwik-Frame," Fred said. "Where by coincidence Manny works, at a task for which he is physically overqualified. That's where my piece was framed, I'm certain."

"What are you looking for, Fred?" Terry asked.

"A man with a squirrel."

The kids put their dishes next to the sink and went upstairs to start appearing to do their homework. Molly would make them work at the kitchen table when she and Fred were finished.

Molly said, "So you go and ask Manny where your squirrel comes from?"

"I can, but the pheromones tell me, Think a minute."

"I don't like those people," Molly said.

"I know it."

Molly went to the sink and ate the remainder of Terry's spaghetti.

Fred hadn't seen Clay all day, or heard from him. His only sign of life had been the index card laid square in the clear space Fred kept on his desk, saying, in Clay's neat Linear C handprinting, "You have the Copley?"

Around noon Fred had telephoned and talked to Roberto, who told him, "I tested it, Fred, after you left. It won't be a problem. No shellac. That's what I always fear."

"So it'll clean all right."

"When I can get to it," Roberto said. "You didn't say there is a rush."

"No rush," Fred said.

"I have people pushing me to finish their things," Roberto said. "They can be very pushy, people like that."

"I know it," Fred said. "And half the time they don't really need it."

"They think you are trying to cheat them, by taking time to do good work."

"I know," Fred said.

"It's why I don't like to work for dealers," Roberto said.

"I can understand that," Fred said. Dangerous ground was entered whenever Roberto introduced the subject of dealers. Dealers needing to recoup their investments, the lifeblood of his trade, always pressed for speed and would sometimes suggest that conservation errors committed on the side of pretty and salable might not be taken amiss.

"They bring you a Corot and want you to goose it brighter," Roberto would say, "until everything is tourist colors. Easter eggs. Miami Beach. Monet in Venice. Not everybody paints that way, using those colors. I tell people this is between me and the picture. I am going to find what the artist painted. If that's not what you want, go somewhere else."

Fred told him, "I thought I'd see how it tested. You let me know when you've had a chance to work on it. I am relieved there's no shellac. No rush, Roberto."

"People who want things fast don't want good work," Roberto said, "I've noticed."

After they'd taken care of the few dishes, Fred pulled out his Rothenstein and sat on the couch in Molly's living room. The lad was a social prodigy; inquisitive, persistent, and omnipresent in

75

his chosen venues of London and Paris. Rather than reading, though, Fred was trying to grapple with the question of how to proceed. Molly came in from the kitchen, where he had half-heard her first taking the side of homework versus Sam and Terry, and then talking with what must be Ophelia on the telephone.

"Fred, do you know a painter named Byron Ponderosa?" Molly asked. "That's Pheely's Denver discovery. He does tennis, cowboys, and historical romance, she says."

"Can't say I know him," Fred said. "But I can imagine."

"I can too," Molly said. "A flat Fasanella with everyone on a diet and no hang-ups about breasts."

"And guns instead of swords."

"I got Cover-Hoover's unlisted number from Pheely," Molly said. "If you want it."

"You're going to call her?" Fred asked.

"I don't plan to. I mention it in case you want to ask her about that painting."

"The framer's the one to talk to," Fred said. "If I can figure out how to approach it. But just the same . . ."

Molly wrote the number on a From the Desk of Mom memo pad Fred had guided Sam to last Christmas. She tore the pink slip off for Fred.

12

"I shall not go to Holland," Clay announced. He sounded like Caesar standing naked on the bank of the Rubicon and noticing how cold and wet it seemed. He had called Fred on the house phone Monday morning after he heard Fred come in. "There is a show at the Metropolitan I must see," Clayton continued, "although it means traveling to New York."

"There is?"

"Flemish paintings. Earlier than Vermeer but pertinent nonetheless. Incidentally, Fred, where is the Copley?"

"With Roberto," Fred said. He listened for the explosion. From the earpiece of his receiver he heard the measured tap of graphite on dull blue china activated by raised white Greeks in decorous activity.

"I would have advised against it," Clay said. "But I suppose it is your project."

Fred listened to the pencil tap. "I shall find a noon train," Clay said, "and stay at the Carlyle. The exhibition is said to go into the methods of the Flemish painters."

"Never put off tomorrow what you can put off the day after," Fred said.

"What's that?"

"A maxim of Molly's mother's," Fred told him.

"I have not had the pleasure," Clayton said. His pencil tapped. "I shall look at the Vermeers of the Frick and the Metropolitan with renewed interest."

"Let me know when you get back. For the hell of it, take a peek at the Christie's East European sale. There's a little Zorn . . ."

"It is on my list," Clay said.

Oona's call did not come until after noon. "Fred Taylor?" she asked.

"Right. Wait. Is that Oona?"

"Don't come before ten, but if you come after ten I might have something."

"The same people?"

"Come at ten o'clock, Fred Taylor. Tonight."

Molly called during her lunch break and Fred let her know he might not be back tonight. Depending what developed with Oona, he could decide to sleep on the office couch.

"I got Cover-Hoover's new book from the library," Molly told him. "*Power of Darkness*. We're not supposed to, but I jumped the line. It's the sort of book you can follow by reading the chapter titles and subheadings. It's full of graphs and statistics, which nobody will pay attention to, and footnotes nobody will read. It looks very academic until you get to the junk food, which is what's selling the book—the confessional illustrations. If you're fast you can have it after me."

"That's OK," Fred assured her.

"Speaking of popular culture, we also have the best-loved works of Byron Ponderosa," Molly said. "For this there is no line. It just came in. Ophelia sent it, and it's not cataloged yet. Ophelia wants to know your opinion of the art, which I promise you can give her sight unseen." Fred heard a hesitant note in Molly's voice: the note she used when she was keeping something from him.

"I might as well tell you, Fred. Ophelia is definitely thinking of going into production with Cover-Hoover."

"It figures," Fred said.

"It's why she's been pestering me to talk with the Doctor. I made her come clean after the meeting I went to. I know Ophelia well enough to see how her mind's moving."

Given the Copley fragment's absence, Fred had hung a Watteau sketch for Gilles (now called, by the refurbished Louvre, *Pierrot*)—in which the clown was nude—where he could look at it. Ass's head coming up from behind a hill following a naked man in pudgy middle age. One of the nicest things Clay had. Clay had the misfortune to let himself believe sometimes that painting was about stories or emotions, rather than about demonstrating or flouting physical laws. The Gilles study concerned the tendency of flesh to defy gravity. Clay could neither see nor understand that.

"Ophelia wants to join the powers of light?" Fred prompted.

"She definitely sees a TV series in it," Molly said. "Cover-Hoover is more photogenic than Jesus to start with, and she has a compelling presence. She has the backing of the wise and the scared, as well as a ready appeal to what Ophelia calls popular wisdom. Fox Twenty-Five could do great things with Cover-Hoover. Run her around the country with stops in Buffalo, Topeka, Missoula. Ophelia sees it in a tent, like a revival meeting or Chautauqua. Cover-Hoover yells, 'Approach, all ye possessed,' and the wretched folk crawl out, weeping and groaning and delivering themselves of prurient witness. It's a natural, Ophelia says. It's all sex."

"Safe sex," Fred said. "Puritan, backward, smoldering, repressed, bewildered, retroactively fantasized sex. And nobody gets wet."

"Right," Molly said. "Sex for the Moral Majority. The hell of it is, I can't make Ophelia see the damage it can cause. The fallout from the entertainment—Ophelia doesn't understand we're not just nailing imaginary villains here; we're talking real people.

"Whether or not Cover-Hoover's sincere in the doing-good department, that doesn't make her any less vicious in her effect. She's scary, and I'd say she's evil, if you can judge from the testimony of the wasted families she brags about, which she leaves groveling in her wake.

"So I'm stalling and looking for a way to keep Ophelia from adding the benefit of her talents and making the Doctor's crusade into a landslide."

Just after ten o'clock, Fred walked along Charles Street, which was only mildly festive on a Monday night. The shops were closed long since, but revelers worked at gaiety in the bars, and diners in the restaurants lingered over dessert, attended by impatient servers.

Oona's was dark and locked. Fred pressed the buzzer next to the door. He looked through his sizable, plain reflection in the window. The temperature was forty degrees or so, but he hadn't bothered to put a coat on over his jacket for the short walk from Mountjoy Street.

His reflection fell between a stuffed ostrich and carved wooden screens against which leaned primitive farm implements. His square face under its short bristle of hair surveyed him. The eyes of his reflection were black and said, She's late.

He waited half an hour. There was neither life nor light in the shop, nor in the upstairs apartment where she lived. Fred went back to his office and dialed the shop's number, and listened to it ring. At eleven-thirty, wearing a coat now, he walked over again; and again at one-fifteen.

The telephone woke him at four-thirty. He'd left a light burning on his desk, and wasn't really sleeping so much as visiting with demons. He lifted the receiver, telling it, "Fred Taylor."

"Please come." The voice was hoarse and foreign, but not Oona's. It was Oona's voice the demons had been telling him to expect. The demons were wrong.

Fred said, "Where shall I come?"

"Oona's. Come to the shop door. I will admit you." It was, Fred thought, a young man's voice. Dismay trickled like sweat down his shoulders and chest. The voice had serious trouble in it. "I am Marek, Oona's nephew," the voice told him. The Hungarian color in his syllables was much stronger than in Oona's. "Oona has been visited by a grave accident."

"I'll come now. Should I telephone for help?"

"No, no, no, no, no," Marek said, blurting the denial through the agony of a young man's tears. "She is beyond help."

Fred was pulling on his socks as he talked, having gotten his khakis on one-handed already. "Three minutes," Fred said.

Oona's was still dark, but a darker shape moved toward him at his quiet knock. Dawn light, not visible in the cold, overcast sky, reflected up from the river that lay a long block behind the shop. It made a luminous fog eddy around Fred's ankles while he watched the young man approach. He was dressed like a waiter, in modified tuxedo, but with white tie. Fred watched him through the door, fumbling with the locks. The bell chinged. Marek reached up to silence it, closing Fred inside with him.

"Oona is dead," Marek said. He was the shockingly handsome young man Fred had noticed several times walking along Charles Street or drinking coffee at Chico's, or, once, talking to Oona in Hungarian in the shop doorway. But Fred hadn't known Oona had family. "Is she here?"

Marek led Fred through the dark shop into the back room, where a lamp burned. He closed the door, sat on the table, and motioned Fred to take Oona's leather chair.

"I work late," Marek said. He rubbed his hands together, warming them. His black hair was longer than a waiter's needed to be. "You are Oona's friend."

Fred nodded. He'd let the boy pace this as he must, within

81

reason, but if a corpse lay upstairs in the bathroom, they shouldn't delay the next step too long. Fred noticed a nice piece of silver on the desk, a cylindrical container with a hinged top. Tea caddy. Engraved shield on top.

"I didn't know what to do," Marek said. His face, round and well formed, was wan. "This note was on her desk."

IIe held up the square of white paper on which Fred had written his number at Clayton Reed's, in red ballpoint, with the message "Telephone. Fred Taylor."

"As if she had a presentiment; because I will not believe she did this to herself," Marek said.

"Marek," Fred said firmly. "What happened? Where is she?"

Marek put his head in his hands, shook, and wept. "She is my mother and my lover," he said. Fred reached and rested a large hand on the young man's knee. Marek sobbed. Fred looked around the room. He saw no sign of disturbance, though the timbre of Marek's grief was mingled with the shock that should accompany violence, for instance an armed robbery that went wrong. Fred put the note Marek had held out into his shirt pocket.

"I live upstairs," Marek said. "She gives me the third floor. When I came home after almost midnight, the police were calling."

"She's not here, then," Fred said.

"In Cambridge. What must we do, Fred Taylor?" Marek took his hands from his face and looked at Fred before he wiped his eyes with a white handkerchief he pulled from his left sleeve. "What does she want us to do?"

"Marek—what happened?"

"She is crushed by a train," Marek said. He shuddered and shook. "At ten-seventeen. The police know the time exactly. I was at that very moment playing Chopin's Scherzo number Two in b-flat minor, opus thirty-one, for my second encore. Jesus, Jesus. Suddenly all I can hear is a great roar. I think it is more applause, too soon. Or a stroke making the blood rush in my ears and I must die. But it was the train I heard, crushing her gallant spirit from her body with tons of iron."

Fred said, "I'll drive you to Cambridge."

"I have been to Cambridge already. I identified her poor body," Marek said, "by recognizing the earrings she was wearing. She is disgraced. Her head, her poor head . . ." Marek shook his head and moaned. "Now all my future is a black chasm filled with thunder."

"How can I help?" Fred asked.

Marek stared. "Her message says telephone you. That is her last wish."

"What did the police tell you?"

"They think she is drunk. They will cut her apart to prove it. They say she leaped or fell in order to be destroyed by the train rushing toward Concord."

"Where did this happen?"

"Oh, the disgrace! The idea of Oona drunk! What was she doing in Cambridge? Slivovitz in her coffee, yes, I admit, always."

"Where in Cambridge?" Fred asked.

"There is a Kentucky's Chicken," Marek said. "The road is named after one of your writers. A bridge."

Fred said, "Yes?"

"They take me past the place. I see her car. Oh, Jesus, her poor car. She cannot leave it there." Marek trembled and wept into his white linen. "What will become of her car?" Marek spread his arms and stared hopelessly around Oona's back room. "I cannot be responsible. Was that not the meaning of her note? Fred Taylor? That you will be responsible?"

"It is a terrible thing," Fred said.

"She believed in me," Marek said, tucking the handkerchief back into his sleeve. "She pays for me to come to your country. She bought my instrument. She supported my lessons. She is to pay for my debut." Marek shook his head, rose from the table, and stood near the door, tearing his hair with supple fingers strong as vines. "She cannot destroy herself," Marek said. "She had everything to live for."

Fred said, "Sleep. I'll talk to you tomorrow if you want."

Marek said, "I shall go upstairs but I shall not sleep again. Never."

Fred put a hand on Marek's shoulder.

"Never," Marek said. He opened the backroom door and let Fred into the dusky shop. Crystal shivered on its shelves. "Take this with you," Marek said.

He handed Fred a large shopping bag with hard internal corners, and with one of Oona's squares of paper stapled to the top. "Hold for Fred Taylor." The irony that is the sole spiritual essence owning certain immortality, chuckled.

"What is this?" Fred asked. His flesh crawled.

"There will be lawyers and police and the tax bandits and I do not know who else comes in your country after the person dies in such disgrace," Marek said. "This has your name on it, so take it. It is between you and Oona. Settle it with her, Fred Taylor, if you are her friend."

Fred said, "Marek . . ."

"Find who killed her," Marek demanded. "She is no strip-teasing acrobat to leap from bridges or balance along railroad tracks at night in—Oh, the shame of it—in her underwear!"

"In her underwear?" Fred exclaimed.

"You see exactly why I shall believe nothing they say," Marek announced. "Oona was never in her underwear!"

"Walden Street," Fred guessed, as Marek opened the street door to the tolling of the bell announcing movement of the customer.

"Yes, yes," Marek said. "A bridge over the tracks. Walden. Henry Walden, your most famous author. I knew I would remember his name."

"Lock the door and sleep," Fred said. "I'll talk to you later, Marek. Later today. I am sorry about Oona."

"Sorry, yes," Marek said. "You may be sorry. I, I am destroyed."

13

Before he looked into the bag, Fred locked the door between his office and waking Mountjoy Street. The triumph of expectation warred against the sinking knowledge, It's too small.

"Like Clayton on a monument," Fred complained against himself, "smiling at Greeks bearing gifts, as Molly's mother would say."

He tore the bag open at the staples. He'd already felt the profile of the familiar Mexican frame, and knew what he would see in that respect; and he was not disappointed. The canvas, backed by gray shirt cardboard, showed a tabletop in shadow—wooden top, round table—the canvas buckled and bent around the stretcher, and bunched under the cardboard. On the table's surface was a calm still life: what Fred would say was a silver inkwell; several papers on which the inverted writing could not be deciphered; a quill pen; and a china cup. Behind this was darkness. The visible fragment was smaller than the first, but Fred had no doubt it belonged with the squirrel. Again, more painting existed here than showed in the frame. The way the cardboard had been stapled into the back covered the nails holding the mounted canvas in. It bulged. There was too much bulk folded in there.

Fred had breakfast at a New Bedford diner—linguica and eggs and blueberry muffins laid open and fried on the same grill. He'd driven straight down, not touching the new fragment, not even to take the cardboard off the back, or remove the canvas from the mocking frame. Roberto Smith's habit was to start working early, but Roberto wouldn't want to see anyone unexpectedly. Fred drank coffee and looked at the paper until eight-thirty, when he called Roberto.

"I will put coffee on," Roberto said. "This is a nice surprise."

Roberto's studio smelled strongly of coffee and solvents. "I cleaned the squirrel yesterday," Roberto said. "That is your reward for not being in a rush." He lifted a cardboard sandwich from a table near the hanging instruments and, keeping it horizontal, brought it to the big worktable in the window, lifting the upper cardboard to show Fred the surface he had worked on. There was color now: not observed color (that wouldn't come for another hundred years), but carefully modulated and justified heraldic color, emphasized by the turnings of the forms as realized in a language growing out of the vocabulary of the engraver—black and white.

"Some yellow in the highlights on the squirrel's fur," Roberto said with pride. "A lot of people would clean that off, because it's a glaze. Stripping the varnish from a painting where the artist suspended a series of pigments in varnish glazes—that's when your heart is in your mouth, Fred."

"It's amazing," Fred said.

"I varnished it so you can see the color," Roberto said. "All that crackle, and the holes—I'll fill those when we line it, if you want me to line it."

"We were right to wait," Fred said. "Look." He let Roberto take out the fragment Oona had bequeathed him.

Roberto held the frame in both hands and carried it to the window, staring at it and making his eyebrows rise, his mustache lower, in a quizzical frown. "Is it extortion they are attempting?" he asked, turning the object over. "Send the ear, then the little finger, then the thumb? You are dealing with kidnappers?" He shook his head. "Who would do this? Were the parcels mailed in Lebanon?"

Fred said, "I didn't touch it, wanting you to be the one to take it apart."

"Solomon," Roberto said. "It is as if that woman had not stood in the way of the wisdom of Solomon." He felt the ballooning of excess canvas gently where it pressed against the cardboard backing, as if the cardboard were charred skin over flesh that might yet be saved. He carried the object to his worktable. "Normally I prefer you not to be here while I work, Fred," he said. Fred looked out the studio window at the damp sun shining through mist over abandoned mill buildings. "But if you don't mind standing quietly, and will not expect this to be a precedent, you probably wonder what you have."

Fred said, "It crossed my mind."

"And you think you should be rewarded for not taking matters into your own hands. Forgive my asking, do you want to keep the frame?"

"For a souvenir maybe, but it's nothing I want. As that same woman might have said to Solomon, Don't save the bathwater if it means letting the baby drown."

Roberto laid the fragment on its face, resting it on the gilded cheesery of the frame. Roberto took diagonal pliers and lifted the staples out of the gray sponge of cardboard, one side at a time, pulling the legs up straight without levering his tool against the cardboard. "The way the canvas is folded in," he said, "we don't want to crease it worse."

When the backing was lifted and set by (Fred saw it had no

writing on either side), a nailed jumble was exposed, folds laid and folded over folds.

"The bastards used common nails," Roberto said, scandalized. "Look what their heads have done."

"It was the same with the other," Fred said. "It's someone who knows what he's doing and doesn't give a shit."

Roberto was concentrating on getting the nails out with the pliers, using the same procedure Fred had on the first fragment, with the same concentration Fred had seen used to disarm explosives.

"It gives me a shooting pain in my heart," Roberto said. "I worry for your safety if you do business with a monster such as this." He tried to lift the square, double-sided canvas package from the frame. It was jammed in too tightly. "I may destroy the frame?" he asked.

"Be my guest," Fred reassured him. Roberto carried the thing over to his woodworking tools, in the instrument-making corner of the shop, and started in with a chisel, unjoining one corner until he could bend the frame apart.

A flight of seagulls crossed the window. Fred looked at the first fragment where it lay. The links of the squirrel's gold chain were as exactly rendered as he expected, and no link showed fewer than three colors. The patch of sunlight on the floor gave the squirrel a red-gold ground to stand against.

Roberto brought the canvas back and took his time lifting the staples out of the edges. "Hurry and you have trouble," he said. "Pour yourself coffee, but stand clear while you drink it." Fred took the hint. It was like the moment when the nurse, frustrated in many attempts to discover a friend's vein, suggests you might visit the restroom across the corridor from Intensive Care.

Fred held his cup and stood looking out the window, listening to Roberto talk to himself softly. "How not to make things worse? . . . Right through the finger. How could he? . . . All right, there's the knees." It was like listening to a breech birth on the radio. "No, no head."

Fred turned and strolled back, leaving his cup on the table next to the hotplate.

"He's holding out for the big payment," Roberto said. He'd laid the fragment out. It was the same width as the first, and about the same height. But the folding and stapling had been more complex and more harmful, because the canvas had been forced onto a smaller stretcher—this one eighteen by twenty inches—so the excess canvas had been bunched before the staples were fired. In this case, because the canvas did not fit the frame easily, the staples had been pounded flat with a hammer, which had caused more damage. Furthermore, the image selected to be displayed for sale to Oona had not allowed use of even that original left tacking edge.

Roberto slid the new fragment to lie above the first. This one would not lie flat because of the places where its folds had been hit by the framer's hammer. The tabletop, meeting the left edge of the canvas, hovered above a man's knees in gray britches. The subject was seated, one hand (his right) resting on the tabletop in shadow and reflected dimly into the wood's finish. The other hand, holding the end of the squirrel's chain, rested on the figure's thighs in the shadow beneath the table.

"Those hands are Copley's," Roberto said. "I won't swear to it, not if this is a legal matter; but it's what they are." Beside the table the man's plain waistcoat, and the gray jacket of his suit, rose to his shoulders where again the knife or razor blade had done its work. "Who hates Mr. Reed enough to torture him this way?" Roberto asked, awed.

Fred said, "It's worse. It's ignorance."

"I'll put heat on it," Roberto said. "But I can't make it go flat without lining it."

The edges of the canvas matched exactly. The feet and calves had knees and thighs and trunk now; the squirrel had most of a captor. Fred had two-thirds of a painting.

"People like that—" Roberto started. "Although I do not believe in capital punishment because I do not myself care to be a murderer, nor do I wish to be a citizen of a country in which human life is so officially despised by law; still, in a situation such as this . . ."

"I have to see a man about a bridge," Fred said. "Roberto, do what you can to protect this piece and start reversing the folds."

"On my hot table I can line them both, putting them together so successfully you will not see the join unless you look for it," Roberto said.

"I'm going after the head," Fred told him. "Thanks for letting me come at such short notice."

"As long as there's no rush, you are always welcome," Roberto said.

Fred left his car next to Clayton's in Clay's space off Mountjoy Street, rather than prospect for an opening on Charles. Driving past Oona's he had seen the hand-lettered sign in the door, "Closed due to death of Oona." He should let Marek know he'd created what some might take for a joke in poor taste.

He'd called Molly from New Bedford in the morning to touch base and warn her things were moving, that he might not get to Arlington for a day or two. There'd been nothing in today's paper about Oona's death, but it was too soon, and perhaps the death was not interesting enough. But Fred asked Molly to see what she could pick up from Dee.

"Poor woman," Molly said.

Fred would not call the Carlyle to clue Clayton in that they were closer to what looked like a Copley, since the possession of two-thirds was more infuriatingly unsatisfactory than having the first section alone. It seemed deliberate, malicious, and inexorable. Also, Oona was dead, of inexplicable violence, and Fred would just as soon not go into that with Clayton on the phone.

"I am filled with grief and worry," Marek mourned when Fred got through to him on the telephone. "I shall have her body burned, and cast her ashes on the Christian Science monument in that cemetery in Cambridge. It is a pretty place she loved. What do you think?"

"Let's look at where she had the accident," Fred said. "If you are free? I'll take my car."

"I shall practice until two," Marek said. "Oona would wish it. Her spirit tells me I must work. We will go at two."

Fred picked him up at Oona's shop door. Marek was dressed in blue jeans, white turtleneck sweater, brown leather jacket, and black leather gloves so thin that Fred thought, That's kid. The jeans were slim and accentuated a well-sculpted matinee-belt bulge. Marek was strikingly beautiful. He looked like a man who must continually fend off passionate advances. He certainly dressed for it. Marek sat in Fred's car, glanced around the inside, and sniffed.

"I am mastering the second movement of Ravel's *Gaspard de la Nuit*," he said. "It is too good for the criminal who has destroyed my mother's sister and my patron."

Fred said, "I don't know it."

"*Le Gibet*," Marek said. "From which you would gladly hang such a person, who violates a lady's precious honor."

Because there was no wind the sun made the car warm. Fred drove along the river. Marek sat speechless beside him, now and again letting his gloved fingers burst into frenzied sequences as if he were rehearsing in his mind a passage of music he needed tactile reinforcement to recall.

Fred said, "It's the railroad bridge on Walden, near Mass. Avenue."

Marek nodded. "Yes, it shall all be mine. God help me, I don't want it. What shall I do with an antique store in Boston when my life must be travel?"

Fred repeated his question.

Marek said, "I am capsized. I was thinking of something else. Miles away. What was I saying?"

"It's all right," Fred told him.

14

"That's Oona's car," Marek observed, pointing out a green Volvo wagon parked on Walden Street, not far from the bridge, on their left side as they came from Mass. Ave., and on the far side of the bridge. Several tickets fluttered under the windshield wipers.

"She shall not pay," Marek proclaimed.

Fred was confirming what had first impressed him when Marek told him of Oona's death early this morning. The Walden Street railroad bridge was eight blocks at most from the Kwik-Frame at Porter Square. Fred parked in back of Oona's car, near a small variety store, on the corner of Richdale Avenue.

"You'll want to drive it back to Charles Street," Fred suggested.

"I have no keys. Also, I do not drive."

Several children, released from school and carrying sodas and snacks from the variety store, stood on the bridge and reached up to toss their wrappers over the solid iron barrier, painted a turquoise green—almost the only green in sight. The afternoon was dark and cold. No, there was also green in the plastic awnings, green-and-white striped, over the windows of a house for sale diagonally across the street and bridge. Fred and Marek walked up the hump of the bridge and looked down onto the tracks, fifteen feet below—almost twenty if you measured from the top of the barrier.

"They want to believe Oona, my mother's sister, who was broad as she was high, and advanced in years, forgot herself so far as to strip her clothing and climb high as her head in order to do herself this thing?" Marek exclaimed.

The neighborhood was generally built-up but not prosperous, and thoroughly mixed-use, and lacking self-definition: a part of Cambridge in which people could still afford to have children. It was possible to look a long way down the tracks in either direction and imagine oneself almost anywhere in the country on a gray day between seasons.

Fred asked, "Did they say where she was hit?"

"Swept like a bird in wind," Marek said. He pointed north and west along the tracks, which ran in a broad gully between wooded banks. An office-furniture salesroom and warehouse backed onto one side, and houses with yards fenced in high anchor chain ran along the other.

A good distance along the tracks on the Mass. Ave. side, next to the northbound track, was the circle of yellow plastic police ribbon protecting a dark patch of crushed weeds. Marek's gesture pointed there.

"I saw that," Fred said. "I wondered where she was hit."

"The train's driver said impact was at the bridge," Marek said. " 'Impact' is his word. He says she came from nowhere. It is a lie." Marek led Fred across the bridge to the side where the cars were parked, including Oona's wagon. "She comes from Hungary," Marek said.

"I say her enemy threw her across this what you call a barrier," Marek said.

Given Oona's size and her potential for fury, what Marek

thought of as a one-man job would require at least two enemies. For that matter, it was not easy to imagine a single enemy getting Oona out of her clothes against her will.

On this side of the bridge he saw a gap in the anchor fencing that generally protected the tracks from idle visits. Fred strolled down the bank next to 56 Walden, a three-decker. Marek, keeping his black loafers inviolate, stayed on the sidewalk.

"Anyone could reach the tracks this way," Fred called up. At night the weeds and undergrowth would give reasonable cover. The person seeking a rendezvous with death at this particular barricade would have to drop down a five-foot cinder-block wall to reach the ground, then get across fifteen feet of open flat to the tracks. It seemed too far for an unwilling subject to be pushed, even if she were small and fat.

"It is muddy?" Marek asked from the sidewalk.

"Yes," Fred told him.

"You see footprints?"

"I reckon. It's the only obvious access to the tracks. Everyone must have passed up and down this way after the engineer called the accident in: police, ambulance medics, all that. Curious persons like us as well."

"There's nobody in that house," Marek said. "Number Forty-five is for sale." Fred climbed up the bank and crossed to the house he had already noticed, the small white one with the green-striped awnings. The children, who had been watching the two men, gathered closer to Fred while he looked at number 45. There were six of them, between ten and fourteen. One of the older girls asked, "You looking about the lady she went off the bridge?"

"Yes."

The empty house was small, with a steep backyard ending in tall weeds and volunteer scrub saplings. Its chain-link fence looked whole—enough so the mother wouldn't have nightmares in the kitchen while the little ones played outside. Growing up in that house you'd hear trains running all the time, filling your head with the romance of possibly being somewhere else.

The children, or a voice from among them, asked, "Whycome did she do it?"

Fred said, "What do you people say? You must have thought a lot about how to get somebody in front of a train at the right moment. They try to make it hard for you."

Fred gestured toward the barriers and fences.

Marek went back to sit in Fred's car. Fred talked with the children, listening to their ideas; listening also for suggestions of what they might have heard.

"Say you wanna push the guy off the bridge, or if she's gonna stand on the rail waiting on a train," a boy said, tossing his Twinkie wrapper over the barrier, which was level with his eyes. "Problem is, there's people on this bridge all the time, driving or walking, one."

"They'd see you," everyone agreed.

"Me, I'd wait underneath the bridge," a girl said. "That's how I'd do."

"My Dad saw the body," someone said. "Like she was bare naked."

"Bare naked like shit. Don't listen to Denetha," another voice tossed in.

"She was too. She was a mess. Blood all around," Denetha insisted.

Fred joined Marek in the car. "You are a pianist. You were playing a concert last night?"

Marek nodded.

"Where?"

Marek stared out the window at the children, now moving in a ragged pack down Richdale Avenue in the direction of Concord—the direction Oona's body had been carried. "I prefer not to say."

Fred prodded, "Not a public concert?"

"Public art is a contradiction," Marek said, "which you Americans deny."

"You mentioned applause. How private was this concert?"

95

"I prefer not to say."

Traffic, sparse but regular, crossed the bridge in both directions. Marek stared into the lowering afternoon. His gloved hands rested on his knees.

"You want to tell me what the program was?"

"Scarlatti, Schumann, Chopin, and Ferenc Liszt," Marek said.

"A private concert. Is that not like a secret proclamation?" Fred asked.

Marek looked out the window and said, "I do not follow you. I must go. All Oona's friends will demand a service. I must decide about her body, and the rest, and waste time with her lawyer, Mr. Bartholdi, an American."

"They are releasing the body so soon?" Fred asked.

"They find she is full of alcohol," Marek said bitterly. "Gin, which she never drank. An empty bottle in her car, they said. They have it. They say she is drunk, therefore she is unclothed. They keep her handbag. Police everywhere are the same. Now drive me back into Boston." Marek leaned back and closed his eyes, his mouth set in a narrow line.

Fred said, "I have an errand in Porter. The Red Line will run you to Charles. I can't leave my car on Walden, since I'm a nonresident and they'll ticket me if they can, but I'll ride you toward the T until I find a meter."

Marek frowned and opened his eyes. Fred had betrayed him. "I do not care for the subway," he said.

"You will allow the police to cover this over?" Marek asked. "You are the same as them?"

Fred had parked at a meter from which he could point out the entrance to the T, under public art that, he agreed with Marek in this instance, was more public than it was art. He enjoyed Maggs Harries's bronze gloves inside, though, cascading down the slope between the up and down escalators, and pooling toward bottom. It was a funny gesture, tender and humane.

Marek said, "Her note to you, and your friendship, oblige you to be interested."

Fred said, "I don't oblige easy, Marek, and not on cue. It is almost five. I'll call you tomorrow or the next day."

Marek said, "I shall take a taxi. I see them at the supermarket. In the subway I risk my fingers. I shall take a taxi if you refuse to drive me."

"I refuse," Fred said. Marek climbed out to the sidewalk and tried to slam the passenger door petulantly, but Fred's car did not take on the displaced emotions of its passengers. Fred had parked across the street from Kwik-Frame, and down a block, to watch the doorway. He would like to learn more about young Manny, discover what he could before he made his interest known. He would not enter the shop today. He tended to make the same impression, Molly said, as the Commendatore in the last few minutes of *Don Giovanni*.

Mass. Ave. was at one time the principal artery connecting Boston, with its Atlantic harbor, to Cambridge, Arlington, and Lexington. It was the route the British army took that morning a couple of hundred years back—through farmland when they got past the village of Cambridge and reached what is now Porter Square. A slaughterhouse stood here, long after the Revolution; and Porter's Hotel, which served its guests famous steaks.

Fred saw the disappointed woman with red hair come out of Kwik-Frame at six. She wore a tan raincoat and held a red umbrella she did not open. She crossed the street and entered the T stop. Half an hour later, Manny came out, wearing brown tweed jacket, white shirt, red necktie, and khaki pants—in battle dress, like Fred. Manny locked the glass street door's top and bottom, checked them, and turned. He stared at the street, then shrugged and hunched his shoulders, loosening them in their tweed; or loosening the tweed itself. He crossed the street and entered the subway station. Fred followed, pausing to lock his car. It would be all right where it was until the meter started racking up violation points at 0800:01 in the morning.

The subway was attracting a good crowd. Manny chose to go inbound, and Fred shadowed him from the next car. He stood at the passage and watched Manny lolling through Harvard,

Central, Kendall, and Charles stations, then poising to make an exit at Park. At Park station both fought the crowd up one flight to the Green Line and boarded a trolley destined for Arborway. The cars were crowded. Fred was obliged to shove his way into the car in front of the one Manny chose, and to watch at each stop to see where his quarry would get off.

They jounced noisily through Berkeley, Clarendon, and Copley, until the Symphony stop on Huntington, where Manny shouldered his way out. Once on the street, Manny was fast, shadowboxing, moving his feet like a fighter and making a good deal of room for himself on the sidewalk.

"He's on his way to the Gardner," Fred muttered. "To revise Titian's *Rape of Europa*. We can get rid of that bull. Titian didn't know from bulls anyway; we'll make it look like the little lady's taking a bath in her nightgown, like a nun."

Fred dropped back far enough to keep a low profile while he followed Manny along Huntington Avenue, past the Northeastern University complex to the massive brick edifice that is Massachusett's public college of art. From a short distance down the street, Fred watched Manny talking to the uniformed and comfortably seated guard, who was well inside the entrance. After Manny went up a short flight of stairs and turned a corner, Fred entered.

For an art school, there wasn't much art to be seen at Mass. Art. But there were lots of posters. Fred walked over to the guard. Inside his slouched uniform he was a pinkish gray presence needing a shave. "Satanon meeting here tonight?" Fred asked.

"What?"

"I think I got the name right," Fred said. "Satanon. Like Al-Anon but . . . It's Cover-Hoover's group. A doctor; a shrink."

The guard said, "What I do, I check IDs. I wouldn't know what the kids are doing, half of them, or the perfessers either. The things they get into, I don't know. These days you call it art, it's art, it don't matter what it is. Put a sign on it it's art. That's democracy." The guard folded his hands. "Your tax money and mine, buddy," he said. "You want to show me some ID?"

"I may come back later. I thought there was a Satanism meeting, or group, here tonight, with Doctor Cover-Hoover? That name ring a bell?"

"Maybe somewhere, but I can't hear it," the guard said.

"The man I just saw go upstairs," Fred said. "I've seen him at these meetings."

"I do not know from Satan, being Catholic, which they take care of that themselves. The heavyset guy, he's meeting somebody. Go on up if you want."

"You want ID?"

"You're not going to steal anything," the guard said, waving him past. "And if you're hoping to see naked chicks in the life room, be my guest. There's nothing up there tonight but a guy, and he's old."

15

The building housed offices, classrooms, and bulletin boards crowded with lapsed opportunities. There were eight floors, and no one vantage point from which to view who was coming and going—all the building's exits could not be covered. Fred's best bet was a random search, starting on the second floor and working his way up. He used the stairs, leaving the elevators uncovered. Some classrooms were dry and empty; others were for wet work, and smelled like Roberto's studio. In the evening only a few classrooms were occupied, and Manny was not in any of them—not even the one where the old guy, sprawled naked on red cloth, was being painted by about thirty continuing-ed students, using easels or wooden horses.

Some floors held faculty offices, all of which were closed and locked. Fred searched the whole place and, after he'd finished with the top floor, took the elevator down to the lobby again.

"Find what you wanted?" the guard asked him.

Fred shook his head. "That guy come down again?"

"With someone," the guard said.

"Kind of a gorgeous woman?" Fred asked.

"I would not say gorgeous," the guard said. "No, I'd say the reverse."

"Did you happen to notice which direction they went?"

The guard shook his head and, after some mental effort, said, "Say, what is this?"

"A student?"

"You want to show me some ID?" the guard asked.

Fred shrugged.

"You want to pick up girls, go somewhere else," the guard advised.

Fred looked up and down Huntington Avenue. Manny had left with someone and Fred had missed him. He should have waited at the door maybe, in which case it would turn out Cover-Hoover had a meeting upstairs.

We'll pick him up tomorrow, Fred said. He took the subway back to Porter and, before retrieving his car, had something to eat at the Indian place next to Kwik-Frame. He hadn't eaten since morning, in New Bedford.

After eating, Fred walked back to the bridge overlooking the place where Oona's body had been thrown. It was shortly after nine, and the lights of cars and buildings fought against the night.

Marek, with his combined self-pity and self-possession, made him uneasy. The young man was overspecialized: out of his element on a sidewalk or bridge, or confronted with the possibility of getting mud on his loafers. He didn't want to say where he had been the previous night. He broadcast his conviction that Oona had been killed, and gave more than a strong hint that he was to be Oona's heir. Oona had been eliminated by ruthless force.

The fact that Fred had the second fragment of the painting proved that a person or persons, pleased with earlier success, had brought it in to sell and Oona had snapped it up, setting it aside for Fred and expecting to collect twice as much for the second piece as she had for the first. She'd have paid less, saying it was dark, and small, and had no squirrel.

What next?

Fred walked back and forth on the bridge and looked out in both directions. The heavy riveted iron of the barricade on either side made a cold chasm. Suppose Oona had convinced the seller to let her come look through the rest of Granny's attic? But this wasn't a part of Cambridge where people had that kind of granny. Walk down Appleton Street at twilight, yes, before the people pulled their curtains—from the top of the hill toward Brattle and the river, you saw pretty nice pictures in the houses that way. But not in this part of town.

Fred spent an hour walking the neighborhood. He followed Richdale Avenue to its ends, going in both directions—first in a swooping curve that met Upland Road; then in the other direction, west, past a jumbled sequence of vacant lots and warehouse and office space, and housing, some of which was decrepit, some newly refurbished, as far as the complex of apartment buildings that served as a dead end. Then he started at the bridge and walked down Walden, looking up side streets, until he reached Masse's corner and the hardware shop across from Paddy's Lunch. It was a series of originally modest, even humble, neighborhoods in the simultaneous process of slow collapse and gentrification. The streets were busy with cars. The children he had talked to earlier were right. You would not stand or sit on the bridge railing alone, or in the company of an enemy large or numerous enough to overpower you, without attracting interested attention—especially if you were old, fat, female, and in your underwear.

Fred was on the bridge looking south when the purple-striped ten-seventeen toward Concord passed under him, picking up speed after its stop at Porter. You want to do it from the darkness under the bridge, Fred thought. The girl had been correct. She had talent and would go far.

From a public phone at the Dunkin' Donuts in Porter Square,

Fred called Marek at Oona's number and told him, "I'd like to come over if it's not too late."

"It shall always be too late," Marek mourned. "I shall descend. Ring three times and then two. Others I am not admitting."

At ten-thirty Molly would be drowsy but not sleeping. Fred called to let her know he wouldn't be back this evening.

"Dee says Oona Imry was half naked, and full of gin," Molly said. "Everyone's agreed, and the nephew also, that she got drunk and put herself in the way of the train."

"The nephew agreed to this?"

"That's what Dee says. If he was making trouble they'd have to leave it open a while, and make inquiries."

"Interesting," Fred said. "You and the kids OK?"

"Why wouldn't we be?"

"I'm going to have a sit-down with the nephew," Fred said.

"You are obliged to learn what happened to her," Marek insisted. He had opened the shop door and now locked himself and Fred inside. He winced at the door's bell's ringing. They moved gingerly in darkness. The shop seemed less filled with things.

"I will not invite you to her apartment," Marek warned. "That would be obscene. Come to the back room and we will have light. I do not like them to see me from the street." Marek had pulled a navy sweater over the white turtleneck. Wearing the black gloves, he looked like a burglar. "The taxi cost me twenty dollars," he complained.

"Subway would be eighty-five cents," Fred told him.

They sat as they had in the dark hours of the morning, Marek on the table and Fred on Oona's leather chair. The jumble of items set aside in the room—books, china, prints, a Japanese kimono—looked like a lifework for the legatee.

"You told the police you were content to let this stand as an accident?" Fred asked.

Marek shrugged.

"It seems awfully quick," Fred said.

Marek announced, "The nature of police is corruption."

"We are not in Hungary."

"We are in the world."

"Marek, where did you play last night?"

"There are reasons." Fred waited. "Reasons of honor," Marek said.

Fred noticed an engraving of a British horse race. He would not have guessed it special enough to keep in the back room.

Marek said, "I want you to find the person; you yourself, Fred Taylor."

Fred said, "You don't know me."

Marek opened a wooden file cabinet and took out a bottle. "Slivovitz," he said. "In Oona's honor." He went into the front of the shop. Fred heard stealthy fumbling. Marek came back with a pair of cordial glasses in Bavarian crystal, each of which bore a paper sticker reading "$25.00 the pair." Marek poured and they drank, leaving the stickers in place. The liquor was too cloying for any purpose other than nostalgia.

"Did Oona speak about her work?" Fred asked.

"I did not listen," Marek said.

"She didn't tell you why she went to Cambridge? Or who she was going to see?"

Marek shook his head, frowning at his empty glass. "It is like the rest of my country," he said. "What rots in a certain way can last forever."

"If she went to buy something, would she carry cash?" Fred asked. "Did she have cash with her when she left? In her purse or her car?"

"If she did, the police have stolen it. There was no money in her purse, they say, but again, the police . . ."

Fred said, "I imagine she kept cash in the office, to buy from people?"

Marek shrugged. "Three thousand dollars in the desk," he said. "That much I find. Are you saying I must pay you to help me?"

"That's all right," Fred told him.

Marek said, "After the three thousand is gone I do not know

what I will do. Taxis are expensive in your country; also restaurants."

"If you don't mind," Fred said, "I'm going to see if I can get an idea what she was doing in Cambridge. She might have made a note about a meeting."

"I know she will trust you to look," Marek said. "Please."

Fred looked around the room. It seemed less cluttered, but if Oona had made notes to herself and hidden them, there'd be no finding them. Therefore he'd look only in the obvious places—desk drawers, and next to the telephone. While Fred searched, Marek stroked the cylindrical silver canister Fred had noticed early that morning, which he had seen before—and, he suddenly realized, making allowances for generic similarities, which he had recognized from the still-life section he had carried to New Bedford.

"You found something?" Marek asked.

Fred shook his head. "I'll take her Rolodex with me," he said. "I don't recall the object you are holding, Marek, being here when I was in last week."

Marek shrugged. "Bartholdi says I must have everything appraised," he said, "except what she has given me as presents over the years. My poor aunt. How she loved knowing more than everyone what everything is worth. For me, I can say that if I saw this last week or the week before, I do not know it."

Marek put the piece down. To Fred it looked like a nice bit of old silver. Clayton would understand it, but Clay was in New York.

"If she went to Cambridge to see more of a collection that this piece came from, for instance," Fred said. "If that is what she was doing . . ."

Marek interrupted, "Then who was it? Someone living near that bridge? Or would they not rather be criminals living in Brookline or the North End of Boston, who say, 'We will take this old woman and kill her in Cambridge to lead the fox away from the nest'?"

"True," Fred said.

"Her car is on Henry Walden Street, but that is exactly what the fox will do," Marek went on. "She will drive Oona's car to Cambridge and leave it for everyone to say, 'This proves Oona Imry drove herself to Cambridge drunk to die under a train, maybe for love.' The person who killed her," he finished. He stared into the darkness of an ending to his sentence that he did not speak aloud.

"Why would a person kill her?" Fred prompted.

Marek explained, "I do not care why. You Americans, you are always asking of each other the question 'Why?' about a criminal villain, and listening with sympathy to the answers you tell each other, for comfort. For me, I do not care why. I want to know *who* did this. Then I will kill him." The fingers of his gloved right hand executed a quick arpeggio on the surface of the table, followed by a brisk chord, almost an afterthought—the flick that does for the fly. "The question why is sentiment and nonsense," Marek said. "For persons who talk when they should act."

Fred asked, "May I take the Rolodex?"

"You want her watch?"

"The addresses," Fred said, pointing to the spool of cards.

"Sure. Take it."

Fred would work through them at his office. "I'd caution you against killing people, Marek," Fred cautioned.

"Because of my career," Marek said, biting the red plumpness of his lower lip, "you are right. Once we know who, we will decide. Fred, you must do it."

"Speaking of foxes," Fred said, "this evening would not be the first time I had a drink with someone who turns out to be a killer."

Marek winked. "If I put poison in the slivovitz, who would know? The horrible taste it has . . ."

16

Clay, calling from his temporary quarters in the Carlyle the next
morning, said, "The Zorn is disappointing. Christie's fiddled with
the color in the photograph, and it's thin even for Zorn. It's been
skinned."

"Too bad," Fred said.

He'd come back last night and immediately started going
through Oona's addresses, recording all names within reach of
Porter Square. The proximity of framer and Bob Slate to the site
of Oona's violent death was too much to be coincidence. It was a
triangulation. Fred had not thought to sleep until first light. Clay's
call had stirred him from the old leather couch.

"This evening, after the Frick has gotten rid of its visitors, I
shall examine the Vermeers, together with their curator and
conservator," Clay said. "Their library is, as you know, unparal-
leled, and in the meantime, during the day, I shall gather information about the other known Vermeers, including Boston's. The

procedure I have outlined, though requiring patience from us both, is sound."

"Ah," Fred said. "You feel hesitation is justified?"

"Exactly."

"That must be reassuring."

Fred took his list of Oona's clients to the Cambridge Public Library, stopping at the reference desk to tell Molly what he was doing. Molly was busy with an older man in jeans and denim jacket looking for guidance on how to locate articles published in car-oriented periodicals in the 1950s. She was looking unusually severe in a black suit.

"What's the occasion?" Fred asked her.

"Howdy, stranger," Molly said. "Fred, talk to the kids and tell them how come you moved out."

"Moved out? For God's sake, Molly, it's been two days."

"I can't make Terry stop asking, 'How come Fred moved out?' "

"What are they thinking?" Fred asked.

"You think I know what they're thinking?"

"I assumed you would explain . . ."

Molly closed a reference book in a thorough manner.

Fred said, "I'll call. Can you tell me if you recognize any of these people? Clients of Oona's from Cambridge."

Molly said, "It'll have to be tonight."

Fred checked his Timex. "You got a lunch date?"

"Someone to meet," Molly said. She glanced over the page of names and addresses. "Nothing leaps out," she said.

"I'm going to drive around and look at the houses," Fred said. "Just to get acquainted. I'll get back to Arlington this evening or tonight, I hope, Molly; or if not I'll call and talk to the kids. I want to pick up Manny at Kwik-Frame and do a better job tailing him this time."

"I'll see you when I see you," Molly said.

Fred had taken seventeen names and addresses from Oona's Rolodex. Because of her system, it was impossible to judge which were new additions, since not all had notations and the notations were not dated. He didn't expect results—Oona's client with the squirrel had, he believed, been a new walk-in who probably remained anonymous, at least until the second visit; on the second visit he might have left a name.

Of the addresses he had chosen, none fell in the immediate vicinity of the triangle that was the center of his focus—the area between Kwik-Frame, Bob Slate, and the Walden Street railroad bridge.

I might as well see these places, Fred thought.

He found occasion to walk past Kwik-Frame and, looking in, saw that the discouraged woman at the desk was holding down the fort. He stepped in and asked, "Manny not here today?"

"His day off," she said. "We work Saturdays. You know Manny?"

"I was passing by."

"You decide to bring in that piece of fabric?"

Fred told her, "You know how it is. I decided to do it and then forgot. Isn't that the way it goes every time? Got all the way here and then remembered, 'I forgot it.' "

"No rush," the woman said.

Fred said, "Give me your card. I'll put it on my dash so I don't forget next time." The card said KWIK-FRAME, with the address and phone, no names. Manny was still just Manny.

The weather Arlington had chosen for today was cold but almost dry. Fred found Terry and Sam at the park. Sam was shooting baskets with a couple of taller friends and Terry was throwing pop flies for herself to try to catch. Sam saw Fred get out of his car and continued shooting baskets. Terry came over. The wind from the pond, on the far side of the playing fields, blew directly at them.

Terry's face was red, her hair matted and awry. She wouldn't close her outsize orange parka. She looked like an orphan. "You want to play catch, Fred?" she asked.

"Does the Pope chew tobacco?"

Terry tossed the ball to him with exaggerated mildness.

"Did your mom tell you why I was away the last couple days?"

"Someone died?" Terry said.

"And I'm helping her nephew out. He's the only one she had."

"That's what Mom said."

"You want high balls or fast balls or curve balls?"

"Curve."

They played catch a while. It was getting toward six. Sam's friends took off with the basketball.

"Yo, Sam," Fred called.

Sam wandered over. He picked his glove up from the fence where he had hung it, next to the parking lot. "We ought to get back," Sam said. "Can we ride with you?" Sam's face and hands were red. He wore his old black parka open. The new (last winter) down jacket Fred had given him had now become, by default, no one's but Molly's. Fred closed his door and started the car, prepared to take no side in the scuffle over who would sit next to him in the front seat. Sam and Terry both climbed in back.

"We could use some spring," Fred told them.

Molly heated franks and beans, which they ate together. Molly hadn't changed out of her black suit. Instead she put an apron over it that boasted "Gloria Flour" in red script on a white field. She was distracted while she put supper together and presided over it. Fred tried to start general table conversation about where in the world people would like to travel if all things were equal.

"Maybe Charlestown," Sam said, mumbling it into his plate.

Silence followed until Fred said, "I'll take you some time."

Sam looked at him. Terry looked at him. Molly looked at him.

"I'll wash up," Fred said. "You kids have homework."

The kids upstairs, Fred exploded. "Listen, Molly, whatever you want. You want me out of the house, just say the word."

Molly went white. "What's going on?"

"Exactly my question. You in the funeral suit, and the kids— who put them up to that, making snide comments about my place in Charlestown?"

"I don't know how they even heard about it," Molly said. She put a kettle on for coffee. "As far as the funeral suit . . ."

"And you all three act like I'm cavorting with strange women," Fred said. "My work takes me away, Molly, for God's sake. That's not too hard for you to explain to them, or to understand yourself."

Fred put the dishes into hot water. Molly took out cups and instant coffee deliberately, not speaking but arranging two cups. "You want some?" she asked. Fred nodded. Molly went on evenly, "As far as the funeral suit goes, I chose it for my meeting with Cover-Hoover, and the meeting shook me. I'd like to tell you about it. Over coffee. In the living room. After I get the kids settled at the kitchen table with their homework. After you're through."

"Right," Fred said.

"As long as my rival is a painting," Molly said, "or poor Oona Imry, I am content. As for the kids, that's between you and them."

Fred waited in the living room for Molly, drinking his coffee while it was hot. Molly liked hers lukewarm or on the cold side. Molly came in and closed the door to the kitchen, carrying her coffee and still wearing the suit. She looked like a bank examiner with bad news. "Ophelia did not tell me everything," she said.

"She couldn't tell you everything and also retain her identity as Ophelia," Fred said. "Molly, I'm sorry I blew up. I always remember I'm a fucking foreigner."

111

"Yes, you remember that more than anyone else does. In the meantime, I went to . . . Fred, you haven't described the second part of the squirrel painting."

Molly's 180-degree midair change in direction threw Fred off balance. She was zigzagging across the field fast, heading for friendly thickets of razor wire.

Fred said, "Terry complains I don't have any stuff."

"They worry about that. It makes you seem not real when you're gone. Nothing left to bump into except Fred's sneakers and a few clothes in my closet—maybe the library book you're reading next to my bed, and your Copley books. But none of that is where they trip on it."

"I can't stand having stuff," Fred said.

"Even if that's reasonable, Terry and Sam don't think so, and they don't trust it."

If they didn't trust it, they didn't trust it, and arguing with Molly wasn't going to change that. Fred described the second Copley fragment and made a rough sketch of what the two parts represented and how they fit together. On the same page he drew a blank third segment and explained, drawing with his pencil, how he inferred the painting might conclude.

"So whoever took it apart—it's like drug dealers, strangers to each other," Molly said. "They have to match the parts of this thing in order to trust the strangers who show up somewhere and say, 'I'm your new partner.'

"For the sake of argument," Molly said, getting up from the couch where she had been sitting next to him and crossing the blue mass-produced Chinese rug to sit in an armchair, "how much would the complete painting be worth if it is a Copley?"

"If it's complete? And before it was damaged, and if it's not hot, but not signed? Also I have to tell you that we haven't found a record of it," Fred said. "So it's a thousand problems in one basket even if I find the rest of it. Given all that, before it was cut apart, maybe a quarter-million bucks."

"Hm," Molly said.

"If the sitter's an important man—a George Washington,

112

say—then commercially the issue involves a tussle between the fact Copley's historically important and the fact that nobody wants a portrait, especially if it's a picture of a guy. The trade is driven by fat old men who crave paintings about their lost youth, those sunny days when they were fawned over by pretty young virgin women whose underwear you *know* came from a place so nice you and I never heard of it."

"Made by contented spiders," Molly added.

Terry put her head in the door. "Dee on the phone, Mom," she said.

Molly sashayed into the kitchen. Fred considered her idea of the painting's being divided in order to provide mutual identification to three strangers. How had two portions found their way to Oona's? Molly came in from the kitchen and handed Fred a slip of paper with a phone number and, in her Catholic-school handwriting, the name "Bookrajian."

"Dee says that's the detective assigned to the Oona Imry killing."

"Killing?"

"Her very word. Dee says call in the morning, after eight," Molly said. She sat stiffly in her chosen chair in her chosen corner. "He's at a game tonight."

Fred, standing in the center of the room, testing the wind, which seemed to be blowing simultaneously from five directions, remembered, "Tell me about Cover-Hoover."

17

"I thought I was saved by the bell," Molly said.

Fred said, "She really got to you, didn't she?"

"Given a chance, there's not much she wouldn't get to," Molly said. "You wouldn't know she'd gotten inside until she started expanding, and it would be too late." Molly took a sip from her mug of cold coffee, brushed imaginary crumbs off her breasts, and shifted her hips in the armchair. "I didn't know how badly Ophelia set me up." Molly shuddered. "It wasn't so goddamn awful," she said. "But the woman got under my skin like one of those egg-laying insects, and the larvae are already crawling everywhere, looking for where they'll bore their openings to get air."

"God, Molly." Fred walked toward her but Molly waved him off, gesturing toward the couch, his usual place. Her normal post was at the other end, using the other lamp.

Molly said, "Part of it is I'm so upset with Ophelia." She folded her hands in her lap and started. "My first plan was, especially when your interest had bumped into this operation, to make a fair evaluation for Ophelia, the way you, in your place, might go so far as to examine an original painting by Byron Ponderosa if you had a sister contemplating doing serious business with him."

"Byron Ponderosa?" Fred asked, and then recalled the name from earlier conversation. "Sorry, I remember."

"Then I heard the woman, and had a look at her book, and frankly, Fred, I concluded, unless she could convince me otherwise, however sincere and well motivated she may be, Cover-Hoover is carrying a potent, deadly virus, and she should be stopped.

"So I called her unlisted number early this A.M. before work. Eunice—she prefers to be called Eunice—wanted to know right off why I had resisted her initially.

"I told her my reason for holding off was I was in denial. That term, *in denial*, is generally used to cover those who do not agree with the program. I said I wanted to consult her professionally but I had not been able to bring myself to admit it. Her little ears pricked up. You could almost hear them on the phone, pop, pop, one after the other.

" 'I'll make time to see you,' she said, and gave me two hours at lunch. That's where I was going when you stopped by."

"So your initial contact was as a prospective patient? Where's her place?" Fred asked.

"She's got an office right in Harvard Square. In her business the ideal client group comes from among the fortunate. She's got a third-floor suite, more or less above Nini's Corner, the newspaper and candy bar and dirty-magazine place."

"I know Nini's," Fred said. "It's where a lot of us did most of our studying while I was at Harvard for about five minutes."

Molly put her mug down. "That's Andy Warhol's line, isn't it? Everyone gets to be at Harvard for five minutes?" She had a potted poinsettia struggling on that side of the room, making an odd red note in a blue room. Terry screamed at Sam about something in the kitchen.

Molly continued. "I walked over, cutting through Harvard

Yard. Yesterday and this morning I'd done some research—it doesn't take much, her own book gives you the guidelines. That's the advantage of having case histories. I prepared enough symptoms to get through an hour I figured, as long as I added some confused stalling. I planned on winging the second half.

"Her suite's a two-room deal with its own john and a sign on the door, brass plaque, giving her name and the initials she professes; and another, paper, sign asking you to ring. You stand in the hall waiting for her to talk through the intercom and buzz you in, at which point you are in an empty room. There's nothing but a gray carpet, two chairs; no magazines of ancient news, fashion, or exploration. The room is fifteen feet square. Not even a window. No place to put your coat. Aside from the door you entered, there are two other doors, closed. You can't help thinking it's a test. You are supposed to guess which door.

"Immediately you feel watched. It's a genius setup to put the client at a disadvantage. A voice has let you in, and there's no person. It's like finding yourself in midair. Not knowing which way you are supposed to fall, you fail even to fall. You lose substance. You look at the two doors, you look at the two chairs, and you think, I'll choose the wrong chair. You think, She's spying from somewhere, sizing me up; you eenie-meenie and sit on Mo, the winning chair, and wait, making a bet with yourself which door is going to open.

"Suppose, like most of the poor goofs coming in, you are already disoriented or emotionally hard-pressed? That's the method-acting approach I had worked up. I was planning to play the scene like, maybe, Diane Keaton in *Annie Hall*."

Molly was no actress. But if she were, Fred would advise her to try for something closer to where she started from, like Holly Hunter in *Miss Firecracker* or *Broadcast News*.

"I must have sat five minutes," Molly said. "The room was lighted from the ceiling, and otherwise, except for cleaning fluid from the carpet, the place was a sensory-deprivation chamber. The walls were bleached beige, the doors wood painted white. Not a sound got into the room. No sound in, no sound out.

"So I sit with my bag on my lap, rehearsing my part, until a door opens and Cover-Hoover strides across the room toward me. She's dressed in a plain, nice blue silk dress with white spots, no big deal, just a pro, the Doctor.

" 'You are safe here,' she says. That's the opening gambit. I must say I respond better to a frank, 'What's up?'

"Her office looks out on Brattle Street. Big windows full of sun and geraniums, her desk with a phone, and papers, and serious dark books, and a nice vase from a place, with thirty-five bucks' worth of fresh flowers. You stand there feeling sick and shabby and filled with envy at the way this woman has gotten everything together. You are ashamed you come from a blank room with nothing in it but gray carpet and two chairs you can't choose between. It's genius.

"Eunice showed me a place on a small couch to sit, and before she sat down on a chair four feet away and slightly higher than mine, she offered to close the blinds. 'It will make you feel safe.'

"Thinking it would help my act, I mumbled, 'Please, close them, close them.' She reached up and did that. She has a gorgeous body, good breasts—like the vase of flowers, something you are supposed to notice, study, want, and envy." Molly fumbled her hands together in her lap. She smiled at Fred, looked down at her perfectly adequate and pleasant bosom, and shrugged.

"Say something," Molly demanded.

Fred said, "I'm afraid I'll break the spell."

"OK," Molly said. "Thanks. So this fucking woman sat waiting for me to open my fool mouth, until I did. I told her, 'I came to your talk the other night and I was moved. I have been resisting you. I am afraid. For years I have struggled with a memory that has no shape, only a weight—nothing to see. And it's been growing.' "

"That's good," Fred said. "It's ominous and vague and offers her room to be the smart one."

"The person who defines the force," Molly said. "That was my thinking. So I told her what I had prepared—chronic trouble sleeping and, when I do sleep, waking and experiencing the strong sensation of another person, or a strange being, in the room."

"Unless he's sleeping on Clayton's couch," Fred said.

Molly stood and took off the black jacket of her suit and draped it over the back of a side chair. She wore a white blouse under it, and pearls. She ran her fingers through her tight curls and sat down again. "I mentioned the constant sense I have of being always next to a serious, impending danger. Sensation of flying. And the scar I cannot account for."

"What?" Fred asked, startled.

"That got her attention too," Molly said. "She said—her first words after she asked me if I wanted the blinds closed—'Show me.'

"Now Fred, you know me. I'm not one of these Vagina-of-the-Month Club women that gets together over coffee and everybody talks up their episiotomy, like the new *Our Bodies, Ourselves* pretends; all smoke and mirrors in my opinion. But it was my own damned fault. You mention the symptoms, you have to be able to demonstrate them, and everything else I had offered was in the ectoplasm field. So the only scar I had to show is where the stob went in when Pheely pushed me out of the apple tree."

Fred grinned. "That put you at a tactical disadvantage," he allowed.

"I had a choice between two tactical disadvantages. One, I refuse and immediately my story goes up in smoke—unless I can be convincing about scars only I can see, of which there are numerous examples in the literature—or, two, I drop my pants."

Fred said, "And you can't afford to look like you're planning your next move. You have to respond fast."

"Exactly. So the doctor sat there waiting, gentle, smiling a little. Not pushy. She had all the time in the world to watch which door, which chair, or which mistake I was going to try. I figured I had to raise her, so I took off all my clothes, deliberate, and challenged her: 'Many deny they see his mark on me.' "

Fred said, "That's really good. It gives you center stage, but it's a bit extreme . . ."

118

"I wanted to challenge her."

They heard, from the kitchen, the sound of Sam and Terry fighting about who got the bathroom first, to brush their teeth on the way to bed.

"I made her come onto my turf and look me over, me testing her now," Molly said. "It was not the way I had imagined spending my lunch hour. Cover-Hoover, being a true psychic, or adept, or whatever, found the old ragged pinch of scar on my left buttock. She hissed in when she touched it and said, 'Does it feel hot?' "

"Mmm. She saw you and raised you, Molly."

"Meanwhile, playing for time, I made her swear she truly could see and feel it," Molly said. "Then I sort of collapsed and told her, 'I can't remember anything. I'm afraid.' "

" 'He's long dead,' Eunice said. 'He can't touch you again.' "

"She was absolutely convincing, working like water that insinuates itself into every opening and is going to damned well drag itself to sea level, and you along with it. As soon as she said, 'He can't touch you,' I started manufacturing visions of who this *he* might be.

"It was as if I'd hypnotized myself, almost, standing there, as Terry used to call it, barefoot. I was surrounded by a violent aura of fear I couldn't put a villain to, or see, or recall—I was inventing it after all—but the sensation and the emotion were real enough to bottle and sell. With this thing lapping around me like a fog, I put my clothes on again—got through that gracefully enough, I think—before I thought of asking her, 'What do you mean he's long dead? Who's long dead?'

"I don't know why the poor old man who came out to the house that night was the first person I thought of. Because he touched me with an intimate fear, I guess.

"Eunice said, 'No need to rush this, Molly. May I call you Molly? Please call me Eunice. You did right to come to me. No human power by itself can withstand the darkness that has reached its long finger into your body.'

"It's embarrassing, Fred. When she said that, I felt the long finger of darkness reaching into me through the old scar on my ass. Which I know for a fact came when I was ten and fell out of a tree. My mother thought I'd got my period.

"Listen, I can't go through the next hour line by line. I am absolutely furious with Ophelia. Do you know how she set me up? Do you know what she did?" Molly started shaking.

"She told Cover-Hoover that she, Ophelia, suspects her older sister, Molly—me—was used in witches' Sabbaths by my poor old dad, before the accident in the warehouse that killed him when I was eight and she was six.

"She told Eunice she suspects Dad was head witch in regular satanic worship on some blasted heath in Newton Lower Falls. God, did I walk into that one."

Molly burst into what was either laughter or tears; a noisy, generous fury of emotion that lasted a full minute and then was gone. She stood, wiped her eyes with a napkin, blew her nose, and said, "I'm taking a long hot shower, Fred. The bugs of fear and loathing and self-pity are all over me. That woman's Typhoid Mary. I've never met anything like it."

"I'll come up with you."

Molly put a hand on his arm. "Fred, I'm sorry. Do you mind? Use the downstairs couch tonight? I can't stand being in the same bed with anyone. I'm crawling all over."

"I can sleep on your floor," Fred offered. "Do you mind if I take a look at Cover-Hoover's book?"

Molly smiled wanly. "Better sack out downstairs," she said. "My poor old dad, who went to the red-eye Mass every morning of his life, at six-thirty, before he came back to the house to give us breakfast."

"It's always who you least expect," Fred said. "That's one of the rules of fiction."

18

Fred woke at five, walked through the village of Arlington, and breakfasted at Dunkin' Donuts. After looking through *Power of Darkness,* he was bemused and interested at the situation Molly had gotten herself into. She had walked into a trap baited with the most persuasive pheromone known to the human spirit: Eau de Soupçon.

The premise of the book was reassuringly simple, arguing from effect to cause and starting from a series of symptoms of malaise like what Molly had described. Add to that the following guidelines: If you *think* you might have been abused, you were; and failing to recall it likely proves it, because that's exactly what *they* want.

Ophelia was a fool playing games with such a subject. You can get the person out of the woods, but you can't get the woods out of the person. The fear that's in each of us will be believed under any of a million names, because the fear itself, the prime evidence, is always real.

The worst of it was not the theoretical basis of the argument, or its scientific trappings; the worst part was the implications the sad stories of abuse, so proudly presented, had for the lives, the families, and the identities of the self-proclaimed victims. The role of victim must for some become a full-time occupation. Cover-Hoover, if her pioneering theory was to be proved, must be able to point to a stable of willing guinea pigs who would announce themselves as "broken" individuals now (and forever) in the healing process.

It was unpleasant and sad, Molly said, and *very* soft science, like that book *The Bell Curve*, big a couple years back, which while pretending to measure intelligence quotients was nothing more than a long way of complaining that black people had failed to remain at home in Africa. "Do not send to know for whom the bell curves," Molly had remarked at the time, tossing the book onto the floor. "It curves for thee."

Fred had little company at Dunkin' Donuts: two solid Greek girls behind the counter, a sweating male who was probably the father of one of them cooking in back, and two men, like himself, drinking coffee. Fred bought a dozen donuts and more coffee and took it all back to Molly's. Terry preferred donuts that squirted, and Sam liked chocolate on chocolate. Molly claimed no interest in donuts and would eat whatever the kids left. Fred made the kids drink milk to offset the sugar.

"Sorry about last night," Molly said after the kids had left for school, as she was putting herself together. "The woman put me in a tailspin."

"How did you leave things with her?"

"I honestly don't know." Fred leaned to kiss her good-bye and she jerked away like a girl with brand-new breasts starting. "Sorry, Fred," she said. "It's just . . . well, sorry, I guess, is all I know."

"OK," Fred said. "I'll clean up here. I'm waiting to go into town until after I talk with this detective, Bookrajian, since Dee says I should." He saw Molly out the kitchen door into the garage, heard the garage door heave open and close again, and Molly's Colt putter away into a cold gray morning.

"You left a message I should call?" Bookrajian said when he called back at ten. Fred by this time was pacing Molly's kitchen, cursing himself for putting himself in hock to a telephone. He wanted to pick up the matter of Manny. Every departing minute threatened to take the head end of the Copley portrait farther into the distance.

"Yes. I did business with Oona Imry, and I understand from Dee Glaspie, who writes parking tickets for the city . . ."

Bookrajian interrupted, "Go on."

Fred said, "I understood you people were satisfied the death was an accident. The nephew said you were ready to release the body."

"Are you kidding?" Bookrajian's amazed bluster caused Fred to hold the receiver away from his ear. "Oh, the nephew. That fucking snake son of a bitch? You a friend of his?"

"Not really."

"You want to come in and talk?" Bookrajian asked.

Fred told him, "My dance card's pretty full today, unless it's urgent."

"We're gonna nail the little fuck," Bookrajian said. "And you can tell him I said so."

"To be frank, I was surprised you were happy with the accident theory," Fred said.

"Are you kidding?" Bookrajian said again. "That turkey won't even tell us where he was that night between eight and midnight—which is when we finally got through to him on the old lady's phone. If you're a friend of his, tell him how that looks to some of the dumb, crass, plain old born-American assholes working my department," Bookrajian said.

"I'll let him know."

"Anything else I can help you with, sport?"

"That'll do it. Thanks," Fred said.

"No problem."

When Fred called the Carlyle Clay was out, leaving no message. If Clay were willing to enter the twentieth century, Fred would have had a machine on his desk to take messages. But Clay was convinced such a convenience would "let them know what we are doing." Fred drove into Cambridge shortly after noon and was just in time to spot Manny leaving Kwik-Frame, and to follow him down Massachusetts Avenue toward Harvard Square. Manny crossed Linnaean Street and took himself into a Mexican restaurant, where he ordered at the counter and then sat at a tippy Mexican revival table to wait for his refried or otherwise reconstituted lunch. Fred ordered iced tea, carried it to Manny's table, and sat across from him.

Manny looked up. He'd been studying the inlaid chips of colored ceramic making a semi-Olmec style design on the tabletop.

"Do you mind?" Manny said belligerently.

"Business," Fred said. The man behind the counter called out, "Twenty-three."

"Table's taken," Manny announced, getting up. He strode the seven strides to the counter and returned with a loaded tray from which fat steam rose, wafting an afterthought of bean. Manny stood, holding his tray, staring belligerence. He himself smelled strongly of something intended to keep a person from smelling like sweat when aroused.

Fred said, "I noticed you work at Kwik-Frame and I want to ask about a picture you framed."

"I'm on my lunch break." Manny tucked into his tortillas, fajitas, burritos, enchiladas, or whatever they were, with meat.

"Please go ahead," Fred said.

Manny stared at him, his eyes gobbling.

"A painting of a squirrel," Fred continued. "The person said you did the framing. Of the squirrel."

Manny swallowed. He took a drink of orange soda, using a

straw. He sucked a long time, watching Fred. He picked up something brown, took a bite from it, and chewed. "The person? What person?" Manny asked.

"Person I got it from," Fred said. "You recall doing the squirrel? Old picture on canvas. A lot of extra canvas bent around back."

Manny swallowed. He took a bite of something else that started brown but oozed green in protest when he put pressure on it. "We do a lot of squirrels," he said. "Cats. Other animals. Mostly cats. The people go for cats."

The storefront was loud with customers giving their orders, the cooks slamming dishes, and people making conversation over hasty lunch. Fred drank from his tea.

"Why do you care?" Manny asked.

"It could be worth money to the person who helps me find the owner of that picture."

"You say you are the owner?"

"The one you framed it for," Fred said. "Maybe they have the other part. The picture of the squirrel was cut from something bigger."

Manny said, "I can't help you. But if I could, how would I find you?"

"I come by all the time."

"You have an idea what the information is worth?" Manny asked. "Or what you're looking for if the other part of this canvas should come in, or if I hear about it?" Manny ate a piece of lemon. He was dressed for cold weather, wearing a deep-blue down jacket, open, over the yellow Mickey Mouse T-shirt he was working in today. "I don't like you following me here," he said.

"Ten thousand dollars," Fred offered. "If it's in reasonable condition. My guess is a guy at a table, dressed like George Washington, you know? He could even be wearing a wig."

"I'll ask the other person in the store," Manny said, through a large amount of something that had become tan. "You stop in sometime when I'm working, maybe I'll know something. Unless you want to give me a number, or like that."

"I move around so much," Fred said. "Out of state half the time. You'd go crazy trying to reach me. I'll stop over when I'm in the area."

Fred finished his tea and stood. Manny had a long way to go to clear his tray. The only way to maintain show-muscle like that was by wasting enormous amounts of energy.

Manny looked up and swallowed painfully. "That's a lot of money," he said.

Fred shrugged. "Maybe in your business," he said. "Not in mine."

Fred drove into town along Charles Street, past Oona's closed shop, and parked next to Clay's car off Mountjoy.

When Clay telephoned at three, Fred was taking counsel with himself over the question of how, and how soon, to stop by Kwik-Frame again. The prospect of ten thousand unexpected dollars had settled firmly into Manny's head by now, and he'd be worrying how to maneuver his knowledge of Fred's quest into the best possible position for himself. When Fred assured Clayton that it was indeed himself at this end of the line, Clay said, "Concerning the research you are engaged in—your project, I fully acknowledge—but as long as I had the opportunity, I have been looking into the matter of the Copley fragment . . ."

Fred interrupted, "That's fragments now. Plural."

A stunned pause on Clay's end. "Excellent, Fred. You made that woman sell us the rest of it? What does it look like?"

"It's not that simple," Fred confessed. "Unfortunately. This will take some time. First you should know that Oona Imry is dead."

It required twenty minutes to fill Clay in. Clay understood immediately that what he owned now was a grotesque. His passionate responsibility to the pure cause of art would prevent him from keeping the fragments separate and enjoying the expurgated details. He would, in due course, be obliged to have the two parts joined, and should they be unable to find the last part, no one would hang and enjoy the headless man with a squirrel. Its missing element would intrude too much. It could be seen only as an illustration.

"At any rate, Fred," Clay continued, "as a matter of interest you might want to take these down as being of possible relevance—American portraits we know Copley executed but which are lost or thought to have been destroyed."

Fred jotted down the information as Clayton reeled it off.

"There's Thomas Ainslie—too early to be ours, painted in 1757, but I might as well mention it. Then Benjamin Andrews of 1773. The wife was done in a companion piece, also unlocated. We know of them from Andrews's own letter to Henry Pelham, who was supposed to paint alterations in some of the landscape detail."

"Pelham the half-brother and apprentice," Fred said. "Maybe Pelham hocked them and . . . never mind."

"The three-quarter-length portrait of Governor Francis Bernard which du Simetière saw hanging in Harvard Hall in 1767—that is missing. Wilkes Barber, of 1770, is not located. But that was a boy of four. A Mr. Barron was painted in New York in 1771, but I doubt ours is a New York portrait because there is no reason for it to have migrated north. But the thing to note in this case is that we know the size, fifty by forty inches, a standard size for Copley. Those must be the dimensions my painting had prior to the assault.

"But here, Fred, you might want to think about these three paintings said to have been destroyed in the Boston fire of 1872, by which time they belonged to a Peter Wainwright: Dr. John Clarke seated at a table and wearing a white wig; his wife, née Elizabeth Breame; and their son William."

"Clarke," Fred said. "That's the family Copley married into, isn't it? Wasn't his wife Susanna Clarke?"

"Same name but different family," Clay said.

19

Clay careened down his list. Fred noted only the known portraits, acknowledged to be unlocated, that had any likelihood of corresponding to what they had: adult, male, originally fifty by forty inches, and painted in the Boston area reasonably close in time to the paintings containing the squirrel motif Copley was using in the Pelham and Atkinson portraits of 1765.

Captain Tristram Dalton of Marblehead, painted in 1767, was gone, missing (along with Mrs. D). Fred liked Dalton, and starred him. James Flucker he dismissed as too small, too late. Maybe Peter Oliver. He noted a missing John Hancock whose size and date were not recorded; a Benjamin Greene (no date) also destroyed in the 1872 fire.

"Never mind John Lane," Clay said. "The evidence is conclusive that the Brooklyn Museum Copley called *Gentleman with a Cane* is in fact John Lane; hence Lane is not unaccounted for. Like many others who seem to have fallen from the face of the earth, he simply went to Brooklyn."

Eliminating a string of missing New York portraits, Fred made note of Miles Sherbrooke (no date but the right size); G. W. Schilling (right date but the painting was last heard of in Utrecht, in 1769); James Scott (1766); Peter Traille; Joseph Webb; Joshua Wentworth (probably too late, since it first entered the record in 1774).

"I have to tell you," Clayton concluded, "that of all these the one I favor is Captain Dalton. You will use your own judgment, Fred, but if I were to make a suggestion I would recommend looking for Dalton's trail in Marblehead. Being a captain he would have social standing and may be in the record, with his heirs."

"I had him starred too," Fred said. "But being a captain he might also have been British or Tory, and left town."

"Drat the Revolution," Clay said. "It is regrettable about that woman. Please, if you can do so without attracting attention to our interest, present flowers in an appropriate manner to her family. She does have family?" Clay had followed some turn of reasoning from the Revolution back to Oona Imry.

"Are you familiar with a young Hungarian pianist named Marek Hricsó?" Fred asked. "He is her nephew."

"I have heard him play," Clay said. "The man is a genius with his hands. By all means, give him flowers."

"An eccentric individual," Fred said. "Would you agree?"

"The word I prefer is 'genius,' " Clay said. "It is true he will not play in public."

"But you have heard him."

"By invitation. I am not the public."

When Manny left Kwik-Frame, Fred fell in behind him, wearing the Irish hod-carrier's cap Molly had given him, and, to complete the disguise, his red plaid jacket. The framer had changed to his bodyguard outfit of tweed jacket, white shirt, and tie. Fred was prepared for another dodging sequence on the subway. Manny, however, ignored the entrance to the T at Porter and stayed on the far side of Massachusetts Avenue. Fred followed a generous block behind as the man made his way toward Harvard Square, passing the site of his Mexican lunch without giving it a glance.

It was cold for March, dark for March, and wet for March—in fact, typical March. Traffic was heavy and slow. Manny marched toward the center of Harvard's metastasizing sprawl and hooked right along the edge of the Common (UNDER THIS TREE GEORGE WASHINGTON . . .), jumped a fence, cut through a soccer game being played by eight-year-old girls, and pushed across Garden Street at Appian Way, skirting Radcliffe admissions buildings and the grad school of education.

"Left on Brattle," Fred muttered. "And take me to your leader."

Manny moving through pedestrian traffic made Fred think of a cow grazing—steady and relentless, though a good deal faster. He made his way past the small shops and the office buildings, until he found a doorway next to Nini's Corner and strutted into it. It must be the building Molly had visited yesterday, where Cover-Hoover had her office suite. Fred hung a block back and watched. After ten minutes Manny came out again in the close company of Eunice Cover-Hoover.

The doctor was tall, graceful, and elegant. From the newspaper photograph, and after Molly's description, there was no mistaking her. She wore a long black coat that gave a capelike impression. Anjelica Huston trying to pass for Tonya Harding, Molly had said. Or had Fred said it to Molly? Manny looked up and down the street with exaggerated caution before he gave Cover-Hoover a nod and the two turned left. They did not speak to each other. Cover-Hoover moved along the sidewalk like a lady traveling with a bodyguard from a rental agency which should be preparing to receive a nasty note from the customer. Manny fawned like a beaten dog who smells bacon on his master's hands.

Fred stayed behind them. He had hoped Manny would lead him to the remaining portion of the Copley, but this detour would also have some value, giving him something to contribute to Molly's research. They took the first cab in rank in front of the Harvard Coop, across from Harvard Yard.

"I'm interested where that pair is going," Fred told his driver. "If you don't mind keeping a couple cars behind them."

The driver nodded an angular gray face leading up to yellow hair in a single braid she had looped over her right shoulder. She was in her middle thirties and drove like a stock-car racer in traffic. She did not take her eyes off the road ahead, or off the cab Fred wanted followed, as they moved into the stream and went with it around the elbow at whose crook sat the Charles Hotel; then down to Memorial Drive and left at the river. Without looking back the driver said, "You got any idea where they are going, in case we lose them at a light?"

"Not a clue," Fred said, leaning back.

"I've seen the woman around," the driver said. "She stands out."

"She does," Fred said. "You know her?"

His driver shrugged. "I don't. But that woman looks like *she* knows who she is." She followed her colleague's left turn at a garden shop.

"Now's where you make the choice," she said. "Which is more important in your book, staying with them or not being seen?"

"I want to know their destination."

There was no one else much on the series of side streets they took, wangling their way toward Putnam Avenue, where they turned left. Manny and Cover-Hoover, sitting in the backseat, were talking together, their heads in profile, Manny on the right, Cover-Hoover on the left, looking like lovers quarreling.

Fred's driver dawdled, allowing a few cars to fall in back of the one Fred wanted followed, to give them a screen. She turned onto Putnam, shaking her head.

"He doesn't, or they don't, know what they're doing," she said. "You'd get here faster turning left on Mount Auburn, from where we started."

Fred agreed. "I'd say he was trying to lose us, except . . ."

"He hasn't checked his mirror once," the driver said.

At Putnam Circle the Cover-Hoover cab turned left and into Harvard Square again.

"If he's running up his meter he's picked a strange time and place and way to do it," Fred's driver said.

They saw their object hesitate across the barricade that interposed between them and their starting place. Only a kiosk selling newspapers and the entrance to the Harvard T station prevented them from coming full circle.

"He'll turn left here," Fred's driver said, herself moving into the left lane before the driver of the lead taxi made the same decision and turned left on Dunster.

"Doesn't know where he's going," Fred's driver said. "Great, now we're on our way back to Putnam."

The lead taxi had turned left, which was all it could do since Mount Auburn was one way. At Hay Street they turned right. The meter ticked to seven-fifty. "Back to Mem. Drive," Fred's driver said. "I guess you could say that figures."

The lead taxi slowed. Fred said, "Stop here. It's been a pleasure."

He slid a ten over the driver's shoulder and got out quickly, moving into the shadow of a dormitory building and watching his taxi swing around the one where Cover-Hoover sat still in the backseat while Manny got out and climbed the steps to the porch of a small three-story house.

Manny stood on the stoop and poked with his finger at the buzzer. Cover-Hoover sat in her cab's backseat. Fred stood in his cover. Manny shook his head and came down to the sidewalk as Cover-Hoover leaned across the seat and rolled down her window. There was conversation between them. Manny climbed the stairs and tried the buzzer again, then the next one down, and then the next. The person they wanted was on the top floor, therefore. Manny waited until the door was opened, and it was clear from Manny's distant dumb-show that the question being asked was, "Do you know where he or she on the top floor is?" The door was answering, "Search me," to which Manny replied, "Then can you tell me when he or she will return?" The door's impatient answer: "Honey, I just live here. This is not my problem."

Manny, as the door closed, went back to the taxi, and after talking through the window he opened the door and climbed in. The taxi drove away, down to Memorial Drive, where it turned right. Turn right again on J.F.K. and go three blocks, you'd be at the Harvard Cooperative Society again. That'll be seventeen-seventy, ma'am.

Fred, after a suitable pause, ambled to the house Manny had blessed with his unsuccessful attentions. The top bell or buzzer he had first tried was labeled BLAKE. A woman, then, keeping her first name to herself.

Fred went back to his cover and waited for two hours. Students moved in and out of the building in whose protection he was standing. No one took notice of him. At nine-thirty a slim woman in her late twenties walked past, glancing toward him briefly. She wore a heavy tan duffel coat and a gay hat imported from an exotic land compelling free labor from its prisoners. She climbed the stairs to the building's entrance, used her key in the lock, and went in.

"Blake," Fred said. "Unless it's the one on the second floor."

He gave it five minutes before he pushed the top button. She clattered down the stairs. He could see, through the door's glass, that the woman Blake had taken off her hat and coat. She had long black hair to the shoulders, and a nice face—round, and still bright pink from her cold walk. She was wearing a blue denim dress, black stockings, and black sneakers. She opened the door and raised her eyebrows.

"I want to ask you about the power of darkness," Fred said.

The woman shrieked a thin whistle, turned sea gray, and fell.

20

Fred caught the woman's head and shoulders before she hit the ground. Keeping down, he moved around her into the hallway and closed the street door, checking the pulse in her neck. His experience, in memory, was warning him of snipers. Her pulse was strong. There was no blood. She only seemed dead. The lady had merely experienced a sudden, irresistible urge to depend upon the kindness of a stranger. She was breathing in a shallow, distant way.

I sure look like a rapist-murderer, Fred thought, standing and scratching his head. The sound of her shriek going down was still loud in his ears, but it had not raised the interest of tenants on the first or second floors. He held the woman's left hand—a narrow and bony one, sea gray as the rest of her—and watched her eyelids flutter open, and then stare and roll. "It's all right," Fred told her, "I'm just a guy."

Strands of pink came into her cheeks as if she had been slapped. "Don't mark me," she pleaded.

"OK," Fred told her.

The woman eased into the world, shaking her head from side to side. She let her eyes come into focus on Fred's. She made an apparent effort—a stage effort Fred would have said—to pull her left wrist out of Fred's grip. "Victim of Satan, child of God," she whispered, barely moving her lips. Fred had to squat down to hear her. Her breath smelled burned. "Say it," she commanded in a tense whisper.

"You want me to put your hand down?" Fred asked.

"Say it, unless you mean to have me here." *Have* meaning both *possess* and *hump*.

Fred said, "If it will relieve your mind. Victim of Satan, child of God."

The woman sighed and let her eyes close. Her hand relaxed. Fred put it down. Anyone stumbling onto this scene would take her immediately for his victim.

"Take me upstairs," Fred's victim said.

The hall floor she lay on was dull green linoleum; the walls plaster, papered before the paper was painted off-beige. The door to the downstairs apartment was closed.

"You want me to carry you?" Fred asked.

"I can't move."

"I'll help you stand. You'll be all right. You only fainted."

The woman glared. "I am paralyzed," she said. "For an hour I will not move. It is how he takes me. I am in his grasp." The woman's black hair, spilled around her face on the floor, accentuated the pallor of her face. "I'm cold. There's wind. There's wind. Carry me upstairs."

Fred put his arms under her, shoulders and thighs, and lifted her slack weight. She had not lost control of her sphincters (thereby preserving an aspect of her beauty even in a state of unconsciousness); but she was serious about exhibiting loss of control of her voluntary locomotive muscles. There was not a helpful or compensating twitch anywhere. Even her head sagged back. He'd carried dead men who were more cooperative.

"If you want I'll call an ambulance, or rescue."

135

"Upstairs," the woman gasped through her stretched neck. Fred shifted his right arm to give her head better support. "Third floor."

Fred took her up. The stairs creaked and smelled of disinfectant. They were inlaid with the same green linoleum, and edged with twanging metal. The apartment door on the second floor was closed. Fred's burden had left her third-floor door ajar when she came down to meet him. Fred edged inside, leading with her head, leaving the door to the hallway open.

The room was furnished with an odd assortment of old furniture worthy of being called furniture, as well as gleanings from the sidewalk. A couch looking as if it would open into a double bed, and covered with heroic Herculon in double plaid, took the woman's body after he kneed books off it—paperbacks of a pink Romance persuasion.

"My name is Fred," Fred told her. He took a red blanket from the floor and spread it over her. She lay completely still. One end of the room gave access to a kitchenette with a table in it, and one chair, off which seemed to be a bathroom. A closed door would give entry to her bedroom, then. This room was heaped with rugs, both stretched and rolled; a desk; Victorian rosewood chairs and a love seat; a file cabinet with her coat thrown over it; and a set of gilded side chairs, four of them, next to each other along one wall under a badly foxed print of Napoleon at Waterloo. It was as grim a place as Fred had been in for some time—like a garage sale postponed indefinitely on account of rain, or war, or both.

"My name is Fred," Fred repeated. He discarded the idea of using one of the gilt chairs, which he'd likely shatter, and went to the kitchen instead for the one at the table there, which he brought back and sat in, at the head end of the apartment's occupant.

"Sandy," she said.

"Sandy Blake?" She nodded.

"Sandy, you took a dive when I mentioned the Satan business."

136

"They won't let go of me. I'm afraid. They will kill me. He will kill me. He will win. I can't get free."

Fred said, "I'm taking off my coat and hat." He tossed them onto the file cabinet, to join Sandy's duffel coat. It was hot in the apartment. He asked, "Do you want me to call someone for you?"

"I don't have a phone. They use it to find you."

Sandy Blake felt about telephones as Clayton Reed did about answering machines. "It is Satanists you are afraid of?" Fred asked.

Sandy struggled to shudder. Fred scratched his face, worried. The woman in front of him was in trouble and needed help and/or a good kick.

"What do they have against you?" Fred asked.

"Because I left them," Sandy said. "She put me on the road of loving-caring. And I ran away. No one knows where I am."

Fred volunteered, "I saw a jar of instant coffee in your kitchen. You mind if I make us some?"

He went into the kitchen and got busy. The place smelled derelict and damp, almost unused. He puttered angrily, rinsing out a couple of mugs and checking the staleness of the milk in the fridge in case she wanted some. If she did she was out of luck.

Fred heard a gasp and turned to see Sandy standing in the kitchen doorway. She had forty minutes left of her promised hour of paralysis. "What are you doing in my apartment?" Sandy Blake demanded. "Who are you? How did you get in? Get out. I'm cold."

Fred told her, "I carried you upstairs."

"Out of my apartment," Sandy Blake said fiercely.

"You got it," Fred said. He turned off the gas and moved toward her. She swayed in the doorway so that he had to push past her. Blundering in a disoriented fashion, failing to notice the door he'd left open into the hallway, he opened the other door into a bedroom filled with rancid clothing festooned over boxes, trunks, and heaped furniture and silver. The bed was isolated, single, narrow, and empty as a nun's. Otherwise the room was full of things, giving an impression of captured wealth hoarded by barbarians who could think of no way to use it, or which way up it went.

"If you must take me, do not mark me," Sandy Blake said behind him. She stood in the room's doorway giving a good imitation of a sleepwalker who has got herself into a corner.

"I don't take people," Fred said.

"He takes me in the air," Sandy Blake said, speaking in a little voice, almost in baby talk. "He spits me like a little bird and flies with me. I am ruined. I am ruined."

Fred said, "Sandy, none of this convinces me. I don't buy it. You're working too hard."

"Tell me how you found me," Sandy Blake demanded. She pushed past him into her bedroom. There was a narrow passage between chests and upended escritoires, all festering with clothing that seemed to cling to life in symbiotic relation with the junked wealth. She sat on her bed facing him, her knees together, her denim dress in order, looking like Saint Theresa, the Little Flower, arriving early for a scheduled vision.

Fred said, "You know a man named Manny?"

Sandy Blake trembled and bit the ends of her fingers. "No," she said. "Her and Manny. I figured it out. They're fucking."

Fred said, "Tell me about Cover-Hoover's operation."

"You are Satan coming to take me again," Sandy said. She used a new voice, a rich one, full and operatic. "Because I left the loving-caring."

"That's horse shit. Satan never took you anywhere. It's none of my business, but get a life."

Sandy Blake stood, angry. "I will show you his mark," she threatened.

"That's OK," Fred said. He had moved somewhat toward her, following her into the room, attracted as to an accident victim it is equally dangerous to help as to abandon by the road.

"You raped me," Sandy Blake said.

The woman was pure trouble, the loosest of loose cannons. He'd seen as much as he wanted, and turned to go.

"I'll tell them how you raped me," Sandy Blake warned, behind him. He heard what sounded like a woman's clothes being removed or disarranged. But he stood fixed in his own paralysis, transfixed by what met him when he turned. It was the head: the head he wanted. He stared. It was pinned to the wall next to the door—a loose oblong of canvas with a raw lower edge.

Back of him was the sound a woman's denim dress makes crawling angrily over her head. He stared at the last portion of the Copley. It could not be by anyone else's hand; the head and shoulders of a young man of great beauty, in three-quarter view. No wig. No window.

"You raped me," Sandy screamed behind him. Fred swiveled. She was down to her skin, hissing, standing, balling her fists, shaking the long dark lashes of her hair from side to side as if they could work on him like serpents. She came at him, screaming and clawing at her full breasts and her cheeks.

"It wasn't a moment I could tarry and ask, 'Do you want to give me a price on what's left of that painting?' " Fred told Molly.

"What did you do?"

"Picked up my hod-carrier's hat and my coat and hit the stairs," Fred said. "We like to keep a low profile, Clayton and I, which was starting to seem hard. So I know now where the rest of the painting is, and I'd rather walk blindfold into a pit of wolves than go into that place again; though I'll go back in a minute if I can figure a way to do it. That's an important picture. We're right about the date. But it's the sitter! The sitter is a young black man. There's nothing like it in the early Copley."

Fred had walked back to Porter Square for his car, called Molly on the way, and learned he was not expected and he might as well pick up something to eat on the way home if he was hungry. He'd grabbed a sub and was eating it now, with a carrot from Molly's fridge, while sitting with her at the kitchen table. The kids were already upstairs.

"So that's my day," Fred concluded. "I made my offer to Cover-Hoover's henchperson; I followed him and his boss to the house of my new friend, or friends, Sandy Blake, who's more fun than a snake in heat; I found the remainder of a painting Clayton would rather have than be appointed Baron of Beacon Hill, and I doubt I'll get near it again; I learned the Cambridge cops think Oona's nephew killed the lady; and I have eaten the left half of an excellent meatball sub, which you would qualify as a contradiction in terms. Tell me about your day."

Molly, sitting across from him, was wearing her red terry-cloth wrapper, and her brown curls were wet, which rendered them almost black. She'd been in the shower when he returned.

"I read the rest of Cover-Hoover's book," Molly said. "The book is full of platitudes couched in go-go phraseology designed to impress today's nonreading public. It begs the central question whether Satan is real, because it's devil *worship* that's the crime, and the crime depends not on the devil but on the worshipers."

Fred said, "So many blasted, blighted middle-class lives."

"It's the blasted and blighted families I notice," Molly said. "It's wicked. The whole thing.

"The problem is," she continued, wrapping her hair in a towel she'd been carrying with her, "since yesterday, talking to that woman, I feel absurdly filthy, infected outward from the inside. It won't wash off. It's amazing you found the painting. The Blake woman's a patient, I suppose—recovering."

She got up, unwrapped the towel, and dropped it on the floor.

"Not much of a recovery, is it?" She went for the stairs. "See you in the morning, OK?"

21

Fred, drinking coffee in Molly's kitchen next morning while the kids noodled over their Flix and Tweetos and Molly ate toast and eggs, telephoned Clay at the Carlyle at seven-thirty, when he would be up but not out.

"You took the whole list and Xeroxed it, didn't you?" Fred asked him. "All the names of the sitters for the American portraits from Prown's book?"

"There'd be no point committing such a list to memory. I am not preparing an invitation list for my niece's wedding."

Sam grabbed the Flix box from Terry, who had been studying its backside. "I'm not finished reading," Terry screamed.

"I'm not finished eating," Sam declared, winning.

Fred said into the phone, "Does the name Blake crop up anywhere?" Excitement fluttered at Clay's end. Hope is the thing with feathers. Suppose it squawks and shits, there's still something about the clap of its wings on an early morning that lifts the spirits.

"You found it," Clay said. "That is excellent."

"It will be a major problem to get hold of it," Fred said. "I'll describe the situation to you in due course. But yes, I found it. I've seen it. What the next step is I don't know, but . . ."

"Don't let it escape us, Fred. The elements must be remarried."

"I'm with you," Fred said. "Also the avalanche must be diverted."

"When you begin talking of avalanches, Fred, or other natural phenomena, I do not follow. No matter. I shall return to Boston. Do nothing before we confer. Expect me by the first convenient train."

"Meantime," Fred reminded him, "for the sake of argument, is there a Blake on your list?"

"I am searching as you catalog your avalanches. I wish you had said Oliver. Since we talked yesterday I began to consider the possibility of Peter Oliver. A Miss Ware of Cambridge, in 1892, was said to own a full-length portrait of that Chief Justice, which is not located—but no, he is in his scarlet judicial robes. It would not be our painting."

"Our man is African," Fred said. "Or African-American."

The hope at Clayton's end of the line screeched like a phoenix scenting camphor and sandalwood. "Amazing and unheard of," Clay whispered. "It is signed, then?"

"Can't say." Fred waved the children out, listening to Clay's distant pause of aghast dismay.

Clay ventured, sipping orange juice and Perrier at the Carlyle, "I am surprised at you. But perhaps there were reasons, Fred, why you did not examine the object closely enough to discover a signature?"

"We'll talk about it later," Fred said. "What Blake do you have?"

Molly went upstairs to dress. Fred poured more coffee into his mug.

"I am looking for Blake as a maiden name among the female sitters," Clay said, "endeavoring to be thorough. I shall occupy myself with that on the train. Meanwhile the only Blake in the record is an oil on copper, five by four inches, of Joseph Blake, painted between 1765 and 1767, which is last recorded as being owned by Winthrop Gardner Minot of Greenwich, Connecticut. I am not familiar with this member of the Minot family."

"Undoubtedly an impostor," Fred said.

"What was that?"

"It's the right date, anyway," Fred agreed. "Copley could have done a three-quarter-length portrait at the same time, except, well, we still want to factor in the wild card of the sitter's color. And as we both know, there's no reason an unlocated Copley portrait would not also be unknown—unrecorded."

"Don't make an offer on it until we discuss it in Boston," Clay said. "I must dress."

Fred drove into town, thinking. For today he would leave Manny to make the approach to Sandy Blake. He reasoned that the day before, Manny, attracted by the prospect of ten thousand dollars, had consulted with Cover-Hoover, the boss of his moonlighting operation, and told her whatever he told her; and the two of them had gone to collect the final fragment from Sandy Blake, who, as Molly had concluded, had to be a patient or former patient or aspiring acolyte of Cover-Hoover.

That was an awful lot of stuff in Sandy Blake's apartment, some of it looking like real value. Nothing Sandy Blake had said— it dawned on Fred, Oh, that was a multiple-personality disorder manifestation act I was witnessing, was it? Right there on Hay Street?—none of it could be relied on in any way.

His only firm conclusion of this morning was that he could not hope to accomplish anything by presenting himself again at Sandy Blake's door. If Manny failed him, could he send Clay, or perhaps Molly, to make an offer on the keystone of the violated portrait? If Oona were alive . . .

That was another element he should not allow to disappear from his field of vision. Sandy Blake had volunteered vague, ominous, gelatinous hints about death by violence, suggesting some

143

"them" or "him" meant to do her harm. Who wouldn't? The lady ought to select one personality and go with it.

Fred hadn't been in touch with Marek for a day or two. Finding a free meter not far from Oona's, he docked his car and dropped in quarters. There was no movement back of the glass door, and no response when Fred pressed the buzzer. Marek had taken down the homemade "Closed" sign, replacing it with Oona's usual one. Fred went to the nearest pay phone and called the store's number. It rang without being answered. The shop phone had an extension in Oona's upstairs apartment; if Marek was there he was not answering. On a hunch Fred called Information and got a residence number for Imry, Oona, on Charles Street. "Madeleine, I am almost dead with longing to hear your voice," Marek said, answering sleepily on the sixth ring.

Fred said, "It's Fred. I want to see you, Marek."

Marek looked bleary and tousled and hungover. He was wearing black jeans and a black sweater, and the gloves. "I cannot get warm," he said. "I am not nourished properly without poor Oona to cook for me. She will be desolate to see me suffering. Come in, Fred. You have found him?"

Fred entered the store. Marek locked the street door, wincing at the bell's habitual ching, and complaining, "It is off pitch."

"Why don't we go upstairs?" Fred suggested.

"Not in Oona's apartment," Marek said.

Oona's back room was definitely less crowded. "They will not let me burn her," Marek mourned. "Therefore her ghost is here. Why will your law not allow me to burn her?"

Fred sat in his usual chair. Marek paced in the small space allowed between the desk and the objects Oona had been keeping for special clients. He said, "They think you killed her. Who's Madeleine?"

"An old lady who is an Old Lady of Boston," Marek said, simpering. "I have learned the young women of America offer no variety. They are all the same, never surprising. On the other hand, those who are seasoned . . ."

Fred asked, "Where were you the night Oona was killed? With Madeleine? Playing for invited guests in her living room?"

"We refer to such a chamber as a salon," Marek corrected him. He limbered his fingers in their thin gloves.

"I cannot get warm," Marek complained. "Not Ravel nor Chopin can these fingers kiss this morning. If what you claim is true and the police believe I killed the pelican from whose very breast I have been fed—that prevents them interfering when you go to kill him for me. Who is the person, Fred Taylor?"

"I regret our laws do not permit us to kill this person if we find him," Fred said. "Also it is for the police to find this person. It is for us to do the things we do."

If Marek found all American women to be bland and unsurprising, maybe he'd appreciate an introduction to Sandy Blake. If the fellow were not himself such a wing nut ("genius," as Clay would put it), Fred would suggest Marek visit the Blake apartment, identify himself as Oona's partner or successor, and ask to buy the remaining piece of the puzzle.

What was the rest of the treasure she was using to air her underthings on? And how did she come to have it?

Fred had wanted to sit in front of Marek one more time in order to ask himself if there was any useful function he could execute. But Marek's priorities were too narrowly focused. "I have nothing to tell you," Fred told Marek. "Beyond, Good luck with your piano playing." He left Marek gaping, locking the street door behind Fred while reaching to silence the off-pitch insult to his ears.

Mountjoy Street was cold and wet and grim. Clayton would be back later in the day and Fred wanted to think, before he reported, about what he had seen tacked to the wall in Sandy Blake's bed-storeroom. First, on an impulse, he checked for the name Blake on Oona's Rolodex. Nothing. Kwik-Frame was not listed either.

Fred started looking through Clayton's Copley books. He would not try Manny until this afternoon.

Molly was not at the library when he called to see if she would have lunch with him.

He drove to Arlington to see if she'd left Cover-Hoover's book next to her bed. There was no sign of it. He wondered how much of his momentary preoccupation with Cover-Hoover was based on her presence on the outskirts of the portrait's head, and how much on the fact that she had managed to interpose her offices between himself and Molly Riley. Molly's distress, and her instinctive distrust of the doctor's self-appointed mission, had made Fred spend more time than he normally would have with Cover-Hoover's *Power of Darkness* the night before. She sounded like a guru adding class and definition to a fringe fad Fred wouldn't have thought worth worrying about: something that catered to people with enough wealth or prospects they didn't have to worry about the next meal; dogs without fleas who are going to damned well keep on scratching until they open a sore.

Since Molly had asked for it, Fred tried the bookstores in Harvard Square for copies of Cover-Hoover's first book, *Culture of Abuse.* It was out of print. None of the used-book stores had it either; and Widener Library's copy was withdrawn by an officer of the university and not due back on the shelf for six months.

Fred drove down Hay Street and checked Sandy Blake's windows. If he trusted her madness—it was too self-indulgent to be real—he might risk trying her door in the hope she would not recognize him. But he was not going to fool with that now. He watched her house for a while. What was it about the irrational that made it so attractive, and so infectious?

Fred stopped at the Cambridge Quilt Company ("Formerly Tumbleweed") in Harvard Square and picked out a yard of patterned cloth Terry might like. It was decorated with eccentric animals resembling goats or lizards. He had it with him in a bag when he went into Kwik-Frame at four-thirty. The discouraged red-haired woman in the ticking apron was not evident. Fred did not need the cloth in order to explain his presence. Manny walked toward him out of the work area.

"I was in the neighborhood," Fred said.

"I see you," Manny said. He glared. The muscles in arms and neck and jaw bulged and frisked around the smiling Mickey on the pink T-shirt.

"Ten grand worth of Mexican food is a big pile," Fred reminded him.

Manny crossed his arms, saying, "You want to tell me why she's worth that kind of money to you? You want to tell me who's willing to pay that kind of money to find her? You think I'm dumb enough to listen to this shit about a painting? You think I'm pissing crazy?" Manny bounced on the balls of his feet like someone who has seen and believed many films about martial arts. "I'm warning you. Leave her alone."

"Leave who alone? I want the rest of a picture I bought. I'm not looking for anybody. Good luck to you if you find her."

Manny started bulling toward Fred, using his overinflated chest as a battering ram. The man displayed the kind of bulk that is grown to match the fantasies of solitude. It was comic-book stuff.

"I'll stop back some time when you're not busy," Fred promised. "The offer of ten thousand is good, but it is not for a person. Your clients are your business. The offer is for a painting."

"This painting means fuck-all to me," Manny said. "I don't know squat about it. Don't come back. I'm warning you."

22

Fred met Molly as she was coming out of the library at five o'clock. "I have my car, Fred," she said. "Or did you want a ride?"

"I have wheels. Just wanted to say hello."

"Hello, then." Molly wore Sam's red coat with the hood down, so the cold drizzle beaded in her dark curls. Fred looked for the green of her eyes to reflect in the drops of water falling between himself and Molly.

"I have to meet with Clayton," Fred said. "I don't know when I'll get back."

"You can sleep in Charlestown," Molly said. Fred walked beside her to the parking lot next to the library, where their cars were parked across from each other. "If you're embarrassed or hurt sleeping downstairs." She opened her car door, which she would never lock, and got in.

"Why don't I sit with you a minute and visit?" Fred suggested.

"A minute. The kids expect me."

Fred folded his body into the front seat next to her. "If we're having a fight I wish you'd clue me in. I don't know where to start. I can sleep on your couch, or the couch in my office, or uproot whoever is squatting in my room in Charlestown, or under a bridge as far as that goes. I'd rather be in your bed."

Molly stared out the windshield at the traffic on Broadway, and at people maneuvering in and out of the grocery store on the opposite side of the street. "I'm willing to fight if you tell me what we're fighting about," Fred went on.

"There's no fight, Fred. You're posturing and I am being irrational. Put that aside a minute. Do you know Cover-Hoover's operation has been accepted by the attorney general of the Commonwealth of Massachusetts as a nonprofit foundation? Not only tax exempt, but capable of receiving charitable donations?"

"It figures," Fred said. "So they have a board and the rest of it? You've been looking into the corporation?"

"Cover-Hoover's the executive director, as well as president of the board. She draws a salary. That's in addition to whatever Holmes College pays. And the income from her books."

"Ah," Fred said. "Thus she affords her disinterested generosity toward her clients, who also provide her with salable stories?"

"The stated purpose of the foundation," Molly went on, "is to sponsor a halfway house for abused children who have become adults. It is called Adult-Rescue, Inc. She goes in for hyphens. There is no mention of devils or devil worship in the charter— which would have made it harder to get past the lawyers and IRS types, I don't care how snowed they might be by the trappings of good works. The charter sounds like clean, misguided social work."

A couple of elderly women in scarves and raincoats came out of the library into the parking lot, looked for a car, laughed at the mistake they were making in trying the wrong one, and finally selected one they could get into.

"A friend of mine, a good friend, whom I hadn't talked to in a couple of years, called me recently and told me he lost two kids in a scam like this one, out in San Francisco," Molly said. "Similar story but without the devils—the same theme, one generation turned against another, in a mess where you can't tell which is which between delusion and evidence and precious *feelings* that are symptoms offered in proof of forgotten crimes. We are all prone to gravity, Fred." She was not answering him, but enunciating a tangent that might apply if Fred was patient. "Aside from gravity the biggest threat to a human person is self-delusion. I don't care if she's paid for it or not, what that woman is doing is perverse, because it pretends to be conversation. But the proper function of conversation is, or should be, that each side of it continually makes a balance or correction for the native self-delusion existing in each of its participants. It's our job as humans. It's the contract we must assume between each other. If I feel something imaginary crawling up my cheek and you point to it and scream, 'Look out, a bug!' I'm going to believe it. I'm going to jump and smack my face."

"So what did I say?" Fred protested.

"Don't be such an asshole, Fred," Molly said. "I'm not talking about you. Listen a minute. I'm ashamed of myself. I've got this creepy undermining going on that started with Doctor Loving-Caring and Ophelia and found a willing playmate in my native scheme of self-delusion. I can't help it's there. I can't shake it.

"I'm preoccupied with the ridiculous notion that my poor old dad, after a night hauling and lifting crates and barrels in the warehouse in Watertown, used to come flying home and drag his daughter out to fuck with goats and kill babies at crossroads and the rest of it, all the seventeenth-century junk Cover-Hoover has been withdrawing from her clients' revived memories. I can't stop shuddering with fear and loathing at the idea."

The bare trees scratched against the wet darkness, on the far side of the library's lawn in front of the stores on Broadway. Molly said, "I can't stop asking myself, 'What does Ophelia know I don't?' Even if it's all made up?'

"I'm going to stop that woman. She was so convincing when she touched my stupid scar and jerked her finger back, saying 'It's hot.' I feel it myself now, two and three times a day. It's hot."

Fred said, "I will sleep on your couch until you feel like having a visitor in your bed again."

"The children are talking," Molly said.

"That's OK."

"They think one of us is a heel and they can't decide which."

"That's fair."

"They think you're going to leave, Fred."

"Not until we have a fight and one of us loses."

Clay invited Fred up to his living quarters. "The occasion of your discovery calls for strong drink," he said on the house phone. He'd been listening for Fred to come in. It was almost seven. Fred had not been upstairs for several months. He was basically aware of which paintings came down from Clayton's walls, and which were selected to replace them. The circulating exhibition in Clay's rooms was handled, under Clay's supervision, by the husband-and-wife team that came in twice a week to polish Clay's spotless quarters.

Clay met him at the top of the spiral staircase. He had removed his suit jacket and replaced it with the scarlet dressing gown that proclaimed him to be in an advanced state of leisure. "Congratulations, Fred," he said. "Have a glass of crème de menthe."

"Let me join you in spirit and accept a beer if you have one," Fred said. "Or ginger ale or soda water. Anything wet."

Clay disappeared into his kitchen. Fred looked around the living room. He'd never heard Clay's grand piano played. The portrait of Clay's wife, born Prudence Stillton, who had died so quickly and so tragically after their marriage, gazed out of her silver frame, which stood on the Kashmir shawl that draped the piano. The room was done in reserved Boston Antique: a style that falls between French and English, and between the eighteenth and the nineteenth centuries. From Fred's brief glimpse of the furniture and china vases and ormolu clocks beneath Sandy

Blake's underwear, she could have provided things to complement or match Clay's.

What stood out, and the only part of the setup Fred was kin to, were the paintings hanging on the stolid green walls of the large room. The current program included an early female human nude by Chase, looking like the young painter's homage to Velázquez's *Rokeby Venus*; a Géricault sketch of a madwoman; a huge late-seventeenth-century Dutch flower piece Fred and Clay had despaired of identifying further.

Clay's sideboard between the gold-draped floor-to-ceiling bow windows overlooking Mountjoy Street carried a silver tray with the cut-glass decanter of green liqueur and two snifters to rub it in. Clay had been waiting for Fred before himself indulging.

"It is Amstel," Clay said, entering with a filled glass mug in one hand and a silver bowl of crackers in the other. He poured a glass of sweet green and lifted it in a toast, then sat in an armchair near the window while pointing another chair out for Fred.

"Now," Clay said. "Tell me everything."

After fifteen minutes there was no further discussion as to their first priority. They must get hold of the missing fragment. "It is a shame you could not overpower her," Clay said. "A shame, I mean to imply, about the ethical imperative. It is eight o'clock. We'll go now. At least I can offer a new face, and a different approach."

Clay went upstairs and came down again, having changed back to his suit jacket, and carrying both a checkbook and six thousand dollars in cash. "It is all I have on hand," Clay said, putting on his coat. "I agree with you, Fred, the thing to do is to acquire the fragment now and make adjustments later as needed. We don't want to take unfair advantage, not indefinitely. Not if there is an alternative that's practicable."

Each drove his own car, Clay following Fred in his golden Lexus. They parked and conferred at the corner of Hay and Mount Auburn, and Fred pointed out the building where, if Fortune blinked, Sandy Blake was, unbeknownst to herself, preparing to sell Clayton the final installment on the Copley.

Clay said, hesitating before he advanced to the fray, "Will that young woman expect me to rape her also?"

"On that you're on your own."

"A person who can do such shocking violence to a painting," Clay said, holding back, "it gives one pause. However, as you say, the cause is just. My approach shall be straightforward." He patted the inside pocket of his jacket, where the cash rested.

Standing on the sidewalk they must have looked like anarchists discussing the final details in a plot to bomb or purchase or otherwise dispose of St. Paul's Church, which rose nearby in its brick Italian-Colonial way.

"If Miss Blake is not at home," Clay said, "I am thinking ahead, Fred. In that case would it be wisest for you simply to break in and—no, I suppose not."

The ethical imperative again.

Fred sat in his car and watched Clay approaching the stairs to the building's entrance. He looked elegant and out of place. Fred rolled down the front windows and drove down the block, keeping behind Clay. If Clayton was admitted, Fred wanted to hear when Sandy started screaming so he could pop in and give Clay the benefit of a corroborating witness. Clay climbed the stairs and pushed the buzzer, standing on the porch in his black cloth coat. The wind blew his wad of white hair around. If Sandy was expecting a visit from the Evil One, she might not be surprised to find Clayton Reed on the stoop.

The door opened. Clay talked to the opening. Fred saw him nod, then shake his head slightly. Clay raised his right hand behind him in the gesture he and Fred had agreed on, which acknowledged that it was Sandy Blake, and by herself, answering the door.

Clay went inside. Fred double-parked in front of the building. Sandy Blake's third-floor windows were lit, and the blinds drawn.

Fred recalled Molly's rueful observation in the car, earlier that evening, that sanity and culture are the continuing result of human disagreement expressed in conversation.

Cover-Hoover seduced her patients, if Molly was right, by guiding them in the direction they were already tilting, while at the same time propping them up, and so becoming a structural necessity. Fred had not realized how deeply Molly had been disturbed by her two hours with Eunice Cover-Hoover. Molly was normally a balanced, sane, and cynical observer; but she had predispositions of her own. Whatever old strands of grief, fear, love, hate, shame, anger, affection, jealousy, chagrin, pleasure, or longing existed in the elements of Molly's being that reflected her relation with her father—those had been tweaked and strummed. Ophelia was a fool to hand such an effective opening to Cover-Hoover. And Cover-Hoover was cruel, and maybe something still more common, to use it: carelessly stupid and self-important, as abetted by avarice.

Part of the setup of this caregiving was that it forced or tricked the patient into a child's posture of submission. Sandy Blake had been made not just submissive, but aggressively impotent. It is not invariably the organism's most practical defense to faint when threatened.

Clay had been inside about ten minutes. Fred could see clear down to the river. The body of water itself was dark, and reflected lights moving on the far side, from traffic between the water and Harvard Business School. The length of Clay's absence began to make him uneasy. Clay was in his own fashion a genius at negotiation. He came on as such a nitwit that a person's instinct was frequently to help him, or to take advantage. Whichever approach Clay's targets selected, often enough they found they'd assisted him in buying something they had not meant to sell—and for less than they wanted.

Wind blew straight through the windows of Fred's car. It was cold and wet and dark. He waited twenty minutes before Clay came out alone and put his head in at Fred's window.

Clay said, "She is an interesting woman, more coherent than you led me to expect. She owns a number of reasonably good

154

pieces, none of which I want. However, she is not familiar with the fragment of a painting you described to me. She never saw or heard of it."

Fred said, "You were able to look where I told you? In her bedroom?"

"And she was very well behaved," Clay went on. "You are sure we have the right apartment?"

"Third floor. Blake."

"It was the third floor, but that was not her name. It is Covet or Covert something—here, she gave me her card. Yes. Here it is. Cover-Hoover.

"Fred, from your expression I gather something is going on."

23

Fred beckoned Clay to sit in the passenger seat, and he rolled down the street toward the river until he reached a spot where he could pull in to the curb. Using the rearview mirror he kept his eye on the entrance to Sandy Blake's building.

Clay looked around the inside of his car, interested. "I would not have thought to find one of these still on the road," he said. He sniffed like a dog arriving on an unfamiliar vacant lot.

Fred said, "Something's going on all right. The painting was there yesterday."

"You allowed them to suspect our interest."

"I offered to buy the thing," Fred said. "Of course they know I'm interested. But it was to the framer, Manny, I made the offer. The fragment itself I saw here. Sandy Blake, though she was here yesterday, is not here now. Cover-Hoover also denies knowing the painting. I am going to make Cover-Hoover's acquaintance. Why don't you go back to Mountjoy Street and I'll call when I have something to tell you."

Clay said, "She seemed so different from the woman you described, in many ways—although you did say long black hair. She seemed, in my judgment, not so likely to be raped as to take the upper hand. She is a different person. Women often are."

Clay's observation put in mind a question Fred had meant to ask. "The pianist, Oona Imry's nephew, on the night she was killed, apparently was playing at the home of a patron, an older woman named Madeleine. There may be a close attachment. Do you have an idea who that would be?"

Clay, contemplating the river, answered, "Madeleine Ruppel is not wealthy enough to reward his cultivating. My guess is— Fred, the young man's fingers move like water. His interpretations may be somewhat dry, but that is the taste of this faithless age. The soul is affirmed but not exposed or tested. I suggest Madeleine Shoemacher. She would enjoy showing a prize like that on her arm, and I suspect her of possessing a strong goatish streak. I may be able to find out. Would that help our inquiry?"

"It is a loose end I wonder about. I'd like to know if he did not kill his aunt," Fred said.

"I will look into it. An element of your thinking is that if he did not, someone else did, whom we may encounter?"

"I'm going up to meet the healer," Fred said.

He let Clay drive away before he walked up the stairs to the front door and buzzed next to the empty space which yesterday had carried the cardboard tag with the name Blake. In forty-seven seconds, Eunice Cover-Hoover appeared in back of the door's glass. Her hair was pinned up. She was in jeans and a thin, pink, long-sleeved top looking like a T-shirt designed for a cool climate. When she opened the door to him she wafted a scent of forbidden luxury. Her face was lean, her skin stark white—whiter than Molly's description of her had prepared him for—and her breasts would win prizes if she cared to offer them in competition.

Eunice Cover-Hoover searched Fred's soul while he stood on the porch. She pursed her lips but reserved judgment. "Yes?" she admitted.

"I want to talk to you," Fred said.

"Yes?"

"About your work."

"Yes?"

"Why don't we go upstairs?" Fred said.

Cover-Hoover completed her judgment. "Come up." She led him up the stairs. "There was another man here not long ago," she said, between the second floor and the third.

"There was?" Fred asked.

She closed them into the apartment, and sat on the couch where yesterday Fred had deposited the helpless Sandy Blake. Fred went to the kitchen for the chair he favored for himself. He saw no signs of packing, or of a hurried departure, but the bedroom door was closed. The two mugs he'd intended making coffee in were on the table still, and the instant-coffee jar was open as he'd left it, with the spoon tilted in.

"Where is Sandy Blake?" Fred asked, bringing the chair back and sitting.

"Her slave name?" Cover-Hoover asked. "Interesting. My relationship with her is confidential. She is very much disturbed. She is in a fragile transitional phase. However, she is safe, and in good hands."

"I want to talk to her."

Cover-Hoover said, "The healing process has been interrupted, but it will continue if she is not disturbed. What is your interest?"

"I was here yesterday and saw a painting," Fred said.

"There is no painting," Cover-Hoover said. "The other gentleman also asked about it. With that I am not able to help you. There is no painting." She smiled and spread her arms, allowing her breasts to emphasize the finality of the denial. Her voice was soft, definite, and reassuring. Its cadences presupposed acquiescence.

Fred said, "I know, I've seen your photo in the paper. Your name is—wait a minute, I'll remember it—Cover-Hoover, the author of *Power of Darkness*. Is this one of the people who was offered up?"

What was this woman dressed for? Moving? Was she here to pack a bag for her patient? Cover-Hoover continued evenly, "I allowed you to come up for one reason. I want to make sure you hear me. I do not know what relationship you claim with my patient; but it is deleterious. Stay away from her."

Fred said, "Not to be rude, but we seem to have started off on the wrong foot."

"You are trespassing. I have nothing to add."

"I don't care where she is or how she is," Fred said. "I bought part of a painting I managed to trace here, and I saw another part here yesterday. Upset as she happened to be, I could not offer to buy it. If you can tell her . . ."

"Because I am a physician I can't help noticing that you have suffered, Cover-Hoover interrupted. She crossed her arms beneath her breasts, raising them slightly to observe him better. "You have suffered far more than what shows in the overt scars I see on your face."

Fred hadn't seen it coming, but he knew the routine: the quick shift, soft music, move to the tender vulnerable part if you can find it. Get them to accept your sympathy and you have them by the balls. Caress until the moment comes to squeeze.

"Scars?" Fred asked.

"On your cheek and chin."

"Not when I shaved this morning."

"I got nowhere with her," Fred told Molly. "I presume she's got my informant locked away somewhere, playing Go Fish with her other personalities. I don't exactly want to start following Cover-Hoover around town. I am not going to land that painting either by guile or by duress. They have it sequestered, like the patient. It's infuriating." He'd called to see if Molly and the kids were hungry for pizza. "I suppose she has a legal means to spirit a person away like that?" Fred added.

"Loving-caring rises above legal."

"I'll have another look at that railroad bridge. Then I'll come back to Arlington. I haven't seen much of the kids. Maybe there's a game I can watch with Sam."

"He's watching one now."

Fred had driven to Porter Square after his dead-end talk with Cover-Hoover, and was talking from a pay phone in the vestibule of the Star Market. "Just now, when you used that phrase loving-caring," Fred told Molly, "it brought an image to mind: a piece of fruit, maybe a pear, falls to the ground and starts rotting where it's bruised, making pheromones the caregivers can't miss. They crawl all over the thing: wasps and flies, all taking their little pieces while the structure of their host dissolves."

Molly said, "When you get in with the pizza—make it pepperoni and onion, will you? Terry can give me her onions. Take a look at the incorporation papers. I made you copies."

Fred sat with Sam in Molly's living room joining the basketball game in progress. Terry stood around for a while, trying to enjoy it, but she could not become immersed. She was already in her Red Sox pajamas. "Are you getting taller?" Fred asked. "Or are my eyes getting lower?" Fred had the couch. Sam lay on the rug not far away, but far enough to keep his independence.

"They just go back and forth," Terry complained. "In baseball at least you go somewhere."

"Shut up," Sam told her.

"Have a seat," Fred said.

"How come you're sleeping downstairs now, Fred?" Terry asked, sitting beside him.

"Shut up, Terry," Sam said, outraged at her directness.

"It's OK," Fred said. "You know how sometimes you like to go in your room and slam the door?" Terry denied it. "Your mom's the same way. Everyone is."

"That's how come Fred has another place," Sam said.

"You have children over there?" Terry asked.

"Shut up, Terry," Sam said.

160

"It's what you *said*," Terry protested.

"I said 'I bet,' " Sam answered. "I never said he *does*."

Fred said, "Can you two give me thirty seconds of your attention while the TV is on?"

"Wait for a time-out or a commercial," Sam advised. "Then you'll have a minute." They waited until the game was interrupted by commerce. "OK," Sam said.

Fred told them, "OK. I have no children. That's one. Two is I plan to live here unless your mom asks me not to."

"That was fifteen seconds," Sam said. "Not even quite. Let's watch the game."

Molly had gone to bed before the game finished, and Terry followed her. Sam saw the game through, staying up since it was Friday night. After he'd gone to bed, Fred sat at the kitchen table with a cup of coffee and read the incorporation papers pertaining to Adult-Rescue, Inc.

"Survivors," Fred grumbled, shaking his head. "Survivors, survivors. If everyone's a survivor how can anyone be singled out? How do we distinguish who's had real trouble? The most robust are always first at the trough of mercy, shoving the weak aside."

24

Saturday morning Fred should have been free, unless there was auction business pressing, but he was not; and in any case, Molly told him, she would not have lunch with him. "Errands to run and fish to fry," she said. "A woman's got to keep her mystery." She smiled and looked distressed.

They dawdled over coffee. At around ten o'clock Terry came down still wearing her pajamas. She sat and confronted a bowl of Choco-Flix.

Fred looked up from the paper. "It's interesting, your business and mine coming together from different angles. Cover-Hoover's foundation has three trustees," he remarked to Molly. "They all report the same address on Brattle Street."

"I saw that," Molly said. "They all used the same address as the office. Must be the corporate address. All three officers perform executive functions. Cover-Hoover directs, Boardman Templeton is treasurer, and the recording secretary is listed as Ann Clarke. Terry, I want you to have milk with those."

Terry was eating her Choco-Flix dry, one at a time. Fred poured a glass of milk for her. She made a face and drank it like medicine.

"Founded four years ago," Fred said. "Do they have to place their tax reports and other financial records in a publicly accessible place?"

"How come you don't have anything, Fred?" Terry asked. "It's like you don't live anywhere."

Molly said, "I'm finding out. The incorporation documents I got anticipate an initial deposit of ex thousand, and they are obliged by law to spend five percent of their capital value every year—which leaves them room to add to their capital out of earnings if they want, depending how much better they earn than five percent. They have to tell the Attorney General and the IRS what they are doing, and supposedly those guys represent us."

"Whatever you can learn," Fred said. "Maybe it helps me get a line on where the painting was, even if I can't find where the rest of it is. Terry, to answer your question: there's not really anything I need. No, wait. I'm wrong."

Terry's face brightened with interest.

"I need a baseball glove," Fred said. "If I had a glove I know right where I'd keep it. I'd hang it by the door into the garage, where your mom keeps the broom." Fred pointed and Terry had to turn to see the place. "What's more," Fred said, "my birthday is next week."

"It is?" Molly and Terry asked.

"Tuesday," Fred said. "March twenty-second."

"How old will you be?" Sam demanded, entering.

"I don't know," Fred said. "Old enough to vote. My parents were kind of forgetful on the year. But they did know the date, March twenty-second. We always had Chinese food to celebrate."

"Unusual in Iowa in those days," Molly noted.

"By then we'd moved to Illinois. Maradocia, Illinois. It was unusual there, too, Chinese food, you are going to say. Right. That's what made it a celebration."

Terry and Sam looked at each other secretively. Sam snatched the Choco-Flix box.

"I wish I had the heart to start figuring out the subject of that portrait," Fred said. "It's hard, given I may never see it again. What kind of game are those idiots playing?"

"What idiots?" Terry asked, offended.

"He's talking about the people he's working with; not you, idiot," Sam reassured her.

Molly reminded Fred as he was leaving that he was in line to spend the evening with Terry and Sam. "Ophelia's back," she said. "She and I have something to do tonight. Tomorrow, if you're free, she wants to introduce you to Byron Ponderosa."

"Byron Ponderosa?" Fred asked. "Oh, Jesus. The painter. He followed her back?"

"They're coming for Sunday tea, which may turn to supper. This is me giving you fair warning, in case you want to be busy elsewhere, such as on the far side of the moon."

At Mountjoy Street, Clay waited until Fred had a chance to settle in. Fred had allowed a backup of auction catalogs and journals, and hadn't examined this week's *Newtowne Bee*. It was almost eleven when Clay made his appearance, wearing a dark blue suit a cut above those favored by His Royal Majesty the Prince of Wales. Clay's shirt was as white and free of care as Eunice Cover-Hoover's skin. His necktie would inspire Cleopatra.

"You would have telephoned had there been progress," Clay assured himself.

Fred nodded. "Either we penetrate their security and locate Sandy Blake, or we figure out the game Cover-Hoover is playing with the help of the wide receiver Manny. Molly's checking the Cover-Hoover foundation, which is called Adult-Rescue, Inc. You've heard of it?"

Clay shook his head. "It may not be the sort of thing I hear of. But I enjoyed success. Last night I conferred with a dear friend who understands such things, and who makes a specialty of knowing the comings and goings in Boston's bedrooms. As I suspected, Marek Hricsó has been a recent fixture in Madeleine Shoemacher's. At his insistence she purchased a grand piano to replace her old one, and she invites a group in once a month to hear Marek Hricsó perform. She will buy him anything he wants. She will buy *him* if he is for sale."

Clay looked over Fred's shoulder at the photograph of a putative Constable landscape sketch being offered next week by a small auctioneer in West Newton. "The guy's got to try," Fred said. "People will come to look at it, and then buy a bureau, or a moose head for the den." He flipped a page.

"You are aware we may lose our advantage on the Copley," Clay said.

"We have no advantage to lose. Except the two-thirds you own, which at best can never be more than flawed—and we have to remember that only the first section was purchased. The second part was handed to me, and it's hard to decide whose it is, since we didn't pay for it as yet. But be that as it may, just to finish up—Marek was at Madeleine Shoemacher's the night Oona Imry met her match?" Fred asked. "You confirmed that specifically?"

Clay shook his head. "I will do it." He reset the white handkerchief in his breast pocket. "I do not know Madeleine Shoemacher well; but that can be my part of this project. The other part—the worship of Satan and so forth—I am uneasy, Fred, being a Unitarian, with issues touching on the next world, or the netherworld, or manifestations of the spirit. They seem an irrational excess."

Clay was a once-a-year presence in the congregation of Boston's Unitarian Chapel of George the Divine.

"Some of us non-Unitarians are with you on that, Clay."

"I have accepted Roberto's invitation to look at what we have collected so far. The other, I have decided, must wait while the two of us are engaged in the present brouhaha."

165

"The other?"

"The Vermeer," Clay said.

"Right. Let's by all means ease up on that. Let's not test the picture or anything rash."

"Very well, Fred, if that is your advice," Clay finished. "It is best we conserve energy and concentrate. You will keep me informed of developments concerning the last part of my Copley?"

Fred nodded toward Clay's departing back.

Clay said, "I would confer with you further but I promised lunch to Roberto Smith. Is there an establishment you recommend in New Bedford?"

"I know a Chinese place in back of the bus station where, last time I was there, you could order a side of gravy with your meal. They gave you bread, too—two slices of Bunny Bread. Most Chinese places are too cheap to . . ."

"Never mind," Clay said. "Roberto will know."

Clay went into the slow wind and rain.

Fred drove to Cambridge and watched Kwik-Frame until the discouraged woman with red hair returned and Manny left for lunch. He gave her a few minutes to get settled and put her apron on before he carried in his piece of cloth.

"Remembered it this time," Fred said, chuckling as he pulled it out. The animals on it were either pigs or monkeys. They were so stylized it was hard to be sure. Fred's portion was a yard square. He spread it across the desk.

"Do you have a style of frame in mind?" the discouraged woman asked. "Or you'd like me to suggest something?"

"Boardman Templeton?" Fred said.

"Gone to lunch."

"That's OK."

So Manny was short for Boardman Templeton, treasurer of Adult-Rescue, Inc. Interesting. Not, by this time, surprising.

"Can you suggest a molding you think might be good? It's going in a room that's mainly green and pink. Or maybe in the blue room." Terry might not like it after all.

166

The woman came out from behind the desk and led Fred to the section of wall where ready-made corners hung for show samples. "You want gold?"

"Something austere. A pink Nielsen? Does the name Ann Clarke ring a bell?"

The woman gave a start; a distinct ping. "Oh," she said, "Manny's mentioned my name."

Fred gestured toward a black wood corner resembling painted bamboo. "Or we could try an Eastern look, to be exotic," he suggested. "That would go with the animals, which are exotic. What do you think they are?"

"They're insects, not animals." Ann Clarke took the corner and led Fred back to the desk. The recording secretary of Adult-Rescue, Inc. showed Fred how his selection would look, criticized his choice, suggested two other possibilities, and finally took his order for the fake bamboo, working out what the punishment would be on the basis of the price per foot, the cost of Boardman Templeton's labor, and the outlay for four thirty-four-inch stretcher bars from Bob Slate Stationer. "You gotta leave room to overlap," she explained. "What we call a tacking edge. That's why it's going to be smaller than the cloth. You want reinforcing crossbars so it doesn't warp?"

"Sure," Fred said. "Oh, shit!" In a moment she was going to arrive at the place on the order where she would record the customer's name, address, telephone. Fred smacked his forehead and checked his Timex. "Gotta ram quarters in the meter. Be right back."

He rushed out.

Clarke is a name on Copley's list all right, Fred told himself, getting into his car. He drove some distance from Kwik-Frame over to the mall at Fresh Pond. He did not want Manny Templeton to see him back in the neighborhood this soon. He sat in his car and looked at the pay phone in front of Brooks Drugs.

I ought to call Detective Bookrajian, he thought, and tell him maybe Marek's covered for that night. But I can wait until

Clay gives me the all-clear. Maybe wait until I have the Copley, too.

He tried calling Dee Glaspie at home, but raised only Walter, who told him, "They've got Dee working the Saturday shift. She's on her beat now. I just ate chicken and chick peas with her. We had a late lunch." It was two-thirty. "It was an Indian place in Central Square and I understand she's working toward MIT on Mass. Ave., Green Street, Franklin—on the river side anyway. I left her a half-hour ago."

Fred cruised the streets between Central Square and MIT until he spotted Dee's small, energetic, and unmistakable body moving briskly in uniform along the main drag, near Metropolitan Storage. Fred double-parked and flagged her. At his invitation she sat in the passenger seat. "They let you register a car like this?" she asked.

"Insured and everything," Fred told her. "Listen, Dee, can you do me a favor? Get on that little box of yours that you check licenses and registrations on, and run some names for me. Can you do that?"

"You can have five minutes," Dee said. "I'm ahead of schedule. It doesn't matter anyway. Someone is getting to the meters with quarters before I can nab the violators. It's today's student prank, working out how I vary my route. I prefer it when they put the president's yacht on the dome of Hayden. We have quotas to meet."

Fred gave her the names Cover-Hoover, Boardman Templeton, and Ann Clarke. "I'm looking for home addresses," Fred said.

Dee fiddled with the gadget she carried on her hip. It looked like a small, state-of-the-art bomb. She said, "See? Hooks right in to the registry. Here's Fred Taylor. You still living on Chestnut Street in Charlestown?"

"Yes, Officer."

"You have an outstanding parking ticket dated January three of the present year?"

"Guilty."

Dee ran a complex sequence of seventeen buttons on her contraption, taking four seconds to do it. "You're all right now," she said.

"Thanks, Officer."

"That'll be five dollars. Just kidding."

Traffic slouched past them in the steady drizzle while Dee occupied herself. "Templeton and Cover-Hoover live together," she said. "La di da, on Brattle Street, no less, except no, a number this low has to be a top-floor apartment in the Square. No big deal."

Fred said, "They've used the address of Cover-Hoover's office."

"The lady has a car, a green Lance-Flamme two years old. She's doing well."

"Registered where?

"Oh, same address. No unpaid tickets. I could put some on her record if you want, so there's a notice out that if we find the car we can boot it. You want that?"

"It's tempting. Maybe I'll pass for now."

"What's the last one?"

"Ann Clarke. Clarke with an *e.*"

"Alexandra? No, here's Ann. Same address. Ménage à trois."

"Sandy," Fred said. Sandy, Alexandra. Blake was her slave name, Cover-Hoover had said, meaning she'd been married. "You saw an Alexandra Clarke?"

Dee caught the movement in his voice. "You want me to pick it up again? Yes, Alexandra Clarke. On Hay Street. At the same address there's Martin Clarke too—no, his license to drive was revoked or expired. There's still a car registered in his name, though, a Ford Temper, blue, seven years old. As long as he's not driving, maybe he'll trade for yours."

"Same address," Fred said. "Martin Clarke?"

"With an *e*, right?"

"Right."

169

"Right, then. Martin Clarke, apartment two. He'd be late seventies. You know him?"

"Oh, shit!" Fred said. "Maybe I do. Tell me, Dee. How good is Bookrajian?"

"He's good. If I follow you, you don't want to tell him anything you don't want him to know."

25

Fred was torn. It was Saturday afternoon at three o'clock. He had a number of directions to go. The name Clarke figured so prominently in the Copley story—it was his wife's maiden name after all—that he wanted to settle down with books and charts and genealogies and get a line on Ann Clarke; and now Alexandra and what had to be their father, Martin Clarke. But his heart was jaundiced with dismay. He didn't want this thing to go where it was going.

He compromised and stopped in at Molly's library, and wrote a note she'd get when she came in Monday.

Molly:
   Here's a question. I have two ends of a string—Ann Clarke, and her sister Alexandra, daughters of Martin Clarke—that maybe connect to the portrait. Copley

*married into a Tory family named Clarke. Question: Who's
the guy, and are my people Copley's relatives?*

Regards, Fred

Marek's assignation with Madeleine Shoemacher on the night of
Oona's death had not yet been confirmed. That was another loose
end. The Cover-Hoover enterprise, and its ability to spirit away a
living person into the bosom of loving-caring—that warranted
attention also.

Fred drove to Hay Street. The top buzzer was still without identifying name beside it. No response. The second floor,
where Martin Clarke was listed by the Registry as owner of a
vehicle, offered the name Mukerjee, and did not answer. First
floor gave him Cubit-Miller-Henry, who showed herself through
the glass window of the entrance door. She looked him over out
of a bright pink face that seemed sleepy: a woman of about forty,
wearing a gold stretch corduroy jumpsuit; and pregnant. She
opened the door only enough so they could talk through the
crack.

"Ms. Cubit-Miller-Henry?" Fred asked. She indicated assent.
"I'm looking for Martin Clarke," Fred said. "I understand he lives
on the second floor."

"He did," the woman said. "Moved out a few years back, I
don't know where to. Daughter's taking care of him. He can't
hack it. Too old. Loony. Mail comes for him but the daughter, she
picks it up. The other one."

"The other daughter. That's Sandy?"

"Top floor."

"She said her name is Blake."

"Was Blake, for about ten minutes. I don't know how that guy
stuck with her as long as he did. Once they were married he
pulled out."

"You wouldn't know where she is?"

"If she isn't upstairs, she's running in circles around the planet
Pluto," Fred's informant said. "The way she carries on, I put my
earplugs in half the time I'm home."

172

"Who's on the second floor?"

"Guy's never here. Lives with his girl. The place is for when his mother flies over. Student. Foreign. Business school. They're gonna own us. Hump like maggots, all of them. You know how they are."

"Blake, the husband, how do I find him?"

"Jeff went back where he came from, which I believe was J.P. Wherever it is he's better off than he was here with that dingbat. I was asleep. Her and her sister both!"

"Sorry to bother you," Fred said. "And I appreciate your help. Would you mind giving me a call if you see Sandy Blake again?"

"I would mind if I did it, but I won't do it," Ms. Cubit-Miller-Henry said. "Mind your own business and let mind your own business is my motto." She closed the door.

"You stole that line from Molly's mother," Fred told the door.

Fred went to his office on Mountjoy Street to think. He had a second reason now to be in touch with Bookrajian, if he could control that—which he certainly could not. He would like to ask, Did anybody identify the naked old man with cinder blocks around his broken neck, who washed up out of the Charles? He'd appeared quite recently, less than two weeks ago, wasn't it? The day before Fred bought the squirrel? Yes, it was in the paper on that day. He had discussed it with Molly.

Who was the subject of the portrait: a man with a beautiful head? Fred had been thinking of the complete painting, and of the man's hands in shadow, holding a squirrel on a chain—so poignant an image it seemed now, given the context of a human's life in Boston in 1765, supposing that human to be African in origin.

J.P. was Jamaica Plain. Fred looked in the Boston and near-suburbs directory and found a Jeffrey Blake listed. He dialed and tripped a recording: "Me and my shadow are in conference and don't have time for you at the moment. If you have a message for

173

Jeff Blake or [a woman's voice] Albion Puttanesca, [now Blake's voice continued] after the tone say what you want. It's a free country. God bless you, and [female voice] God bless these United States of America."

Fred gave the numbers where he could be reached, and enough message to cause interest if he had found the right Jeff Blake. He telephoned Molly's house, reached Sam, and told him he would take Sam and Terry out for something to eat, and something else, at about five-thirty.

"You want to talk to Mom?" Sam asked.

"If she has something to tell me."

Fred heard Sam's voice in the distance, calling. In a minute Sam returned and told him, "Mom says OK."

"You and Terry be hungry at five-thirty."

I don't want to stir things around, Fred thought later, driving past Cambridge on his way to Arlington. Everyone denies that the remainder of the Copley exists. If I keep making trouble they are going to deep-six it. It's what I would advise them to do, given that it is probably associated with murder. Nobody who's dead is going to become less dead if I let things trickle along at their own pace. If I push, I could make everything worse. We'll ease up onto the thing quietly from another direction, if we can.

Clay telephoned Molly's, which he rarely did, to tell Fred, "Not knowing how urgently you wished the information, I talked with Madeleine Shoemacher. She is clear—she is even upset—that Marek Hricsó was nowhere near her house, or herself, last Monday night. She does not know where he was."

"Hmm," Fred said.

"I can't eat and I will not sleep," Clay went on. "From anxiety about my beautiful Copley. I should not have gone to New Bedford to look. It will haunt me until we can complete it. I understand tomorrow is the day of rest, Fred. But given the delicacy of the situation, do you think—also perhaps a need for deliberate speed . . ."

"I have no plan to rest tomorrow," Fred promised him.

He took the kids to Charlestown and showed them Bunker Hill, explained the layout of the battle, and told them if they were interested he'd bring them back sometime when the buildings were open so they could see the dioramas and displays inside. He drove them past the building where he kept his room. He owned the house, along with a pickup group of veterans of this and that—some of whom were now settled elsewhere in the country. They used it, or had used it, or could still use it, as a place to come if they needed privacy to get priorities in order.

"Can we go in?" Terry asked.

"We won't today. It's just a room like yours, where I can close the door."

"Or slam it," Terry reminded him, grinning.

Fred didn't mention that someone else had been sleeping in his room for the past year or more. "Besides, who's hungry?" Fred asked.

They ate fish and chips at Poppy's by the bridge. They found a tedious movie about swords in Somerville. When Fred got them back to Molly's it was almost eleven. Molly's red Colt was in the garage, but Molly was not home.

"Oh," Sam said, yawning, and on his way upstairs. "Mom said tell you she's going in Aunt Ophelia's car, with Ophelia driving, and she'll be late or if she doesn't come back tonight don't worry, she'll stay at Ophelia's in Lincoln. I told her you said that was all right. That is all right, isn't it? You're staying the night?"

Fred looked at Molly's couch, touched and furious. It wasn't Molly's fault Sam had manipulated events, using his position as an intermediary. That even was what touched Fred most, Sam setting things up to leave Fred no alternative. But with Molly gone and himself the surprised babysitter, Fred was obliged to guess his place was, once again, to be the fold-out option.

175

He read Rothenstein until midnight; then lay on the couch without opening it. He had no idea where Molly had gone. If there were an emergency with one of the children he should know. He could not authorize an appendectomy. He was no more than the guy on the couch. At one o'clock he telephoned Ophelia's place. After ten rings a male voice answered, half asleep or three-quarters drunk, and drawling in a marked Western manner, "Yello there . . ."

"Ophelia Finger?" Fred asked.

"Honey, you are plumb blamed out of luck," the voice said.

"Wrong number?" Fred asked.

"You are the wrong number, honey. Me, I'm the right number. See, I am here. She is not here but here is where she's coming to, and when I say coming you better believe it. She is hightailing it back right now to my lonesome, limber dick. Therefore you lose, honey." The voice howled like a wolf before it replaced itself with a click. That would be Byron Ponderosa.

Fred made up the couch.

Fred roused to the kitchen door opening at almost three. Lying in the dark, he listened to the sounds. It was Molly, alone. He knew the way the air changed when she entered the house. She took her raincoat off, shook it, and hung it from the hook he'd told the kids he wanted for his baseball glove. He heard her stand in the dark kitchen, listening to her house. She'd know he was here because his car was in the driveway. She took off her shoes. Her plan was not to wake him, then.

Fred listened for five minutes. Molly was standing still in the center of her kitchen, not moving from the place where she had taken off her shoes. Finally came the slow rustle of her limbs in their clothing moving from the kitchen into the hallway to go upstairs. To be the witness of a lover while she believes herself unperceived—that is more intimate than anything erotic. Fred felt a pang of desire and rage, hearing her shift cautiously up the stairs. He heard Terry's door open and close. Molly didn't trust him with the children then? No, that was stupid; he was just mad at her and taking it out by making her accuse him in his imagination. He heard Sam's door open and close.

The door to the children's bathroom opened and spilled light down the stairs. Molly did not use that bathroom anymore. But she was using it tonight, not going into the new bathroom off her bedroom—the one Fred had given her.

Fred heard the toilet flush: an oasis of noise in the silence of Molly's house in the larger silence of Arlington. She ran water. The spill of light narrowed again. They always left enough to illuminate the hallway in case one of the kids woke in the night, though both were too old by now for that to be a major issue.

Fred's watch ticked near his ear. The house poised. Molly's slow steps moved along the upstairs hall, then descended the staircase in that deliberate, secretive way guaranteed to discover every creak.

Molly stood next to Fred for a full minute, quiet, and tense as an assassin with a conscience. He heard her breath shudder when she decided. She pulled the covers back and climbed in next to him, with all her clothes on but her shoes, and shivered. Her face was wet against his neck.

"You want me to be awake or asleep, Molly?" Fred asked her.

"Just be here, Fred, and be a human grown-up."

"Bad day?"

"Don't move. Don't turn around. Let me hold you," Molly said, curling against his back and reaching around him. "No, don't move. Don't talk. Be asleep, Fred. There's no chance I will."

They lay together like that until Molly sighed and said, "How can it be so many educated people over the age of twenty-five don't understand there's always going to be a war between the sexes? There's always going to be a war between the generations. But Jesus merciful God in wide blue heaven, we're all in trouble if anybody starts winning those wars."

Molly slept, weeping.

26

Next morning Fred stuck to the kitchen, listening to Molly's occasional snore, drinking coffee, and looking across the Sunday papers. He had not actually slept after Molly crawled in with him; but in his time he'd lain awake with worse company. When Molly started moving and complaining at around ten, Fred called in to her, "Your sister Pheely's little friend Byron Ponderosa: he tells me he has a limber dick. I have been puzzling about the claim. Do you think he means limber as in limp, or limber like a fifth limb?"

Molly said, "Ophelia's practically walking bowlegged, she's gone so cowgirl."

"You going to tell me what you were up to last night?"

"Later," Molly said on her way upstairs.

"The way I see the setup," said Molly, washed and dressed in jeans and a big gray sweatshirt advertising Cambridge Rindge and

Latin School, "the deal last night was supposed to work like an initiation and get me absolutely nailed. Ophelia and Cover-Hoover are in a hurry to come to terms, or I wouldn't have gotten this far this fast with Cover-Hoover. She's subtle, able, and careful. But I've given Cover-Hoover the impression I am prematurely ripe for the harvest, and she's tripping over her own eagerness to get something going with Pheely. She makes the mistake of wanting to get everyone on her side; dumb thing for a crusader to do, since it would put her out of business not to have an enemy. Anyway, Pheely was there as an interested observer, informant, and the gal who has the know-how to move Cover-Hoover's operation into the big time."

Molly had entered the kitchen talking. Her hair was damp from the shower. She went to the stove and poured coffee for herself.

"Every time I've been with that woman I come back feeling, Where was I? India? Tibet? Someplace where they eat dogs alive?" Molly sat at the table. She waited for what she was inviting him to say.

"You've seen her other times? More than the first time and last night?" Fred asked. Molly'd been playing a double game. No wonder she'd been keeping to herself.

"Oh, sure. I'm interested to learn the woman's scam," Molly said lightly. "We have a session every lunchtime. She is helping me remember quite a lot." Molly looked grim. "You see, the post-traumatic stress syndrome makes a barrier across the memory which causes the adult to have forgotten horrors in her childhood, which nonetheless have had a shaping function in creating her characteristic flawed adaptation to the world. The therapy finds apertures in this barrier, through which the past, in time, comes flooding back."

"All this for free," Fred said.

"Except for the fact her foundation pays her a salary. And something is supporting the foundation, isn't it? Grants and donations. Does it matter whether it's directly from patients or from others, even institutions, who can write off their payments so the

179

taxpayer covers them? Last night I got a good look at where this loving-caring is supposed to lead."

Fred asked, "You want bacon and toast?"

Molly shook her head. "I couldn't eat. The affair last night was staged for Ophelia's benefit, and to rope me in. They won't trust anyone but a convert, and I am their hole card with Ophelia, Cover-Hoover thinks. Cover-Hoover arranged for Pheely and me to meet her on Hay Street. She warned us that we should expect to be so emotionally exhausted her driver would have to take us home afterward. She dropped more than a broad hint I might want, in order to feel secure, to go straight to their safe house afterward. 'Bring overnight things,' she said. 'In case. My driver will take you.' Her driver, by the way, is that top-heavy guy from the frame store."

"Also treasurer," Fred interrupted. "Called Manny. Short for Boardman. Boardman Templeton. I wish you'd let me know what you were going to . . ."

"You don't," Molly said, "do you? You don't tell me a thing you're going to do. OK. Following instructions, Ophelia and I wait in Ophelia's car until Manny drives up in a sleek French car . . ."

"A Lance-Flamme," Fred said.

"I wouldn't know. Cover-Hoover climbs out her side. Two women get out the back. One's the redhead I saw in the same store as Manny—the lady who looks like she has bought a lot of real estate in the Dismal Swamp from magazine ads. She is called Ann. First names only, by the way. Everyone gets to be anonymous. I assume it's Ann Clarke, recording secretary?" Fred nodded. "The other one, who I haven't seen before, turns out to be her younger sister, Sandy."

"There's Sandy again," Fred said.

"Manny's job is to watch the street, making sure the satanic forces don't get in. Cover-Hoover, for our benefit, so as to stress the aura of danger and mystery, makes a production of warning him to keep his eyes open for someone they call the Stalker on account of the widespread and common satanic movement you and I were not aware of, Fred, flourishing here and elsewhere, with thousands of secret unknown worshipers and adepts and dupes in every major urban center, all of them looking for a chance to rain on Cover-Hoover's parade of hopeful-healing. As we both know from her book, these villains hold Black Masses, kill babies and bury their bodies, eat human flesh, force each other to dance naked—

"Fred, how come—have you noticed?—everyone who spends a lot of solitary time thinking about evil, whether they are for it or against it, fixes on nudity as the keynote symbol, naked people being the sure sign something is going on—

"Anyway, the women go upstairs and Manny sits downstairs looking alert and important and ready for trouble in Cover-Hoover's car."

Fred started frying bacon. He was hungry and this was going to take time if Molly's pace continued. Her upset of last night had crystallized into deliberate rage.

"All right, Fred," Molly said. "Here's the genius of the setup. It's perfect, even for nonbelievers—in fact maybe it's best for nonbelievers, since they have nothing to measure against. It does not matter whether Satan is real. You are not required to accept anything supernatural as a given. If there is a God or none, nobody gives a shit.

"We, the recovering victims of satanic worship, need only accept that anyone we trusted in the past is suspect—the bishop, the crossing guard, the fourth-grade teacher, the uncle, the wicked stepmother, the piano teacher, the acrobat in the circus— whoever might have had intimate access to us. By that person, and by that person's numberless cohorts, who are called enablers, we were betrayed.

"As little innocent children we were taken hostage by dark powers. Now, as adults, we remain hostages until we are ransomed by Cover-Hoover, who gently leads us to mistrust everything we have ever known, and bring to birth the loving-caring self we would have been all along had we not been so abused and betrayed. Turn the bacon over, Fred. It's going too fast."

Fred flipped the bacon with a fork and turned the heat down.

"I saw the rest of your painting, Fred," Molly said. Fred raised his eyebrows.

"Cover-Hoover had brought it with her, rolled in a mailing tube. I forgot to mention it. She carried the tube before her like the Ark of the Covenant, climbing the stairs to the third-floor apartment. I didn't know what it was."

Fred said, "What did they do, worship it?"

"They cut it in half."

"Oh, shit!" Fred said. He put his bacon on paper towels to drain. "Suffering sweet shit! What are those assholes doing?"

"I'm trying to tell you," Molly said.

"These people don't know your connection to me, do they?" Fred asked. He dropped bread in the toaster.

"Not from me."

"Excuse me interfering, but these are not nice people."

"I know it."

"Where are the pieces? They cut lengthwise across the head, I assume? Even though they know the thing's worth at least ten thousand bucks to someone?"

"The cut's vertical, not through the head. Ann did the cutting, with Cover-Hoover holding her hand to give her healing strength, when the time came. They used a Skil-knife and they followed a line already drawn in charcoal. There was method to it, and premeditation. They kept the pieces too, when the ceremony was done. Ann rolled them up together and put them back in the tube. Is that toast for me?"

"I reckon so," Fred said. "I'll make more for myself. Ann Clarke walked away with my last piece, which is now two pieces. Right. Fuck. For the hell of it, if you saw it that close, was there a signature?"

Molly said, "Here's what I saw: 'I. S. C. Pix' next to the head. Beautiful man, by the way. I. S. C. Pix. Doesn't sound like John Copley."

"Wait a minute. You had someone in your library a while back, last week maybe, asking about Pix, remember?"

"I did?"

"You called and asked me about it and I made a joke, one *x* or two?"

"Two. Over easy," Molly said. "Oh. The joke. Yes, I recall. I didn't see the client. Billy handled it. It was a telephone inquiry. We note the question and telephone them back if we get the time and if we find an answer."

Fred broke two eggs into the pan for Molly. "If that note exists, get ahold of it tomorrow, would you?" Fred asked. "Also, I left a note for you, hoping you could help identify the sitter. Ten to one the query only leads to Kwik-Frame; but if not—but go on with your story. I can explain Mr. Pix later."

"Let me start again. It was eight-thirty. Cover-Hoover led the way upstairs. Ophelia, at her obsequious best, followed her. Then Ann and Sandy and then me. We sat on a couch or on chairs, as Cover-Hoover directed us. She had to give a speech, mostly to clue Ophelia in. Ophelia sat there with future TV programs flashing across her eyes. She'd dressed all in black. We all had, following Cover-Hoover's directions. Therefore Sandy stood out. White party dress with frills and a fat sash a girl of ten would be ashamed to wear.

"Cover-Hoover told us, in a we-are-gathered-together intonation, that this was to be Sandy's night. She, the younger sister, had been the most abused one. 'We are here tonight in loving-caring, and hopeful-healing, to set this victim free. From now on she will be known as a survivor. Whatever happens here tonight, Sandy, we will be here for you. And you will be safe. The only way to purge the abuse is to bring it forward.' "

"Sandy started to shake and tremble. My goddamn scar started burning. 'He's here,' Sandy said. 'Not yet, but he will come,' Cover-Hoover told us. 'And when he comes, you will prevail.' "

Fred put Molly's eggs on toast and sacrificed his bacon to her. He started more bacon.

"They really said 'prevail,' " Molly said, taking a bite of fried egg on toast. "We all had to repeat, 'You will prevail,' like cheerleaders from the seventeenth century. Everyone worked themselves into a state. We turned the lights down low—no candles or incense but you get the idea. Everyone watched Sandy moan for five minutes, this being her night."

"You did not take to Sandy?" Fred remarked.

"We were told her traumatic past induced multiple-personality disorder. Of all the ones she tried, she didn't find one I liked. Anyhow, Sandy's function was to be the mascot or medium. I gathered Ann went through a similar process a few years back, though she doesn't show the same histrionic flair. Blasted is more her style. She sat through the whole evening looking like, I told you so, never astonished. She's older than I am, Fred. Really old enough to know better.

"Anyway, the stage having been set, Sandy thrashed in her party dress, lolling on the couch next to Cover-Hoover and groaning, 'I can't.'

"Everyone told her she could, it was the only way, and she'd be safe, no one would leave her. Ophelia ate it up. You could see her thinking camera angles. The victim has beautiful long black hair and a great body."

"I know that," Fred said.

"You understand, the assumption is I am attending this event to pick up pointers for when it's my turn to get the call, after I remember enough.

"Suddenly, down Sandy goes onto the floor, in her white party dress, jerking as if she's been shot, and she moans in a little-girl voice, 'He's here. He's here.'

"Everyone looks around. You couldn't help it, peering into every dark corner of the room. Her terror was so riveting, the way she's rolling on the floor. You see the rest of her costume includes accurate little-girl white cotton Spanky Pants. My scar burns and throbs. Everyone feels an alien presence in the room. He's a big, looming, stinking, hairy thing with horns."

"Everything you want in a guy," Fred whispered.

"The scene called for extensive nudity," Molly went on. "But we were spared. Sandy, in her trance, moaned, 'The dark man. No. I won't. It's too much. It's too big.'

"She gasped and heaved like someone being raped; someone small. It was horrible, Fred. You couldn't help but believe it. I mean, there it was! The poor child. Such suffering. Such anguish. Such hideous abuse. We all sat transfixed by the awful privacy of the little girl's pain. You accepted she was a little girl."

"The dark man," Fred said. "In Cambridge you get this PC circumlocution even in a state of trance?"

" 'Mr. Pix, Mr. Pix,' Sandy whispered in a tiny, wounded, last-gasp voice. That's when Cover-Hoover unrolled the rest of your painting. I almost peed my pants I was so surprised. You'd told me about it but still I was not ready for it.

"When Sandy saw this thing, which Cover-Hoover and Ann held out, the patient went cataleptic. She lay on her back with her legs open, her arms raised to fend something off, staring at the face of Mr. Pix.

"Cover-Hoover murmured in her gentle, gentle voice, 'Annie and I are holding Mr. Pix, dear. If we are holding him, it cannot be Mr. Pix on top of you, dear. Who is it on you, dear? Look at him. Look at his face!'

" 'I can't!'

" 'It's a face you know, dear.'

" 'He'll kill me! He'll kill me!'

" 'Look at him!' Cover-Hoover commanded.

"Sandy crumpled into an agony that seemed, if anything, more real than what she had been showing us. She resisted a while longer but the dominance of the situation she was in, as well as Cover-Hoover's skill and her older sister's prompting, forced it out of her. She stared in a cold, adult way, and screamed, 'I see. It is my father on me.

" 'And all his friends are waiting.' "

27

"Explain how doing further massacre on the painting helps the situation," Fred said. "I gather that's the next event on the program?"

"First we had the blubbering aftermath of breakthrough," Molly said. "And never have I seen so confident an exchange of emotional matter. It was a release, a true catharsis: a good cry. We all joined in, even Ophelia, though she was mostly thinking money because as entertainment this self-help shtick has it all.

"After Ann had taken her younger sister downstairs—sorry, Fred, they had the painting with them—for Manny to take them wherever they go, I could see Cover-Hoover was disappointed in me because I didn't get swept up in the contagion, start feeling my daddy at his priestlike task, and have to make my own retreat along with Sandy back to their halfway house.

"Anyhow, as Cover-Hoover explained later, it is one thing to know the abuser in theory, but until you can add your corroborative recalled emotional trauma, your understanding is incomplete and you cannot be healed. It must be lived again.

"Sandy has known for years she and her sister were offered ritually and regularly—widespread and commonly—in rites of satanic worship. Everyone had agreed long since that their dad was a chief organizer of these chowderfests. But Sandy had to fully experience it herself in order to surrender—Cover-Hoover's term—to the truth of her own history, and to reclaim her body.

"Ann led the way. Then, after Sandy started having her own flashbacks, after Cover-Hoover pitched in to help, she recovered repressed memories of being violated on their living-room rug by a dark, ominous presence who brought with him a familiar spirit—a little animal."

"Oh, come on," Fred said. "My squirrel?"

"It sounded more malicious as Cover-Hoover described it. More like a weasel or a monkey on a chain. They saw a 'dark man,' but they couldn't point a finger at anyone black not having mixed with anyone of that persuasion. That's a lucky break for someone. People haven't forgotten how to do one kind of lynching or another. For every victim there must be a perpetrator. But they put it together that the dark, ominous presence was a picture that hung in their house, and so they had to be wrong about the character in the picture doing these things to them. A picture is worth a thousand words, but there are limits.

"So, they concluded, if the painting didn't do it, somebody else did. That's logical. They looked around, and tried hypnosis and role playing and so on, and sooner than you might think, they found another candidate."

"Daddy," Fred said. "Was your dad in the same satanic group as theirs?"

"Theirs belonged to a Brattle Street coven," Molly said. "And here's where Cover-Hoover may be right to fear reprisals. They are starting, at least among themselves, to name names. They've got perps from the Divinity School, and a former assistant secretary of state: no riffraff, no city counselors or anything tawdry like that."

Molly put her head in her hands and was silent. The silence was like thunder crashing through the room. One moment she had been her cynical, cheerful self. The next, a quiet loomed out from her that filled the house. She sat like that for three minutes. When she spoke again, her voice was dull, and she did not look up.

"You have to be a criminal or hero to deny what everyone around you sees. Most of us are neither. We depend on each other to affirm our most common experiences. It's dangerous what she's doing. That older sister's a zombie, and the younger one, the fruitcake, is heading in the same direction once Cover-Hoover finishes wearing down her independent streak.

"If something else had weakened me already—I don't know, suppose I'd lost my job, or lost a child, or couldn't get loose from a bad marriage. If I were desperate and couldn't find anything better to do, I could see myself . . ." Fred let her silence linger. The kids were moving upstairs. There wouldn't be much time before the nature of the day changed. Molly said, "Once you've decided on that road, what happens next? What about the old geezer who fostered these two late, late adolescents? Does Cover-Hoover think about him?"

"I fear he was a major part of her thinking," Fred said. "I have to find out, I guess, though it's not my job. His name is Martin Clarke; is or, as I fear, was."

"Martin?" Molly said, looking up with big tears in her eyes. "You think that was *our* Martin, standing outside the house at night, looking for the daughter he had misplaced?"

The telephone rang in a timely way. "Jeff Blake here." Fred signaled to Molly that this might take a minute. Molly started rattling dishes. Fred said, "Thanks for calling. Let me think where to start."

"If the subject is my ex, most any place you start will get you somewhere you don't want to be," Jeff Blake confided. He used his voice as if he wanted you to conclude he'd passed the bar but found the insurance business far more stimulating and rewarding.

"Why don't we do this over a drink, or coffee?" Jeff Blake said.

"I'm open until two o'clock. What's the exchange I called you at, Arlington? I'm J.P. Tell you what, my lady is out of town. Conference. I got nothing to do until this after. And I am aching to eat grease. Split the difference. I'll be in the Watertown Diner in Watertown—you know it?—in about thirty-seven minutes, eating hash and eggs. I'll be the one in the suit. If you want to come by and talk, we'll talk. I'm easy. Something comes of it, fine. Nothing comes of it, that's fine too. Like I say, I'm easy. See the suit is because I have a wedding at two o'clock. Did I say that already? And it's no use getting dressed twice when you can get dressed once.

"I'd as soon not talk on the phone, you know? I like to see the whites of their eyes. So. You want to talk, we'll talk. At the diner. Half an hour, give or take a few. That good for you?"

"You bet," Fred said.

Terry and Sam came in, preceded by sounds of intense discussion. They fell silent when they saw Fred in the kitchen. Sam said, "You said you thought one time you would be a pitcher, Fred. In those days did the pitchers use the same dorky gloves they do today?"

"Some did. I always preferred a fielder's glove."

"What color?" Terry asked.

"They all come out about the same after you use them awhile," Fred said.

Sam and Terry nodded. Fred divided the comics into sections and handed Terry the portion containing Garfield. Her week was ruined if she did not read Garfield before Sam did.

"I have to go talk to this guy," Fred told Molly. "After, depending on what develops, I may go check in on Marek Hricsó; or the guy I'm going to see now, Jeff Blake, who was married to Sandy Blake for ten minutes once according to my informant, may point me in another direction."

"Cutting that painting up. I still don't get it."

"They called it weaning, or transimaging," Molly said. "The abused child, revolting against the enormity of what she knew, shifted the blame onto an innocent icon—the painting—and the

189

blame must be shifted back where it belongs, by the ritual dismemberment of the mistakenly selected alternate surrogate."

"And they don't care they're wrecking a quarter-million dollars worth of painting? A real icon?"

"Presumably they don't believe that. Who is Mr. Pix?"

"He's not a problem. I'll tantalize you now so you'll want to stick with me. I'll call if I can't make it back for the hoedown with Byron Ponderosa and Ophelia." Outside the window it was dark and damp. The lilac bush at the foot of Molly's garden looked like a bad dream about insects: not a sign of a leaf.

"Gloomy today," Molly said.

Fred started out to the living room to put the bed up and get his jacket.

"I'll do the bed," Molly said.

Terry and Sam markedly paid no attention.

"Wait a minute," Fred said. "You say Manny was watching for someone they called the Stalker?"

"Correct."

Fred stalked out.

Once you have made it successfully past the age of twenty, it is hard to follow eggs on toast (which Fred, in solidarity with Molly, had eaten for breakfast) with hash and eggs. Fred ordered coffee, sitting in a booth at the Watertown Diner, and watched for Jeff Blake, who should be a man in his late twenties or early thirties wearing a suit on his body and a handshake in his smile.

Blake did not show up until almost noon. Fred knew him right away. He was five foot five and already had a well-advanced paunch, which accentuated the almost-baby-blue double-breasted suit with the pink carnation. Blake's face was less pink than the carnation, but it was working in that direction and, by evening, if the wedding reception went well, who knew?

Fred stood, and a mysterious unseen power, common and widespread, caused him to reach out his hand in welcome. "Fred?" Blake said. "Good to see you. I'm running late. If you don't run, something bites you in the tail."

190

He laughed. The waitress behind the counter looked over. Jeff Blake held his hand up. "They know me here," he said. By now they knew Fred, too. They'd been watching him drink coffee for an hour, wondering if he didn't have a place to live. The waitress came over. "What'll you have?" she asked.

"The usual."

"The usual what?"

Blake attained the color of his carnation. "Hash and three eggs over easy, extra side of home fries, whole-wheat toast, coffee, grapefruit juice," he said.

"I guess she's new," he told Fred. "No offense. See, people remember me. I don't know what it is about me. Women especially. Because I make people feel good, my lady says, and if they don't want to feel good then the hell with them."

Fred said, "I called about Sandy Clarke."

"She still uses Blake, Jeff Blake said. You can t blame her.

"What happened?" This did not seem a person who would respond to less than an accurate blow with a hammer.

"She was a fucking introvert," Jeff Blake announced. "That's to begin with. Then she got turned off of sex. And frankly, between you and I and the bedpost, I did not have time for all the whining. Still, no hard feelings. What does she want?" His friendly, open look was immediately canny.

"I don't represent her in any way."

The waitress brought Blake's order in two trips. He decided not to send anything back or say, Thanks, honey. Instead he took a bite of hash and leaking yolk and said through it, "You talk. I eat."

"My business put me in touch with the family," Fred said. "I need to understand how to handle them. I'm having a hard time figuring out how they tick."

Jeff Blake laughed hash. "They're a bunch of loonies is why," he said. "They don't tick. They go *sproingngng!* What business you in?"

"Antiques."

"OK, look. I was set to give you a hard time. Figured she sent

191

you to feel me out, see will I go back on our deal. But you're straight up, and if you're not she's not getting anything back anyway. We made a deal and shook on it. You got that?"

Fred said he got that. Jeff Blake struck fear into the survivors on his plate. He took a swallow of coffee and signaled for a warm-up. Fred covered his own cup with his hand.

"There was the three of them. The old lady died a long time back, way before I'm in the picture. So it was Daddy Clarke and the loony sister, Ann, who was already divorced and had moved out to I don't know where. We didn't see much of her. They'd used the whole place on Hay Street once, the family did; then as people died and moved out, the old boy took the second floor and rented out the first. Sandy and I took the top. I never could make out how much he had. See, he was well off the deep end then; would wander around in his underwear at night and pee anywhere—Sorry, dear, I didn't see you." The waitress had bowed to accept certain of his soiled dishes.

"Pretty well-heeled, was he?"

Jeff Blake looked at the ceiling. "Nobody was hurting. Except they were all crazy. I'll tell you the truth," Jeff Blake leaned across the table to whisper crumbs of toast, "I blame everything on the older sister, Ann. She got this enormous wedgie nothing could get past, and this is before it got popular—she's like a prophet pioneer; before everyone else started seeing ghosts and whatever like they do today. Like now it's a whole industry I wish I could get in on. Anyhow, Ann'd come roaring in, screaming about how the old man used to sacrifice her to the devil, and eat people's liver and the rest of it. I didn't listen. Till the old guy started to believe it. One minute he'd be as sensible as I am, the next he'd be crawling on the floor moaning, 'I'm sorry.'

"When it got too bad—Sandy and I are married by this time— Ann, the sister, took the old man to live with her, wherever that was. Tell you the truth, I and Ann did not get along. This is about four years ago. Then Sandy starts seeing ghosts too, and wouldn't put out—sorry, honey—and that was about it for me."

Fred watched the waitress struggle away with the remainder

of Jeff Blake's dishes. He asked, "Did you ever see a painting the Clarkes had, an old one, of a man holding a squirrel?"

"Sure. Mr. Pix. Black guy. I'm not prejudiced. Here's how loony old man Clarke is. White as he is, he claims the picture is an ancestor. How is Sandy anyway? She's not trying to go back on our deal? Oh, I get it. You think the picture's worth something. There I can't help you."

"Thanks," Fred said, standing.

28

Marek did not answer the shop bell. He had not answered either telephone. Fred said, "To hell with this." He went around to the rear of the building and let himself in the back door. That placed him in a vestibule giving him access to either the stairs going up, or to the shop's back door. Once in the vestibule, Fred heard the piano upstairs. Marek was practicing.

It was a fluid, graceful, marvelous, and completely disciplined touch. Chopin, one of the mazurkas. It sounded like someone reaching into a stream and tickling trout. "Fingers like water," Clay had said. It was passionate and remarkably cold, looking to conceal its own intent and trap an alien life, in order to exploit it.

"So he's here," Fred said. He started up the stairs, thinking, in the words of Molly's mother, What's good for the sauce is good for the gander. The music's complexity increased as he got closer to the third floor. The door to Oona's apartment on the second floor was open. It did not follow from the shop downstairs. It had the generous, sparse look of a farm kitchen. All Oona's romance was downstairs. This was functional. Fred could look through it later if he wanted, if Marek did not have him arrested.

Fred climbed the next flight. Marek paused and switched to a new mazurka. Fred heard Marek laugh. This selection had a formal, haunting quality that seemed, in a dance, an eerie joke. Marek played it with abandon. It sounded like a king in his coronation regalia falling down stairs. The fall was in slow motion. Odd and unnerving as it was, it sounded exactly like what Chopin was thinking about: the vandalism of something precious, sad, and despised; and beautiful.

Fred eased his bulk onto the landing. The door to Marek's apartment was ajar. Because of the door's placement he could see nothing without poking his head into the opening. He saw only the foot end of the piano—which, by its sound, had cost Oona Imry some thousands of dollars. More arresting was the wobbling white hind end, with zits, of the pudgy young man executing a parody of dance while Marek played.

"Oh, come on," Fred said, walking in.

Marek stood up with a screech and a chord more Hindemith than Chopin. He was as naked as the room's other occupant. The space was large and contained almost no furniture aside from the black mass of the piano—a Steinway. Marek had placed a large Oriental rug from Oona's shop on the floor; around it were a few throw pillows, two antique-looking chairs, and a daybed whose state of undress Fred was in no mood to appreciate.

Marek was holding his beautiful hands, stripped of their gloves, up to his mouth. The other man used his in a more conventional gesture for the first encounter with an unexpected stranger when in a state of nudity.

Fred assessed the situation. Marek was not going to call any cops. Fred gestured toward the pudgy young man who now, defiantly, removed his hands from their easy task of concealing the obvious.

"Your alibi for that night?" Fred guessed.

"Not here. No. Never. Not while Oona might . . ." Marek faltered.

"I'll need your name, address, phone, all that," Fred told Marek's companion in a pleasant, official tone.

The young man was sullen. Fred spotted his shirt, suit, and accessories draped on one of the chairs and went over to them, shaking the wallet out of the suit's jacket pocket—English cut, brown wool, side vents. The suit's most recent inhabitant peeped an objection. Fred flopped the wallet open.

"Sylvester H. Penny?" Fred asked, looking at the driver's license. Massachusetts. Address on Forham Place, not far from here, halfway up Beacon Hill.

The pudgy young man put his hands on his hips. He was a real blond. Marek kept distance between himself and his companion. He looked interested, but made no protest. His was a beautiful, boyish body, like that of Michelangelo's David before the Holiday Fitness Program started working him over.

"Number ten Forham Place," Fred read. "Birth date three, seventeen—say, you just had a birthday! What are you, twenty? And Social Security number—I'll make a note of this . . ."

The young man tottered toward Fred to retrieve his identity: Visa Gold, Diner's Club, American Express, Boston Public Library, Videosmith, Hollywood Voyage Club, Boston Museum of Fine Arts membership, the rest of it.

"I don't mean to embarrass you, Penny," Fred said.

"He is called Hop," Marek said, enjoying the moment. "And yes I was at his home, and yes if his parents discover certain things Hop will find himself in the street as you see him now."

Marek was not posing consciously. He fell naturally into graceful postures designed by a profligate creator to enhance his beauty. Hop, on the other hand—Fred handed the wallet to him—had not been so endowed. He looked like one struck by a change of wind direction in the fourth grade; his childish shape remained, but with bulk added.

Marek stretched luxuriantly. He and Fred watched Hop picking up his clothes. Marek said, "Boston is not kind to those of its sons who exhibit artistic temperament. Often they are driven into a wilderness of exile."

Fred asked, "Hop, was Marek Hricsó with you last Monday night?"

Hop nodded, standing on one foot, pulling tiny yellow underpants around the other foot. Once Hop was dressed, Fred was going to lose this moment's dramatic advantage. Much of the man's backbone was in his suit.

"At ten Forham Place?" Fred asked.

Hop nodded. The change in his balance caused by the nod almost toppled him. He put on the undershirt—Brooks Brothers, sleeveless, long, and sleazy.

"What time?" Fred asked. "Your parents are traveling?"

"At the opera," Hop mumbled. "Eight to midnight."

Marek said, "We were six people who will all deny it."

Hop put the long socks on, then the shirt—white shirt with a pattern of lines forming a hint of check. Marek scratched his right armpit absently.

Fred told Hop, "Your friend may be in a lot of trouble if you won't come forward."

Hop pulled on his pants. He shrugged. His flab fell away. He slung a green silk necktie on with a flourish. "Don't call me," he told Marek, putting on his jacket. He gave Fred an evil look— premature. He was not ready for his exit line, having neglected to put on his shoes. Marek held them up.

"These I will throw out the window unless you tell me goodbye nicely," Marek announced. He smiled and watched Hop brushing creases out of his suit.

"Who is your ugly friend?" Hop asked Marek.

"An ugly friend of me," Marek said. "Here, take your shoes. They have been on the street." Marek dropped them one at a time for Hop to retrieve and put on. They were heavy walking shoes, as British as the suit, and they clumped.

"Don't call me," Marek said as Hop, shod, flounced out. "He is a homosexual fairy," Marek explained loudly as they listened to Hop's shoes descending the stairs. "Now, Fred. We will pretend you knew I wanted to talk with you. I am thinking I want to buy some things Oona sold you."

"You do?"

Marek sat on the chair from which Hop had retrieved his clothes. It was not clear where Marek's clothes were. Closed doors off this room must lead to bathroom, closet, bedroom—or perhaps Marek lived naked. He was at ease in that state.

Fred sat on the green velvet cushion of the piano bench. "What do you want to buy?"

"For three thousand dollars I shall buy the squirrel and the other painting Oona gave you or sold you; or perhaps you did not pay for it, yes?"

"Three thousand dollars," Fred repeated.

"You will have to trust me," Marek said. "I shall have the money soon after you give the paintings to me again. I will sign a piece of paper saying I promise you the money."

Fred said, "The deal is already done."

"So," Marek said. "You have the squirrel."

"You want to tell me what's going on?"

Marek said, "I am not receiving enough money. Three thousand and five hundred more is my last offer."

"How much is he willing to pay to get them back?" Fred asked.

Marek looked open and secretive. The expression went well with his nudity. "Who?" Marek asked.

Fred told him, "I am not at liberty to say."

Marek crossed his legs. His genitals lolled across his thigh, a large pet, petulant.

"The person sold these things by mistake," Marek said. "My offer is six times what Oona paid."

"You mentioned three thousand five hundred."

"Three thousand is enough. When you can bring them. After I get my money."

"No deal, Marek. Listen—the person who wants to buy back these things . . ."

Marek clenched his lips. "I find a note only in my door," he said. "I have not seen these person."

198

Fred stood. "I want to mention that if Oona was murdered, it could be by these persons. And I think it was."

"I shall tell you nothing," Marek announced. "You shall not frighten information out of me the way you did to poor Hop, play-acting you are the big and tough American cop gangster."

Marek followed Fred to the apartment door. "Mr. Bartholdi says I shall have everything. It is written in her will. But it takes many, many months, perhaps a year, maybe more, before I may touch anything, except the many beautiful presents Oona has been giving me in the past. I cannot open her doors and sell, even, as Hop asks me to do so he may stand behind the desk and stroke my beautiful things."

"Be careful of these people," Fred said.

"I must find an appraiser. And I must pay the appraiser. I have no money. It is almost gone. I must eat. I must buy clothing."

Fred said, "Marek, be careful."

"When will you bring the painting of the squirrel and that other one I gave you by mistake, when I was stupefied by grief, being offended that Oona was dead in shame and violence?"

"You have a way to reach these people?" Fred asked. He'd offered Manny too much money. He'd played that wrong, making a strong bid, trying to be fair as well as showing Manny enough slack to work with. Manny had decided—or whoever he shared his information with had decided—that the last fragment was worth more if he put the whole thing back together.

Fred said, "Would anyone think I was a fool if I took a chain-saw to a green Lance-Flamme, cut it transversely into steaks, and undertook to market the slices?"

Marek yawned. He picked his gloves up from the piano's top and started putting the left one on, with as much loving care as if he were settling a foreskin.

"These people are dangerous," Fred insisted.

"I should have told you nothing. You, Fred, who were my friend, will go to them to get more money for yourself, and so leave me in poverty and misery. Therefore, go!"

199

Fred said, "Tell me if you hear from these people. Will you do that?"

"Ho!" Marek exclaimed. "And ho again, Fred Taylor. I tell you nothing. I am not Oona Imry's blood for no reason. She would not and I will not. Marek Hricsó is not everyone's fool."

Fred had not intended to stop at Mountjoy Street, but he was uneasy. Marek was covered for the night of Oona's death. Fred was more than uneasy.

Clayton was out. Fred wrote a note on one of Clay's index cards and put it into the mail slot of his front door, the street door, where Clay could not miss it when he returned.

The people who cut the painting want the fragments back. They are dangerous, I believe. In case I am right, stay somewhere else. If they track me they find you. All best, Fred.

29

Fred stood on Mountjoy Street. The sun came out, thumbed its nose, and evaded. The glistening steep slope, lined with brick sidewalks and buildings, ended at the river. This was all Copley's land in its day; a farm not far from Boston Common. It was four o'clock. Fred went back inside to call Molly, since he recalled that he was missing the afternoon's entertainment.

"Byron Ponderosa here," said a voice Fred recognized, at Molly's number.

"Would you put Molly on?" Fred asked.

"Can't do it," the cowboy artist said.

"Her sister Ophelia there?" Fred asked.

"Yep."

"Would you put her on?"

"Don't mind if I do. I put her on all the time." Fred heard him call, "Yo, Filly!"

"Not much of a party," Ophelia complained. "Molly took the kids shopping. She's not back. Where are you?"

"Ophelia, where's this rest home of Cover-Hoover's?"

"Not even donors are told that," Ophelia said. "Only the victims and survivors. She's made so many enemies doing what she's doing—the perpetrators involved in all these things—there's nothing they'd rather know than how to find their victims and stop them talking. Everyone's life is in danger."

"You believe all this?" Fred asked. He was surprised. Ophelia's general game plan was so cynical he had taken it for granted that she had rejected it. Had Ophelia really bought in?

"I would expect you to deny it," Ophelia said. "Even though you clearly see how Molly's life has been blighted."

Fred tried Cover-Hoover's number for the hell of it, but put no message on the machine. An exceedingly warm invitation to do so followed the opening gambit, "This is a safe line." He tried Kwik-Frame and received no response on a Sunday afternoon. He sat at his desk and drummed his fingers, telling himself, I'm letting this painting get in front of logic. Make the question easy. Most things involving force are easy. If we eliminate Marek as the person who killed Oona Imry, then someone else did it. Then I'm back to the Cover-Hoover crowd. Pretend one of them killed her. Why? Gain? How? Revenge? For what?

How much do they believe their own line? Do they genuinely think people care so much about their fantasies they'll come after the survivor victims?

What about that retired symphony conductor whose son or daughter announces, to the world or any part of it that wants to listen, "My mom used to beat me with a broomstick until my dad would drag me out to be offered up to the full moon and the bats and his poker club."

This was no joke. This could ruin lives. Suppose the symphony conductor has a gun, and can simplify the reason for the fog of grief and accusation he finds himself in to a single target, and call it Cover-Hoover. Suppose he's lost his son or daughter, his reputation in the world, maybe his wife as well, for this could not make her happy; maybe he's not retired so he loses his livelihood; maybe there's been a suit and the jury buys the story and hits him

202

with a penalty of a half-million bucks. In such a case, Cover-Hoover would do well to watch her back. Pressure like that, a parent could go berserk. I think I understand but I'm no parent. I ought to ask Molly what she thinks.

They don't know I'm connected to Molly, do they?

I'll follow Ann Clarke tomorrow after work.

If they are coming after the parts of the painting they sold, their motives are not purely psycho-healing social work. Among them there's a healthy avarice. They understand there's money to be made.

Manny would have no trouble helping Oona catch that train. Forget the question why, for the moment. He has the size, and the character.

Which of them approached Oona in the first place? Or was it more than one?

Fred was still sitting at his desk, hesitating. He had nothing more than Bookrajian's voice to go by, and Dee's assurance, "He's good." But it was time to have a look at the next step. He telephoned the headquarters of the Cambridge Police Department and was switched over to the detective's office.

"Ernie Bookrajian's in Atlantic City getting laid the hard way," Fred was told. "Whatta you want him for?"

"When does he get back?"

"See, he wins a free trip for two on the bus," his informant went on. "Beyond that he pays meals, hotel, limo, booze, and he's gonna bet, right? And he's gonna hafta let her play too, right? We figure that's about three K it's gonna cost him."

"When does he get back?"

"What do you want?"

"Bookrajian and I already talked," Fred said. "Some things we were talking about, you know? It's a continuing conversation."

"He's on like a witness protection program," the Cambridge end of the line claimed. That inspired a scuffle of laughter. "Monday morning he'll be here at eight. I was you I'd wait, call about ten."

"Ask him to call Fred Taylor," Fred said. He gave both numbers, Molly's and his line in Clayton's office. It was nothing that couldn't wait, what he had to say. What was dead was dead. The Kwik-Frame crowd was not going to destroy the remainder of the painting now. They wanted to put it together as badly, maybe, as he and Clayton did.

Who was the subject of the portrait? Mr. Pix, as he was known to his friends. Fred knew of only one African head in all of Copley's work, but it was painted much later than 1765.

Before he left, Fred wrote another note to drop in Clay's door.

The point is I don't know how badly these people want what they threw away. Call me. F

Fred drove along Commonwealth Avenue looking for signs of incipient engorgement in the buds on the magnolias. All this water should be giving them ideas. There wasn't a hint of the first tingling throb. Too early in the year. The magnolias were closed tighter than Oona's shop.

"Things have their own logic," Fred said aloud. The statement had the vacuous ring of American pop wisdom, like the recently best-selling title *Wherever You Go, There You Are.* It was just dumb. Even so, his instinct, speaking aloud in a dumb phrase, urged he not push too hard to turn events while he understood so little of what was causing them.

He'd see where Ann Clarke went tomorrow.

He drove along the gray mud of the riverbank until he picked up Route 2 and swung west and north toward Arlington, saying to himself, I ought to hear the rest of Molly's story. He thought of her shopping with the kids, and smiled.

Ophelia and her cowboy painter lover did not ride into the sunset until well after sunset. They left behind them a presentation copy of the fat book, eighteen by eighteen inches, entitled modestly, in letters two inches high, *Byron Ponderosa,* beneath the smaller *Best-Loved Works of.* The picture on the cover was fake, pale, ill-drawn imitation Remington. "It's not a coffee-table book, it's about right for the bathtub," Molly said, when they were gone.

The only good moment of the evening had been when Ophelia referred to her lover as an 'old cowpoke' and then tittered and blushed and said, "Oh, mercy, I never thought! I didn't mean it that way!"

Terry loved the Ponderosa book almost as much as she had been awed by the man himself, who called her 'Podner.' She sat on the couch with the book in her lap, struggling to manage its weight. "He must love horses a lot," Terry called into the kitchen, where her mother and Fred were cleaning up the aftermath of beer and pizza and a big salad.

"When they start talking horses the next step is the training bra," Molly whispered. "Oh, honey, leave the horses alone a couple more years, won't you?

"You've both got homework," Molly shouted into the atmosphere. "And it's Sunday night, and it's already eight o'clock."

"I'm taking this book to my room," Terry said. "I'm never watching TV again as long as I live."

Sam sidled into the kitchen. "Where is Burma?" he asked.

Molly looked in Fred's direction. Fred started explaining. Molly asked, with interested suspicion, why the question occurred at eight o'clock on a Sunday night.

"Social studies project," Sam confessed.

"Due when?"

"Friday."

"You have a week then."

"Last Friday, I mean. She'll maybe give me an extension. You had to reach into a hat and pull out something and I got Burma."

"How many pages?" Molly asked.

"Five."

"I've been in Burma," Fred said.

"Then you two better get busy," Molly said, drying her hands. She went upstairs.

Fred said, "They eat dogs."

"They do?" Sam stood at the kitchen table in indecision.

"They cook 'em first. Get your paper and notes and books."

"I have paper and pencils. It's not in our textbook; see, it's a research paper. Five pages but two can be maps and art. I can make Terry draw a dog, except it's gonna look like Snoopy, which nobody will believe people will eat. How come dogs?"

"The key to any nation's economy is protein," Fred said. "Get your paper and an atlas. There's one next to the telephone in your mom's bedroom."

"It's old."

"Burma is older than the atlas."

"Did you eat dog?"

"You'd be surprised what people eat when they are really hungry," Fred said. "Get your stuff."

Shortly after midnight, after Sam had jury-rigged a paper that might pass quick inspection, Fred went up to Molly's bedroom. The room was dark and she was sleeping. Fred stood next to her and nudged her cheek until she could understand him.

"Sorry. Don't wake up. Just reassure me. Ophelia drove you back last night?"

"Yes, Fred."

"And my relationship with you has not been a topic of conversation?"

"No. No. You get your paper done?"

"Yes. It's going to rely heavily on informed sources. Sam's tracing a map now."

"You coming to bed?"

"If you want," Fred said.

"You think a person enjoys sleeping alone? It ain't friendly."

"How friendly you want us to be?" Fred offered.

"About like yay," Molly said, and slept.

30

"I'm driving you to work," Fred told Molly in the morning. "I haven't seen you."

"If you'll bring me home."

"Deal." Fred poured himself coffee. Molly went up to wake Sam again. The morning was dark, but looked as if all the rain had been squeezed out of it. The sky was hanging slack and ashamed. The sun was somewhere else. When Molly herded the children into the kitchen at seven-thirty, there was a small commotion. "Close your eyes, Fred," Terry was demanding.

Sam objected, "You're crazy. He's gonna know." He held something bulky behind him. Molly took her scarf down from the hook beside the door to the garage; the scarf with Eiffel Towers on it. She used it to blindfold her lover. "OK, Fred," she commanded. "Hold up both hands."

Fred put down his cup and complied. He heard the children come to join their mother. There was activity in the vicinity of his left hand. He felt the breeze of furtive rustling. Whispered consultation adjourned to the hallway and became heated. There was agreement. Molly removed the blindfold. Sam and Terry sat at the table and poured cereal. Molly went up to get dressed. Fred looked at the newspaper. The sky puckered outside the kitchen window but did not offer rain.

In the car, driving Molly into Cambridge, Fred told her the fragment of recent Clarke family history he had learned from Jeff Blake the day before. "I'm at sea," Fred said. "I realize, much as I hope I'm thinking like your fellow human, I don't know what it is to have a child; in the present context especially."

Traffic was heavy and slow, waterlogged, it seemed, on Route 2. Everything conspired to make it Monday morning. Molly said, "As soon as you have a child you become a hostage. Once you learn to wake in the night and worry, your mind changes forever. A child holds a mortgage on your identity and you don't have control over it."

Fred changed lanes and moved at the same pace in the new lane.

"It's not your life you are willing to lay down for your child," Molly said. "Because that's your life in the child. Of course you want to save it. You'd do anything."

"That's the mother," Fred said. "Here is where I'm stuck. Blake said the father of these two inner girls of advanced years— Ann and Alexandra, or Sandy, Clarke—whether or not he was in his right mind, admitted to participating in these things: raping the daughters, or offering them up. If he didn't do it, why would he say he did? Maybe he did it, or something like it. People do awful things. But if he didn't, why does he confess?"

They reached the traffic circle at Fresh Pond. Molly said, "In a way that would reduce the enormity of the accusation. It's a desperate trade-off. Suppose the child makes the accusation in good faith, believing it is true—and all these stories and fads and memories and recovered so-called *repressed* memories are convincing, so full of detail; anyway, the child accuses him or her of some intimate assault that violates the natural bond between parent and child. The accusation is so awful maybe the only way to bring it down to manageable size, and at the same time free the child from such a weight—because a false accusation of the kind is really an awful crime—is to say, 'I love this child. Therefore it must have happened.'

"And, we can all be moved by the power of suggestion, as long as it finds the right way to sneak in; you see the child jump off the cliff and you jump after, hoping somehow you'll land first and break her fall."

They drove silently for a while.

"The children's father used to say—I'm not talking about him, Fred, but you want to know what goes on in a father's mind. Ask Walter. But my kids' father said once, and I still love him for it, 'A man would do anything for you if you let him get enough of that sour, sweet, milky smell on a little baby's neck, under the chin.' He said that. I'll never understand what happened, Fred. He cared for his own bottle too much after all.

"What happens when the kid is old enough to spot the mileage he can get by shouting at the parent, 'You betrayed me!'? The parent wants the child's success so much, maybe the parent goes along because that's better than to think, 'My child is killing me.'

"I don't know. Sam and Terry are too young. Ask me in ten or twelve years. Today's program is bad enough. Terry wants me to bring her back a 'big, big, huge book about horses.' "

Bookrajian met Fred in an upstairs room filled with pencils and No Smoking signs. His eyes were bloodshot and he smiled crookedly. A man in his late forties, he was thin and tall and dark, and wore a greenish suit that may have started black, and a blue necktie loose at the collar. He chewed a toothpick. "You got something on that lady antique dealer from Boston," Bookrajian said. He had stood to test his height against Fred's when Fred walked in. Having proved it better by an inch of hair, he sat behind his desk again, motioning toward a hard oak chair on Fred's side.

Fred said, "Another thing came up."

"What were you, in the service?"

"Like that," Fred agreed.

"I notice a man comes in the room and spots where all the weapons are," Bookrajian said. "Easy, not making a big deal out of it; but he's got the setup cold before he opens his mouth."

"About Marek Hricsó," Fred began.

"For the moment he's out." Bookrajian took the toothpick from his mouth, looked at it, turned it, and started chewing on the splayed dried end. "Seems the boy wonder is doing an old lady in Boston. She came forward during the weekend, says he was with her that night. Called and left a message I got this A.M. I gotta drive into Beantown and follow up."

Fred said, "Madeleine Shoemacher?"

"So what you got for me?" Bookrajian asked. "I'm busy." Bookrajian grinned. He'd stolen Fred's thunder and gotten laid in Atlantic City, both.

"A question," Fred said.

Bookrajian spread his hands, then checked his watch.

"A week, maybe two weeks ago, an old man's body turned up on the bank of the river. You recall?"

"John Doe." Bookrajian chewed his bit of tree. "Neck broken. In the water maybe three months."

"I heard about a missing person and I thought I'd take a look at the body."

"The body, no," Bookrajian said. "It's too late. Nobody wanted it. Autopsy reports and the rest of it you can see if you get authorization. The body we didn't need. Photos, though, those you can look at. Maybe give us an ID. That would be a favor."

Bookrajian riffled through a pile of manila folders on the right side of his desk. "These are all wide open," he said, choosing a fattish folder and tossing it across to Fred. When Fred opened it Blanche Maybelle Stardust, clad only in a glossy black-and-white eight by ten photograph, gazed up at him invitingly. Molly'd been wrong about those perfect breasts.

"Lighter than air indeed," Fred said. "It's a canard."

Bookrajian, who had half-risen to see Fred's response, turned purple. "Wrong folder," he said. He snatched it back. "Different case. The boys mix 'em up. Try this one. Sorry about that." He tucked the Blanche Maybelle Stardust file into his top desk drawer, next to the matches and cigars.

Fred opened the new folder and looked at the face of the cadaver of the man who had called himself Martin last winter, in front of Molly's house. The face was leaner and more horselike, and, naturally, rendered somewhat more desperate by death and immersion; but it was the same face. Fred kept his own face still, but not too still.

"Know him?" Bookrajian asked. His chewing became lazy.

Fred scratched his face and studied the picture. "Problem is, I didn't know the guy myself. Some people were talking and what they said started me thinking."

"These people have a name?"

I ell you what I'll do," Fred suggested. "If you can spare one of these photographs a day or two, I'll see what they say."

"Are these local people? There's no missing-persons report on file that fits my guy, who is a homicide, incidentally." Bookrajian reached out for the folder.

"If you can't spare a photograph, I can't help you," Fred said.

"A photo you can't have, but I'll get you a Xerox. Wait here," Bookrajian said. He looked at his top desk drawer and chewed. "No, why don't you wait downstairs at the desk."

It took Fred twenty minutes to lose, without appearing to know he was there, the adept young man in blue jeans, white sneakers, and brown leather jacket who happened to be on the Green Street sidewalk, opposite the entrance to the station, when he left it carrying his envelope with the couple of good Xeroxed heads, full face, and profile.

Fred was on foot, having left his car in Molly's space at the library. He put his nose inside and found Molly at the reference desk. "You're not seeing Cover-Hoover again today, are you?"

"It's on the schedule. I got your note and I've been working on your problem. Don't start protecting me, Fred. I'm to see Cover-

211

Hoover with Ophelia. Lunch. We're Cover-Hoover's guests. I can't sink her ship unless I'm in it. Ophelia's ready to brainstorm over big plans she has that include both book and TV series, called *Rescuing Satan's Children*.

"Ophelia's really bought this?"

"Filly—you gotta love that little cowboy artist's attention to detail, don't you?—does not buy. She sells. And yes, she is ready to sell it unless I convince her otherwise. This business is a dangerous flaming pile of horseshit, and Ophelia deserves to get burned. But the rest of the public does not, and anyway she's my sister. I am going to open Cover-Hoover up and show her guts to Ophelia, and suggest an alternate course to equal profit. Look what I've got. In less than five years the Adult-Rescue, Inc. foundation has socked away over a million bucks. They own the property on Hay Street outright. That's worth another, what, two hundred thousand? Their annual report shows shares in Portuguese banks, Euro Disney, and AT&T, and they pay out a seventy-five grand annual salary to Miss Loving-Caring-I'll-Scare-You-Out-of-Your-Pants Cover-Hoover." Molly waved a sheaf of papers. "That's what I have. What about you?"

"It was our guy," Fred said. "I'm sorry."

"Photos?" Molly asked, shivering. Fred nodded. "You need me to look at them?"

"No."

"I was afraid of him. The fear was right," Molly said. "I smelled it. I translated it wrong. I should have feared *for* him."

"We don't know for certain he was Martin Clarke," Fred said.

"No. But we know. They got his house, didn't they?"

Fred called Clay from the pay phone in the library's vestibule. Clay could take a hint, and had moved to the Ritz, having called Fred last night at Molly's to interrupt his description, to a rather awed Sam, of nightlife in Rangoon.

"There's only one African head in all of Copley," Clay said. "It appears a couple of times, but it's much later than ours. What does ours look like?"

212

Fred told him, "Can't talk now. Got to keep moving. You're OK there?"

"I shall try the MFA library tomorrow," Clay said. "I must look deeper into this Copley puzzle. You did say it is signed?"

"It's OK on that front."

He'd forgotten Billy, at the reference desk, who was said to be the one who had talked to someone on the telephone about a picture signed I. S. C. Pix. He went back in and asked Molly, "Did you check with Billy?"

"I'll go through his pile. He's gone to lunch early." She fingered through the clip of pink memo slips until she found the one with the right date and message; she read the phone number to Fred.

"Shit. It's Kwik-Frame. That's no surprise. I wanted the number at their secret hideout. Gotta go. Be careful."

Molly said, "Don't look like that."

31

Fred drove to Walden Street and parked near the railroad bridge. He took his necktie off and tossed it into the backseat. It still wasn't raining. It felt like a different land. It was twelve-thirty, and not warm. Fred was wearing a sweater under his tweed jacket, but no coat. He looked down at the tracks. The police caution tape had been taken away. Oona had been dead about a week—time enough to begin to know the ropes wherever she had landed in the hereafter.

Fred walked to Mass. Ave. and crossed it so as to see into Kwik-Frame from the far side. The view was good enough for him to make out Boardman (Manny) Templeton and Ann Clarke inside, talking at the counter. If Ann Clarke left for lunch he'd follow her and initiate a conversation. If Manny went to sacrifice unnecessary protein to his pectorals, Fred planned to amble into the store and apologize to the despondent woman in red curls for his recent hasty departure. He picked up a sandwich and ate it on the sidewalk, keeping an eye on Kwik-Frame's entrance; upstairs-office windows offered signs that read MARTIAL ARTS and REAL ESTATE.

Manny came out, loosening his shoulders in a black hooded sweatshirt he'd thrown on over Mickey Mouse. He looked like the Teenage Mutant Ninja Turtle Scimunito, named after a justly ill-known painter of the Italian Renaissance. Fred waited, giving Manny time to decide which direction to go to seek his prey. The framer turned toward Porter, crossed the street, and went into the subway entrance. Depending where Manny was headed, Fred might have more than an hour.

Fred finished his eggplant sub. When he walked into the store, Ann Clarke was on the pink counter phone, telling it, "I know." She made a signal to Fred that meant, I'll be through in a minute, or, Your order is ready. She said once more into the phone, "I know," then, "I will. Yes. I'll be careful."

She hung up, looked past Fred, and read the empty words graven upon the far side of the universe; *Wherever You Go, There You Are.* Oona's spirit had read the words already, spat into the elephant leg provided by the management for that purpose, and exclaimed, "I come all this way to learn garbage like this?"

"Your order," Ann Clarke said. "I'll get it."

Fred waited at the counter while Ann Clarke drifted back to Manny's workspace and found his yard of cloth, now stretched to thirty-four inches square and framed in fake black bamboo. She looked the question at him whether it would do. The little fish or sparrows cavorted in a strained way on the rack.

"Perfect," Fred said, tapping his manila envelope on the counter.

"I'll wrap it then."

Fred pulled out cash to pay her. She put the cardboard corners on, then wrapped his purchase in brown paper and fastened it with tape.

"You got rid of those Mexican frames," Fred said.

"At that price people couldn't resist them." She handed Fred his change from the two twenties he'd given her.

"Too bad," Fred said. "I thought I could use one for this—

here, I'll show you." He pulled out the full-face picture of the dead man with his mouth gaping.

Fred had been prepared to run around the counter and catch her, in case sudden collapse under stress was a family trait. She did not move or change color, but stood looking down at the Xerox, which was as clear as the photograph from which it had been taken. Her eyes became wider. Aside from that there was no flicker of life or emotion on her face. "Satan sent you," Ann Clarke said. She stood like a discarded Victorian marble statue commemorating an unhappy virtue like Forbearance. Fred asked, "What did you expect?"

Ann Clarke gaped at the picture of her father. She walked to the front of the store and locked the door. She turned the light out. Fred had stayed with her in case she was heading for the street. "What does he want?" Ann Clarke asked.

Fred took a guess. "Mr. Pix."

Ann Clarke kept nodding. Otherwise she did not move. The moment was hypnotic. She resembled the crouching plastic dog in the back window of the car in front of you, its head moving as if it were interested in the passing world in the mildest way.

"Is it here?" Fred asked. "Does Boardman Templeton have it? Does your sister? Or Cover-Hoover?"

Ann Clarke shook her head and told him, "I am lost."

"Look," Fred said. "I don't have all day." He pointed down at his picture. "That's your dad, right?"

"He was disowned."

"I'll say. He was disowned but good. But he was living with you, right? You tell anyone he was missing?"

Ann Clarke shifted mental gears and focused. "My father was not missing. He was gone. Disowned a long time ago. He was replaced by something else, a shell."

"I'm worried about your sister," Fred said.

"Keep out of my sister. Kill me now. The others are safe." For the first time her face assumed an expression, which was spite. "I will tell you nothing. Kill me. How will you do it?"

Fred said, "Why don't we go someplace and talk this over;

maybe sit down?" Ann Clarke took off her apron. She went into the back of the shop and grabbed a lined tan raincoat from a hook, putting it on over the navy pants and brown sweater she was wearing. She said, "I'm ready."

"Oh, the painting," Fred reminded her. "That's in the shop? Mr. Pix? You remember?"

She shook her head. "Somewhere else," she said.

"Let's go then," Fred said. He followed her to the door, which she unlocked and locked again once they were on the street. Fred carried his wrapped frame job. Ann Clarke carried the envelope with the pictures of her disowned old man. Fred walked her to where he'd left his car on Walden Street. He had gotten a ticket for parking in a spot intended only for residents of Cambridge. He wondered, What happened to Oona's car? He put Ann Clarke in his passenger seat and the framed cloth in the backseat before he sat next to his companion.

"Where will you kill me?" she asked. She showed no surprise, displeasure, or impatience with her situation. She didn't seem drugged, or crazed; just absurdly passive.

"Shall we pick up Sandy?" Fred tried.

"She's safe. Are we waiting for a train?"

Fred's back crawled. "Let's sit somewhere else," he said.

"That woman was trying to find us," Ann Clarke said as Fred started the car. "Now you have found me."

Fred started driving. If Molly were available he would take this zombie to the library to see if Molly's sense could straighten her out before the kingdom of shrinkdom bent her worse. If he delivered her to Bookrajian in this state she'd likely be committed to Cambridge City Hospital's psycho ward, one of whose top docs was continually in the news and TV talk shows for his best-selling published therapeutic work with victims of UFO abductions.

The best spiritual advice Fred had ever heard was from an old cowpoke who suggested, "Lift your tail when you shit." Most other advice he'd heard, however much anyone paid for it, he could pass up. But Ann Clarke was beyond heeding the cowpoke's wisdom. The loving-caring had driven her up to the eyes into her own asshole. No wonder she acted like someone in a dark place.

Fred made up his mind and turned right, toward Boston.

"I said we should destroy him," Ann Clarke said. "Manny wouldn't."

"Mr. Pix?"

"Now I will be destroyed." She folded her hands in her lap. "He will win."

Fred found an empty slot on Chestnut Street and put the car into it. He came around, opened Ann Clarke's door, and helped her out. He took the woman inside. Teddy was at the desk. Teddy was settling down more, rational most of the time. Ann Clarke saw Teddy and nodded. "Mr. Pix," she said.

Teddy looked a question at Fred. They had only a few rules for the house, but those included No Women and Mind Your Business. Teddy even dressed coherently now. Today, for the desk job—some of the guys couldn't rest unless there was a sentry working—he was wearing jeans and a red flannel shirt and a yellow neckrag. His Afro was modified to where, if he had to, he could get work in a bank. He'd remember his last name pretty soon, go back to Atlanta, and pick up whatever he had been studying before he joined the spooks.

Fred told Ann, "This is a friend of mine. He's not Mr. Pix, and he's no relation. Nobody wants to hurt you here, not even me.

"Teddy, this woman's name is Ann. Do you mind if she sits with you till I come back?"

"Sure. Hello, Ann."

"Nobody in the back room?" Fred asked. "If she needs it?" The back room, provided with its own john, could be locked from the outside and enjoyed soundproofing and no windows. They'd put it in for when somebody went off the deep end.

"Sure," Teddy said. "The lady's fine with me till you get back. Suppose she wants to talk to pass the time, is there a subject that interests her?"

Fred went into the kitchen of their building, modified from apartments to its original status as a rooming house. He took a chair and brought it back to the front hall so Ann Clarke could sit across from Teddy. "She may think the devil is trying to get her."

Teddy inclined his head. "I can understand that," he said. "That is one place I been."

He'd thought, driving over, following more or less the Red Line's path, So Manny is taking the T somewhere? Fred did not want to spend so much quality time with Ann Clarke that he lost sight of everything else. She really was safe now, with Teddy—safer than she'd been for many years.

Fred put his car next to Clayton's in the space off Mountjoy Street, and walked down the hill and along Charles to Oona's. The shop was dark, and the old Closed sign Oona had used was hanging in the door, behind the glass. But light shone in the back room. Fred rang the buzzer and, in a few moments, opened the door. No bell rang. It had been ripped off the door. The door had not been locked. Marek always locked it. Fred locked it himself and brushed through to the back room, calling, "Marek?" The room was empty of human life, though filled with its byproducts—which were noticeably fewer in number.

There was nothing here alarming other than the scent of fresh alarm—and the light burning for no reason, and the front door unlocked. Fred took the back stairs up, searched fast through Oona's apartment, calling, "Marek!" Her rooms already had the despondent feel of an abandoned church. Fred ran up the last flight. The silence was wrong. He opened the door and saw Marek stretched on the floor on his back, his arms out, wearing only the black jeans and gloves, his bare feet tied with a black thing on the far side of one of the Steinway's legs. He didn't move; was dead or, no, not conscious. Fred tore off the gag made of the white shirt the pianist had been wearing.

Fred was puzzled. If the intention was to immobilize the guy, he'd just untie his feet when he came to—but then Fred understood the state of Marek Hricsó's hands inside the gloves. The

219

fingers, even the thumbs, were bent and swollen into blobs. They looked like Mickey Mouse's gloves, but on this man were stuffed with a pain that would be horrifying both as physical fact and for its implication. Marek's hands lay on the Oriental rug without a twitch. The guy was unconscious for good reason. Manny Templeton had stopped by to do lunch.

32

Fred watched Marek return to consciousness. It was slow and exceedingly painful. He'd untied his feet immediately, and covered Marek with blankets he took from the ormolu cheesecake of a mad Bavarian prince's wet dream bedroom he found behind one of the doors off this room. Into his bedchamber Marek had crammed everything gilt and curly he could find in Oona's shop: five-foot-tall candlesticks and all. Fred had been obliged to go down to Oona's kitchen looking for brandy or whiskey, but had to settle on slivovitz.

Marek needed medical attention right away. Nice sense of humor Manny had, tying the feet together with their long black socks, leaving the man no hands to free them. When Marek surfaced he was dazed by pain. He choked against the second dose of Oona's slivovitz, and swung his head back and forth on the carpet to look at his extended hands: grotesques in their strained leather. His eyes filled with tears. He opened his mouth and gave a long sob of despair.

Fred said, "There are good hand people."

Marek sobbed again. He gagged and puked next to the right side of his face. Fred slid him gently from the pool. He said, "I'll take you to the best person there is. I called her to expect you, on Oona's phone downstairs."

Marek shook his head. "A clock smashed with a hammer, that is not fixed. Take me anywhere. He is coming back to kill me after he decides I have nothing more to tell him." Marek tried to sit and failed. His face went gray again. The muscles in his arms and chest jerked. Marek lay still. He said, "After you leave that day, I start to think what I am thinking while you are here making Hop hop. I think that one who wrote the note, or you, Fred Taylor— one of you is the one who killed Oona. First I think it is you. Therefore I will not tell you anything in case I must kill you. But now I know it is this other one. And I can do nothing to him with these hands. Help me stand."

Fred thought, The guy has Oona's blood and spirit in him, holding out while that vicious bastard snaps every finger, and— Jesus Christ—the thumbs. If you want a mind-altering experience, try that one.

Fred said, "I don't think you can move yet. I'll go downstairs and call some medics in. I can't splint your hands any better than the gloves are doing now. You're lucky he did not take them off."

Marek shook with agony, realizing what would be laid bare when someone cut the leather off him. "No medics," Marek said. "We must go before that man returns to kill me, who am innocent!"

"You got aspirin?"

"These drugs are no good for you."

It was cold outside, and there was no way Fred could think of to get Marek's upper body into clothes. He made a poncho by cutting a slit in a blanket with his pocketknife, then got him standing. The blood pushed down into his hands by gravity made Marek groan and totter. The man stood with one arm around Fred's shoulder to keep his balance and, raising his right foot, used it to lower the Steinway keyboard cover with a crash.

"We'll put on your shoes downstairs," Fred said. "I don't want you skidding on the way down."

At the shop door, after Fred had got Marek's feet into their loafers, Marek showed him where to find the key and how to set the alarm. "People will steal my things," Marek said. He looked speculatively around the shop, weaving in anguish. "Ignorant persons who are rich pay well for beautiful things," he said. "And I am friends with such people."

Fred walked Marek slowly to his car off Mountjoy Street and put him in the passenger seat. Marek, groaning, balanced the ugly nonsense Manny had made of his hands on the poncho rucked up on his thighs.

"I want to take you to this hand surgeon I found," Fred insisted. "She is the best; people fly in from Europe . . ."

"I do not play again. Never," Marek said. "The instrument is closed. I shall sell it. I cannot be what I was; therefore I shall be another thing. Take these hands to a place that will fix them fast and cheap. From this time on I need these fingers only to pick my nose, clean my backside, and fondle the genitalial parts of my friends—and to count the money I shall make in my antique store on Charles Street in Boston, which I shall call Marek. It is the name Oona would want."

Fred started driving. "Marek, tell me about the man. You told him nothing?"

"Are you crazy? He says he will break my fingers! I tell him everything so he will not hurt me, but he will not believe. He says I am trying to find the place they are hiding some children. He is terrible, terrible nonsense. He says I have a picture of a squirrel and another picture and am using them with spells to find where the children hide. He says I am a friend of the devil. I am the devil. I tell him no, it is you, Fred, doing all these things.

"Only then does he start breaking my fingers. I scream. He ties my mouth and I cannot scream. Each time he says something he breaks . . . he breaks. . . . Let them fix my hands and I will help you kill him."

223

"It doesn't work that way," Fred said, but Marek had fainted. Fred took him to the walk-in clinic in Charlestown and showed him how to get to the place on Chestnut Street after he was finished. "Wait for me there."

It was four-thirty and he wanted to tell Molly that in case he was a bit after five, don't worry, he had not forgotten his promise to take her home. He stopped into the place to use the phone.

"Molly took some personal time," he was told, by whomever was at the reference desk. "Unexpected errand. She left you a message. You want to come by for it or shall I read it to you? It's sealed."

"I'll be there in fifteen minutes. Where is she?"

Teddy looked over at him, worried at the tone in his voice, and said, "She's sleeping in the back room." For an instant Fred thought he meant Molly. The needle registering hope shot up, then plunged. He had forgotten Ann Clarke.

He drove carefully, keeping his anxiety at bay, and had Molly's envelope in thirteen minutes, tearing it open as he made for the library's drafty vestibule.

Fred, here's the best I can do. Copley married Susanna Clarke, as you and Clayton know. She is the daughter of Richard Clarke, a Tory who received most of the tea into his warehouse that didn't go into the harbor and get wasted symbolically. You know how I feel about symbols.

Copley sailed to England in 1774. His wife's family came later, but before the fighting started. You can believe they took as much as they could of what they owned. We have names for brothers and sisters of Susanna—Mary, Sarah, Isaac, Hannah, Jonathan. But that's the white brothers and sisters. The black ones, we don't know.

In Boston before—also after—the Revolution, a person was slave or free depending on the legal status of the mother. Though you could bear your father's name and be a slave. Suppose Susanna's father (or brother—but let's keep it simple) had a son by an African woman who was enslaved to him; and that this man had children in due course, and a sequence of marriages ensued of the offspring of these unions with persons who were of European background, until there was nothing visible left of the African heritage, only the remnant of the slave name to proclaim a nominal identity to this root. What do I know?

Copley went to England and did well. He had a son, and the son died and his things were sold, including paintings he had inherited from his artist father. Among them—do you know the Copley portrait in the Detroit Museum, called Head of a Negro? *It's the same head, a sketch, and was sold out of the son's collection in 1864. Here's how it was described in the sale catalog: "Head of a Favorite Negro. Very Fine." I think your portrait is of a brother of Copley's wife, and, who knows, maybe part of her dowry. Isn't that an awful idea? I think part of the Clarke line stayed in, or came back to, the New World, after the Revolution; and that those women—Alexandra and Ann Clarke—are descended from the man in the portrait, who bequeathed them their slave name: which I fear was wasted on those jokers.*

Molly

P.S. Don't forget your birthday tomorrow.

Fred half-read Molly's note while using the vestibule's pay telephone to call Molly's house. He let it ring until he concluded there was nobody home—though the kids should be there. Alarm percolated in him. He'd hoped the note would tell him where she was, not go on about Clayton's problems. He tried Ophelia's number and got Terry. No, her mom was not around, but Ophelia was. Did Fred want to talk with Ophelia?

"Get her."

"What's wrong?"

"Terry, just put her on." Fred drummed his fingers on the

wall. Ophelia took the Lincoln end of the line, saying, "I'm holding the fort, Fred. I told Molly I'll feed the kids and take them to her place, and sit in case she is late, so nobody worries."

"Where is she?"

"Doing research for me. I decided to change my approach to one of investigative reporting. What I see now is more along the lines of the exposé. Apparently, I have discovered, this group . . ."

"Don't fuck around, Ophelia! These people are dangerous. Where's Molly?"

"She's getting a look at what they call their safe house. We arranged she would lead them to believe she wants sanctuary, and they bought her act. We're going to pull the rug out. She'll call when she can and one of us, you or I, Fred, will pick her up. Where this safe house is nobody knows until I tell the world."

Fred put his sick fear to one side. He telephoned Kwik-Frame. No answer. Manny, at large somewhere, could be with Molly. He telephoned Cover-Hoover's secret unlisted number. After three rings her voice answered, "Yes?"

"Put Molly Riley on," Fred said. His fingers stopped drumming. He felt the silence lengthen.

"I am good at voices," Cover-Hoover said. "We've met. You were looking for a painting. Now, apparently, you have involved yourself with another of my patients. She fears you."

"Put her on."

"Mrs. Riley—that is her slave name—has placed herself in my sanctuary. She is safe. She has reached a critical stage. It is especially critical, I would say, now that I know of your . . . attachment to her."

Fred said, "You may be surprised how little you know about critical stages."

"I hear your concern. Thank you for sharing it with me. Mrs. Riley wishes privacy and I may not ethically violate her wish. I can do no more than to assure you, and her loved ones, that she is safe."

"Ann Clarke is safe too," Fred said. "And she's talking."

He listened to the silence turning colder on the line. "Ah?" Cover-Hoover prompted. "Perhaps we can discuss these feelings in my office."

Fred said slowly, "Wait there. Feelings aside, if anything happens to Molly, you are dead meat."

Fred put the car in the lot under the Charles Hotel and walked to Brattle Street. He took the stairs to Cover-Hoover's floor and pressed the buzzer.

"Yes?" came Cover-Hoover's fragrant, patient voice.

"No games," Fred said into the voice slot.

The door opened to a click. Manny sprang at him with the beginning of an Asiatic roar, very martial arts. Fred met his chin with a head butt that knocked the man out, watched the large mass sliding down, and broke both the bodyguard's arms back quickly at the elbows. He laid him on the anonymous gray carpet of the waiting room before he closed the door into the hall. Manny snorted the deep snore of the suddenly unconscious. When the big man resurfaced he was not going to be cutting paintings apart for a while, or breaking fingers.

With his arms out, Manny would have no further stomach for cute kicks, though he could still make noise. Fred glanced around the waiting room, noticing the two chairs and the pair of closed doors Molly had described. He thought back to the moment on the street, looking up at the third floor. He recollected where the staircase must fall, and the elevator shaft next to it, and how the windows were laid out. The bank of three in a row would be the office, on the left as you looked up. The single, separated by a space of brick, would have to be the bathroom.

Fred opened the door on his left, discovering an antiseptic john with a Japanese decorative theme, into which he propped the snoring Boardman Templeton. Manny's black Ninja sweatshirt rode up, exposing a stretch of tummy as well as the mouse smiling on a green field. Fred had worked in silence, even cutting off Manny's Asiatic roar before it got more than an inch out of his throat. He pushed the privacy lock and closed Manny inside.

Eunice Cover-Hoover was either wondering what had developed in the silence of her waiting room, or she was confident the treasurer of Adult-Rescue, Inc. had accomplished his mission.

Fred opened the second door.

33

Cover-Hoover was at her bank of windows, lowering the blinds, saying, "It will help you feel safe," to the young woman on the couch who started panting and turning green at Fred's entrance. "Don't mind me," Fred said. "Please continue." Cover-Hoover continued turning. The young woman continued fainting, falling sideways on the couch, and slipping softly to the floor. Cover-Hoover remained in her window, the blind half closed. She was wearing a green dress of nubby linen, its color matched by a silk scarf that was keeping her hair up.

"You are not safe," Fred told her. Cover-Hoover's eyes flicked toward her telephone. "I wouldn't," Fred advised. The youngster on the floor moaned. She'd been small sitting, and was much smaller on the gray carpet, in her gray skirt and gray lambswool sweater and gray pallor.

"You are shattering a confidential dyad," Cover-Hoover said. She raised her eyebrows and asked, "Did you notice my colleague?"

"No."

Cover-Hoover studied him a moment before she looked down at her patient.

"Let's go," Fred said.

"I have a responsibility toward my . . ."

"Can it."

". . . people," Cover-Hoover continued evenly. "Many of them are deeply affected by their traumatic disturbances. The abrupt entrance of a stranger into their sanctuary . . ."

"We don't have time for the crap."

". . . may cause them to try desperate measures." This last phrase was spoken with such sweet resignation Fred received it with a chill of worry.

The patient on the floor whispered, "Victim of Darkness, child of Light."

"That's right, dear," Cover-Hoover soothed her. "We have been interrupted by a former patient of mine. His need is pressing. You may go when you are strong enough. I will be here for you tomorrow." The patient stared at Fred with such a grimace of anxiety Fred wanted to strangle someone. Who had done such damage to this person? Cover-Hoover watched him closely.

"I have class at seven," the patient said. "Boardman will take me?"

"Do you mind waiting in the next room?" Cover-Hoover suggested.

"Better she waits here," Fred said. "I don't mind including her in our confidential dyad. Here's what I have. Your people killed Oona Imry, an antiques dealer from Boston, also a friend of mine, for reasons I have yet to appreciate. You or your people sucked an old man dry before you killed him—you got his house, and somewhere around a million bucks . . ."

"I accept no payment from my patients," Cover-Hoover broke in. "Pay no attention, Candace. He is upset."

"You, Adult-Rescue, Inc.," Fred said. "Now you claim your patient-adult-victims are prepared to defend their safe house or some damned thing?"

Cover-Hoover spread her hands and sighed.

"You study at Mass Art," Fred told the student. Her mouth opened with surprise. "What's your major?"

"Art ed."

"Contradiction in terms. Never mind. Your family rich?" Fred asked. "How much does your dad make?"

The art education major stammered.

"This woman here," Fred said, jerking his thumb toward Cover-Hoover, "is going to hit you up, or him, your parents—someone in your family—for a big donation. Not to her. She's too pure, doing great missionary work. To her foundation. Wait. The expression in your eyes tells me your people already started forking over. Right?"

"Not that much," the student said. "Dad believes what my uncle did, but Mom . . . Anyway, fuck them. After what they maybe did . . ."

"This is a precious confidence you are betraying," Cover-Hoover said to her patient, administering mild reproof.

"Shut up," Fred told her. To the student he said, "You live at home or at the safe house?"

"Safe house? I have an apartment."

"OK. Because the safe house is going to be off-limits. And Cover-Hoover is going to be busy. If you have problems—most people do—go to the clinic at your college. Meanwhile, since you have a class scheduled, go to it. Take the T. You don't need Boardman. You'll be fine on the subway. I guarantee it."

The student got up and left. Fred closed the office door. "People believe what they were already going to believe," he said. He cracked his knuckles and rubbed his hands. "Now. I assume your office is soundproofed? What's the story on this safe house?"

A timid tap came at the office door. Fred opened it. "The bathroom door is locked," the student said.

"It's hard to find a toilet in Harvard Square. There's one in the Harvard Coop. Second floor. The Coop's gonna take care of you," Fred told her.

"Thanks," the student said, closing the door again.

231

"Where was I?" Fred went on. "Oh yes, Manny's in your crapper." Cover-Hoover licked her lips and stared. "Let's go to your safe house," Fred said. "We'll take my car."

"Ann Clarke is not to be trusted," Cover-Hoover warned. "She suffers from delusions." Fred moved behind her and pulled her chair back. She rose slowly. "You are impeding an important work," the doctor said.

"I hope so."

Before they left Fred carried Manny into Cover-Hoover's office and laid him, snoring, on the couch. The doctor of loving-caring looked sick, seeing his arms flop backward at the elbow joints. Fred pulled the shirt and sweatshirt down. "Euro Disney stock was Boardman's idea?" Fred asked. "Yeah. Right. He likes Mickey."

"Boardman was horribly abused as a child," Cover-Hoover said. "He came to me, one of my early—but this is no business of yours. It is a wonder he survived. The mouse, its happy innocence, is part of a therapeutic . . . What you have done to the boy will add years to his therapy. Our work together . . . his capacity for trust . . ."

"After Molly Riley joins us we'll arrange for someone to scoop the little fellow up," Fred assured her. They walked down Brattle Street, across the brick no-man's-land filled with pitfalls and traps for the unwary that some designer had inflicted on an honest corner. Fred kept to Cover-Hoover's elbow. Anyone who recognized her would see she had switched bodyguards. She said, "I cannot be held responsible for the actions of my patients. Nor can I be required by law to break the doctor-patient bond of confidentiality. What they do is their business. What they say is mine."

She looked at Fred's car with dismay before she got in. As he drove to the tollbooth to buy their way out she said, "I am under duress, because I understand my former patient, now my colleague, is being held by you and is in danger. I am under duress. You are forcing my hand."

"That's fair," Fred said.

Cover-Hoover had not put on her coat, and it was a cold evening. She did not shiver. She crossed her arms and said, "Can you find Walden Street?" Jesus, Fred thought. The place was nearby. He should have found it. "I have been concerned about Boardman Templeton," his passenger said, looking beautiful. "The dark forces buried within him are powerful. He may yet not escape them."

Fred cut along to Garden, turned right up Chauncy next to the old Commodore Hotel, now Harvard housing, intending to turn left on Mass. Ave. toward Porter. "You may be placing my patient, Molly Riley, in grave danger," Cover-Hoover said.

"What are you, talking into a microphone?" Fred asked. "Making evidence? Or is this a threat?"

Cover-Hoover looked out her window at the dull, cold, darkness of the night.

Fred pulled over in front of a health-food store and, looking to any interested observer like an impulsive first date, gave his passenger a quick search and found the device between breasts well-designed to give it shelter. He tossed it into the backseat, where it slid down the wrapped package of stretched cloth representing dogs or kangaroos. Cover-Hoover did not make a move to stop him or look back. She did her wide white buttons up.

"You'll be more comfortable now," Fred told her.

"Your argument is force."

Fred started driving again after a bus opened a place in the stream of traffic. "Your argument is force also," Fred answered. "Poison is force. What danger is Molly in?"

"She fears you. She fears all men."

"Fraud and murder. That's what you should be afraid of. Being indicted for those things."

"I am a healer. What a patient of mine, outside my knowledge or control . . ."

"We'll find out soon enough," Fred said. He turned left on Walden. "Oona Imry was killed here," he mentioned as they crossed the bridge. She showed no flicker of interest. "Little

Boardman has a thing about bridges. Apparently, according to Ann Clarke, she and Manny forced gin into her until she lost control. Then Manny held her under the bridge until he could get her in front of a train. Say anything you want . . ."

"I am not responsible. I know nothing about this. I am not responsible. Turn right here." Fred turned on Richdale. "It's too late. It is out of my hands." She spoke like someone standing on a mountain and looking down at a rushing sea of mud below her, engulfing everything that lived. Unfortunate as it was, at least it was happening down there. Fred looked ahead of them down the S curve of Richdale Avenue. He passed the office-furniture warehouse and showroom backing this side of the tracks.

"Ann Clarke is the victim of recurrent guilt fantasies," the zombie's therapist confided. "I don't know what she may have said to you . . ."

"Which house?"

Fred had driven along Richdale last week, prospecting generally. It was as mixed-use as a street in Cambridge could be. Cover-Hoover gestured toward a large lot, vacant except for dismantled brick factory buildings. The lot was fenced, but kids had cut openings so they could get in and hurt themselves. At the far edge was a one-story brick building, boarded up, running the whole length of the lot. Fred saw no residential units in the vicinity. It was isolated and looked abandoned.

Cover-Hoover said, "A kidnapped witness will say anything. Ann Clarke will say she is Marie Antoinette looking for her lost head. Templeton knows nothing, except the loyalty of the low IQ. I have given these people something to live for, something to die for."

Fred studied the brick building. They could have it booby trapped and wired. All they'd need was one convert from MIT.

"Let's go in." Fred opened his car door. Rain began activating the dark air. Lights were sparse on this street.

"I cannot take responsibility for the consequences." Cover-Hoover spoke with grave simplicity and understatement. Fred, listening to her mild, sad voice, was invited to imagine ghastly

234

possibilities behind the patchwork facade of the building. A mob of fanatic former victims of Satan stared out from behind the boarded apertures, brandishing weapons.

"We'll see what's going on," Fred said. "According to Sandy Blake you sleep with Manny?" Cover-Hoover glanced at him, her tongue flickering moisture onto her full lower lip. Her eyebrows rose. She asked herself—Fred could see her doing it—if this was a way in, an invitation anted up by Fred's subconscious unselective lust.

"Contemporary therapeutic practice allows broad latitude, if exercised with discretion, and with due respect to the patient's needs and progress. Supposing you, for instance, found yourself to be a patient of mine . . ."

"Thanks for sharing these feelings with me," Fred said. He walked around the car, opened the door, and took her arm. "Let's say hi to the dervishes."

34

They walked in the light rain beside the low building at the edge of the vacant lot. It was an old cement sidewalk underfoot, cracked and soft with weeds. Fred kept slightly behind Cover-Hoover, and on her right; the building was on her left. She was right-handed. She'd provide instant cover if anyone inside had the notion to use firearms. The building paced at forty yards. Fred watched for movement in the boarded windows.

The power of his own experiential memory and fear was growing. Cover-Hoover would rely on that. That was how she worked. She was good enough to smell some of his past. He'd held men while they died screaming. He'd done his own screaming in his day. She'd gotten out of the car with such palpable recognition he wondered, What's her bluff? What does she have waiting?

She had hardly turned a hair when she saw Manny, her demon lover, out cold with his powerful arms gone flaccid. She'd looked him over, seen he was finished, and started planning her next move.

"Boardman is impulsive and excitable," Cover-Hoover said—one professional to another, as if she were responding to Fred's thought and distancing herself rapidly from these wayward patients. They rounded the narrow building. The back entrance would not be visible from the street. Surrounding buildings were too far away, or were warehouses without windows. Cover-Hoover pushed a buzzer next to a heavy iron door and spoke into an intercom grill. "The Stalker is with me. He is holding your sister somewhere."

The door buzzed open. Fred went in behind her, stepping into darkness. He kept his hand under Cover-Hoover's elbow. She turned a light on. Someone had done a half-decent job making a bad place habitable. It was lit by hanging fluorescent work lights, and furnished with camp stove, folding chairs and tables, and four metal single beds. Fred saw a big stilt with dishes in it. The room was as wide as the building, maybe fourteen feet. It smelled like tuna fish.

No crowds of victims greeted them. Cover-Hoover looked around the empty space. "They must be in the meeting room," she said. "We'll go and see, shall we?"

"Where's the door-lock buzzer?" Fred asked.

"One here. One in the meeting room." Cover-Hoover opened a door at the room's far end, giving access to a passage that was dark until she turned lights on with a switch. They were going back the length of the building, in the direction they had come from outside, along the walkway, in the rain. The smell of tuna was stronger. On either side of them the passage offered stall doorways. One led to a bathroom. Some were vacant and tumbled down; others had beds, and a couple of these had stout doors with hasps and padlocks ready.

"You kept the old man in one of these," Fred remarked. "Martin Clarke. According to Ann."

"Sometimes he wandered and required restraint," she said

matter-of-factly. "He'd get loose sometimes, deluded his daughter had been replaced by a changeling. He deteriorated rapidly."

"But he could still sign checks? Or did he surrender his power of attorney?"

Cover-Hoover raised her eyebrows. "One night he simply disappeared," she said. "We feel he went to stay with friends in San Antonio. We never heard. He was a free agent. Anything might have happened."

The woman's aplomb was so impermeable he could not get past the soothing professional veneer. Fred checked each stall for signs of either Molly or Sandy Clarke.

At the far end of the passage was another door. "I'll do what I can to help you," Cover-Hoover promised, easing open the door into a black cavern with small sounds in it. The smell was gasoline, not tuna fish.

"Fred? Don't turn on lights," Molly pleaded from the darkness. Fred was jerking Cover-Hoover's arm down and back. "You'll make a spark. Then the place goes up," Molly explained, her voice shaking with tension. "Fred?"

"Right," Fred said. "I'm here with Cover-Hoover."

"I'm soaked with gasoline. She's next to me. Sandy. Sandy Clarke. Blake. She has a lighter. She's soaked too. I don't know what she wants. I can't figure her out."

"This is Eunice," Cover-Hoover said. Fred watched the light from the hall they had come through stretch slowly into the large room as his eyes adjusted. It was forty feet long or so. Molly was at the far end, kneeling on the floor in front of one of the posts that held the ceiling up, her hands back of her. Molly still was wearing Sam's red down jacket, with the hood up now. She was drenched with gas; the fire, unless it was an immediate explosion, would take her head right away. Her feet were joined on the wrong side of the post. The area was storage space, burned sometime in the past. It smelled charred, once you got past the smell of the gasoline fumes.

Sandy Blake squatted next to Molly, a dark hump of limbs with a pale face that turned toward Fred and Cover-Hoover where they stood in the room's doorway. She held a fist clenched next to Molly's face. Fred could not distinguish the object in the gloom, but Molly would not make a rash misjudgment on so crucial a point. If that's what Molly said, it was a lighter.

"I feel your pain," Eunice Cover-Hoover called into the room, striving to push backward into the hallway. Fred stood their ground. "And I respect your patienthood. Both of you."

It was Templeton's method, to tie Molly's feet and hands around the post. Molly was not one to accept a malignant fate without gesticulating protest. Manny had done the job on Marek, then met Cover-Hoover in Cambridge and taken Molly into safekeeping, and then gotten back to Cover-Hoover's in time to greet Fred.

"I feared such an eventuality," Cover-Hoover whispered to Fred, his colleague now. "I warned you."

"Sandy?" Fred called.

Sandy Blake did not answer. If the woman's intent was to inspire terror, Fred could not have advised her to a better posture at this moment; no pleas, no ultimatums, nothing but silence. Let the opponent engender his own idea of what might come to pass: blinding flash of fast fire; screams of air forced out of lungs in torment; smell of charred flesh. There was no use to think about it. If it happened it was going to follow its own logic, and fast. Fred took his jacket off to have something in hand to use against the blaze he could foresee consuming Molly's head and body.

"Get blankets from the front room," Fred whispered to Cover-Hoover. She'd know it was a chance to run; he'd been holding her by the waistband of her dress, not able to read her quiet. He hadn't let go of it more than an instant, changing hands while he got his jacket off.

Cover-Hoover said, "This is not my concern. I will not, as a trained professional, take sides between patients. It is for them to work out their differences."

She was trembling as the Romans must have when watching the games where lions and Christians worked out their differences. What a paper this would make. Fred shifted his hold to

Cover-Hoover's right arm, bringing it up behind her in a hammerlock. She had been given her chance. "You have a suggestion?" he asked Molly.

Molly said, her voice easy and conversational, not wanting to trip the alarm bells in the woman next to her, "It's quite a puzzle. The one thing I know is, something you want is in the bathroom under the tub. They let me go . . . after Boardman Templeton brought me. Before he—well, before what you see now."

"She doesn't mind us talking?" Fred asked. Cover-Hoover trembled like an idling Lance-Flamme, well tuned. The huddle of crouched women at the far end of the meeting room hadn't changed its profile while they were talking.

"I'm coming in then," Fred said. Sandy Blake jerked her arm threateningly as Molly shouted, "Don't!"

"Send Cover-Hoover," Sandy Blake croaked. "Send Manny's fucking-partner, Eunice." Cover-Hoover went rigid. Sandy Blake stood upright, keeping hold of the hood of Molly's jacket with her left hand and the lighter next to Molly's face with her right. Molly coughed.

"I am your friend and healer," Cover-Hoover said, trembling, but making no attempt to walk into the trap.

"You. I know you, Stalker," Sandy Blake said. "Your name is Fred. You want this woman? I'll trade. Want to trade?"

"Sounds fair," Fred said. Cover-Hoover gave a convulsive jerk. Her perfume struggled against the vapors of fear and gasoline, and faltered badly.

"Bring Cover-fucking-Hoover in and tie her like this one, over there," Sandy Blake commanded, gesturing with the lighter toward another post, ten feet away, between herself and Fred, to Fred's right.

"Fred, there's another factor you might want to consider," Molly said reasonably. "Just so you know, my hands and feet are cuffed, not tied. Manny took the keys with him."

"He gets these magazines," Sandy said, giggling. "He sends away for stuff. Kung fu and that. Stud stuff. The fuck. So give me Cover-Hoover with his mangy sperms all gooshling down her leg."

Cover-Hoover had started babbling and struggling in a serious way while Sandy spoke.

"We know what she wants now," Molly said.

"I want to see her fry and dance. I want to burn her at the fucking stake," Sandy said.

"That's fair," Fred repeated.

"For what she did," Sandy Clarke said calmly.

Eunice Cover-Hoover, struggling, shouted, "I rescued you. I helped you. You and your sister. Both of you."

Fred was obliged to put considerable upward pressure on her arm. He felt the shoulder joint straining to escape, but he left play in the arm. She might yet decide to try doing something helpful.

"You made me a fucking orphan. You took everything. I have nothing," Sandy Blake shrieked.

"How many people do you want to burn?" Fred asked her.

Sandy Blake stopped shrieking as this new idea dawned on her: hope tinged with bitterness. "What do you think? You believe I want to burn myself alive if I don't have to? I got nothing against this other lady—what did you say your name is, lady?"

"Molly," Molly said.

"Molly. There. Nothing against her. She explained it. I knew it but I wouldn't see it, the ride this Cover-Hoover took us on? Maybe Molly burns too, because Manny has the keys, but I have nothing against her. Where's fucking Manny? Bring him. I'll burn him too."

"He couldn't make it," Fred said.

"I am not intimate with my patients, Sandy," Eunice Cover-Hoover announced in a loud voice, "until and unless there has been a marked improvement. . . ." She paused and whispered, only for Fred's ears, "There's a telephone in the living quarters. I'll call for assistance."

"Will you give me Cover-Hoover?" Sandy Blake demanded.

"Sure," Fred said. She'd had an earlier chance to help and

she'd refused it. What she wanted now was only to run. Cover-Hoover heaved in alarm. "What are you doing?" she whispered urgently.

"Trust me," Fred said.

"No whispering," Sandy Blake commanded.

"She doesn't want to," Fred reported. "You still want me to bring her?"

"I don't believe you will."

Molly said, "If Fred says he will do a thing, that thing gets done."

Cover-Hoover shouted, as Fred started moving her into the large room, "Don't be a goddamn fool. She's my patient. Let me work with her."

Fred got as far as the post and told Sandy, "I'm going to tie her with my shoelaces unless you have a better plan." He was close enough to Molly and to Sandy Blake to see the dull glimmer of steel around Molly's ankles and wrists. The fumes were heady; the red gas can sat in a far corner of the room. He held Cover-Hoover with one hand—she trying to bow and escape him—while he stood on one foot after the other, taking the laces from his shoes one-handed. He'd had to drop his jacket so he had nothing left to fight the fire with. He left his shoes on so as not to soak his socks in the puddles of gas on the cement floor.

"Just her hands. Don't tie her feet. I want to see her dance," Sandy Blake said, holding her lighter next to the furze of Molly's darkened curls along the edge of Sam's hood. Sandy was deeply, and sensibly, suspicious. Fred couldn't find an opening anywhere.

"Tell you what," Fred said, working on the laces. "With all the gas around, and the vapor—don't strike your lighter until we're ready, Sandy, OK? We could have an explosion instead of a fire, and you can't watch her burn; I mean we'll all be in it, instead of just her. That's what you want, just her?"

Cover-Hoover, retching and trembling as he forced her hands back of the post and tied them, whispered, one pro to another, "I hope you know what you're doing." The longer they waited, the longer the gasoline had to combine with the room's air. Where the flashpoint was, Fred could not guess. The room could have gone up even when Sandy Blake pressed the door-lock release.

Molly and Sandy Blake watched Fred's work. When Fred was finished, Sandy said, "Get away and let me see what you did." Fred stepped back to the room's doorway while Sandy Blake examined his work. She held the lighter in Cover-Hoover's face and said, easily, "Now look at you. You stole my father and you stole my sister. You stole my husband. You stole everything. You raked it all into a pile and lay down on it and started fucking my Manny."

Cover-Hoover croaked, her voice under strain glowing with the light of pure reason, "Sandy, your father admitted his past actions, and regretted them. He became one of our foundation's valued supporters. He received hours of therapy. We helped him understand that though the actions may have been his, some responsibility for them could be explained by the fact that he himself had been abused as a child. It is a vicious cycle."

"Now pour gas on her," Sandy Blake commanded Fred. "I threw the can in that corner, scared it would blow up."

"Tell you what we'll do," Fred suggested. "Since you don't want to burn if you don't have to—there's so much gas in your clothes, and all around, and what we want is for her to burn, not explode—my suggestion is, put your wet clothes around her feet, which gets them away from your skin, you know? We burn the pile of clothes, and she burns slower. Only if that's what you want."

Cover-Hoover seemed to be saying, "God, God, God."

"Her first," Sandy Blake said, suspicious, pointing at Molly. "Take her stuff off first." She moved between Cover-Hoover and the door, keeping well away from Fred as he walked toward Molly. Sandy held her lighter, ready to spark into flame and throw.

35

Breathing was not easy in the room. Fred had been studying the twelve-foot ceiling, the joining of the beams, the rest of it. By now he could see quite well. The problem was what he did not see: a way out for Molly. One spark in here and she might be finished. Fred worked with his knife, cutting the soaked clothes off her.

"Manny's going to come," Sandy Blake warned. "We better hurry. My Manny's not gonna like this."

"He is injured," Fred said. He'd gotten the jacket off and put it to one side. "He's locked in Cover-Hoover's office."

Sandy Blake laughed. "You with the devil's people?" she asked. "I knew he'd win. You're with them, right?"

"I'm independent," Fred said. He worked on Molly's dress and slip, cutting them away, stooping over her, his blade trembling with caution and the desire to be faster than careful. He'd rather cut her than not get her out of this. He'd rather cut her hands and ankles off, save what he could from the furnace of stupidity these people were . . .

"My underpants. They're nylon," Molly pleaded. "Don't be a prude. They're going to melt."

Fred cut them away and lifted Molly up enough to clear the rest of her clothes away from her, leaving her only the last slick of acrid gas. Her hair was sodden. She was slippery and cold with mortal fear. She said, "Thanks, Fred. That's better." She knew it wasn't much better. The post, though charred, when he leaned against it while he worked, was firm, set in cement at its foot, and well joined to the rafter.

Molly whispered, "You're in my will to be the children's guardian. I never asked . . ."

"No talking," Sandy Blake ordered. "Throw all the clothes over by the doctor's feet. Then you, Fred, get back out of the way."

Fred piled Molly's cut clothes around the excessively pointed high-heeled green leather shoes of Eunice Cover-Hoover.

"One flick of my Bic," Sandy Blake called, capering, waving the lighter.

Molly said, "We don't want an accident. Put your clothes on mine, Mrs. Blake."

"For God's sake, listen to me, Sandy," Eunice Cover-Hoover pleaded. "All this acting-out—I promise there is nothing you have done that cannot be explained. I am here for you. I am working with you even now. I promise hopeful-healing in your future."

"Unless I catch on fire," Sandy said. "You are right," she told Molly and started stepping out of her low black sneakers, laughing. She tossed them one by one at Cover-Hoover. Fred leaned in the doorway again, against the jamb, at ease. "I never undressed in front of a man before," Sandy Blake said, trying a new virgin personality on for size.

Fred assured her, "No big deal. I want to be here in case something goes wrong, Molly being my friend."

Sandy Blake's clothes were doused as completely as Molly's had been. She had not been fooling around, making a bomb of herself. She discarded the green jersey she was wearing, doing it fast and making no opening for Fred to take advantage of the moment the poisonous fabric swished across her face. She kept hold of the lighter. Then she stepped out of the green corduroy pants. She stayed on the far side of Cover-Hoover, between her and Molly, with the lighter ready to use on the piled clothing. Each item of her clothing, once removed, she tossed on the growing pile at Cover-Hoover's feet.

Down to a sleazy yellow camisole, Sandy Blake hesitated. Nothing else covered her breasts. She wore yellow socks and black briefs.

Molly said, "Don't worry about it, honey. Join the club."

Sandy stepped out of the pants and tossed them in Cover-Hoover's face. "That's for stealing my Big Manny." She danced, shimmying as she stripped off her socks, twirled and threw them. Fred, leaning against the doorway, was considering the boarded door on the far end of the room, behind Molly. If the room went, and if he lived, he'd throw himself against the door. It might give. He might find a way to rip that post loose. He'd gotten gasoline on himself, of course, dealing with Molly's clothes. He couldn't help that. He couldn't tell how much was in the room, his own air passages being saturated now.

Sandy, holding the lighter tightly and eying Fred, remembered she was a woman, and beautiful—even voluptuous. She shook out her long black hair. She swayed and let the audience appreciate the shift and shimmy of her body before she slipped her arms down into and under her camisole and lifted it over her head in a fluid motion. She tossed it at Cover-Hoover's feet and stood in the center of the room, naked, and gleaming with gas.

"Now," she said, licking her lips, turning white, smiling toward Cover-Hoover and edging toward Fred's doorway.

"Should we say a prayer first?" Fred suggested, lofting himself across the space between them and smashing the flame, and her right hand, and his, together in one creaking, snapping, fist.

He did not let go of Sandy's crushed hand, but dragged her by it behind him all the way to the far end of the corridor, and through into the next room, until he had it down in the filthy and blessed water of the sink.

"I trusted you. You fuck, I trusted you. You're like the rest of them," Sandy Blake whined.

Fred locked her into one of the furnished stalls. The new personality Sandy had chosen he didn't want to give much independent room. He ran back into the so-called meeting room, where Molly was calling for him and where Eunice Cover-Hoover stood pale and calm as Joan of Arc after the last-minute reprieve, wondering how to justify her divine mission given the intervention of human mercy between herself and martyrdom.

Fred kicked the soaked cloth away from her. He picked up a length of pipe and knocked out glass and boards from the windows on both sides of the room, so they'd start sucking a damp crossdraft. The soaked cloth he threw out a window, along with the gas can.

Molly said, "OK, Fred."

"I thought you were exchanging my baseball glove," Fred said. "Which I know is a surprise. I can't undo the cuffs. I'll get someone as fast as I can."

"Soon would be good," Molly said. "Meantime, maybe something to kneel on? A pillow?"

"Untie me," Eunice Cover-Hoover demanded.

"You interrupted a precious dyad," Fred told her. "Molly, you were saying?"

"Just, my knees ain't what they were back when Sister Rita was training me for Queen of the May," Molly said. "What with all this cement."

"Will do," Fred said. "I'll make you as comfortable as I can. I know you're freezing. But I don't want anything in here that will burn."

"Cold and wet is my favorite," Molly assured him.

"Untie me," Cover-Hoover repeated. "There is still danger."

"Molly has questions," Fred said. "The two of you might as well take advantage of the opportunity, as long as Molly is detained."

It was after eight o'clock. Sandy Blake yelled in her locked stall. Fred used the safe house telephone to call Cambridge police headquarters and made an obstinate stink until they gave him Bookrajian's home number, which was answered on the tenth ring by a sweet, little-girl Southern voice.

"Blanche Maybelle?" Fred asked. "Stardust?"

"Bookrajian," she answered proudly.

"Put Bookrajian on."

The parade did not start arriving until twenty minutes later; but after it started it left little to be desired from the point of view of the children of the neighborhood: rescue vehicles, ambulances, fire trucks, fire marshal, bomb squad, a representative of the sheriff's office, and five squad cars—as well as Bookrajian in his old Diego. Fred had urged strongly that he begin by coming alone, leaving his cigar outside, and bringing tools to deal with Molly's cuffs.

Only with difficulty, and by offering threats of mute non-cooperation, did he cause Bookrajian to hold back the army of occupation, keeping them in a cluster in the living quarters. "See, of the three people detained against their will, only one of them should be at large, and she would prefer, not being of a type who courts the public eye, that I carry in those bolt cutters by myself, and that we give her a chance to become decent. Otherwise you are going to be asking questions for a long time to one very silent man."

Bookrajian sent the fire team and bomb squad outside to get set up and detained the others, allowing Fred three minutes to cut the chains on Molly's cuffs. The cops would get the bracelets off her wrists and ankles later. Cover-Hoover snarled as Fred wrapped Molly in the pink blanket he had found, which, when he opened it, turned out to have a Mickey Mouse head emblazoned in the center.

Molly, her teeth chattering, said, "Thanks for not bringing in the cavalry. I'm not at my best until I wash. Cover-Hoover wants to know if we want a present of fifty thousand dollars. All we'd have to do is go to the Cayman Islands to pick it up."

"Got an account there, have we?" Fred asked Cover-Hoover.

"I told her we have too much money as it is," Molly said.

Cover-Hoover said, "It will be the word of lunatics against mine. My offer was made simply to preserve my work from distraction. I can assure you . . ."

Fred took Molly to the bathroom and left her to it, watching hot water start its rush into the big tub and telling her, "I'll find you something more than that blanket to wear."

Bookrajian, in the living quarters, kept his team at bay and told Fred, "Listen, sport. I figure we got two minutes before the *Chronicle* gets here; three for the *Globe*; maybe seven for the *Herald* and WBZ. You want to give me a clue here what the story is on all these victims?"

"If you'll keep the other two ladies in protective custody, Bookrajian, and bear with me while we waltz together down the fine line between victims and murdering assholes."

"I said we got two minutes. Call me Ernie. It'll save time. Meanwhile I'll be thinking about what kind of custody to put *you* in."

At almost midnight the party had adjourned to headquarters at Central Square. Sandy Clarke, in an incoherent threshold phase between personalities, was on her way, restrained, to make a close encounter of the third kind with the shrink at Cambridge City Hospital. Cover-Hoover was talking to some people elsewhere in the building.

Bookrajian had brought Fred to headquarters in his own car, leaving Fred's on Richdale Avenue to start collecting nonresident tickets. "You're an interesting guy," Bookrajian had insisted, "that I want to keep next to for a little while."

Fred and Bookrajian had picked up Boardman Templeton and

shipped him, strapped to a stretcher and under police escort, to Mount Auburn Hospital. "We like to throw a little of our business to everyone," Bookrajian confided, "so nobody gets jealous."

He'd learned enough from Molly, and from Fred, to call in warrants and seal off the place on Richdale Avenue, as well as Kwik-Frame, Cover-Hoover's office, and the apartment on Hay Street. At each place a team was now working.

"You are a busy guy," Bookrajian told Fred as they watched the medics bumping Manny's stretcher along the corridor outside Cover-Hoover's office. "Two naked chicks restrained, as well as this wicked-witch-of-the-East Doctor Cover-Hoover, who I will lock up permanently if I can; though it's hard persuading a judge to put away a beautiful professional woman who's a full professor and on the board of several big-deal places and the rest of it, and also publishes books. They think it's a vendetta or professional jealousy. Too bad she's not an ugly man. Besides, a doctor— they're gonna say her patients need her and let her out on her own recognizance. Then there's Mickey, who you say did the old man, and that lady antique dealer?"

"It's just a suggestion."

"You did that to his arms?"

"I was pressed for time," Fred said.

"I love it. Understatement. The Greeks have a name for that rhetorical device. They call it dehydrated bullshit. Who else you got on ice?"

"I'd appreciate it if you'd arrange for my friend Molly Riley to be released so she can go back to her children."

Molly, walking stiffly, and wearing a collection of drab and outlandish clothing brought to the safe house for her by one of the female cops—Bookrajian would allow nothing to leave the premises, since everything in the place might become evidence— was driven to Arlington in a cruiser.

After Molly had been sent home, Fred suggested, "You want to talk to the other sister?" They were sitting in Bookrajian's office, smoking cigars like old poker-playing buddies.

"I hoped you were going to ask me that. Meanwhile, you mind letting me have the keys to your car? Save us breaking in with a warrant. Save us even getting a warrant. I am a thorough guy and I like to make sure nothing gets away from the scene of a crime by accident."

Fred tossed him the keys. "Be my guest. You'll find a recording device, maybe under the seats. I took it off Cover-Hoover. Be careful with the picture in the back, though, would you? It's kind of fragile."

Bookrajian handed Fred's keys to a waiting gofer. "Tell the guys to give special attention to the picture in the back. You want to tell me anything about the picture in the back?"

"I'm thinking the animals are snakes or snails. Maybe your people will know. You want me to telephone the place where the sister is, tell 'em we're on our way?"

"I like a surprise. You are gonna stay away from telephones, and you are going to ride with me, sport."

36

Jackie Banner, a huge black-bearded man in rags, was doing the honors at the desk in the Chestnut Street vestibule. He looked up in a question when Fred appeared with the two uniformed Cambridge cops, an escort from the Boston force, and Bookrajian in plainclothes, who had just been remarking to Fred, "This is supposed to be my honeymoon."

"Teddy says wake him when you come in," Jackie Banner growled. "You need help entertaining these people, Fred?"

"They're friends. Thanks."

Bookrajian noticed how Jackie Banner's hands rested quietly on the desktop. "He knows what he's doing," Fred assured Bookrajian. "It's in the top drawer of the desk, and yes, there's a permit for it." The others were looking back and forth, wondering what this was about.

"I'll rouse Teddy," Banner said, and shoved his chair back. He climbed the stairs leading up from the vestibule. Bookrajian stood tense, his eyes alight. "Interesting place," he said.

Teddy came down with the key to the back room. Fred made introductions. Bookrajian and his people stared at Teddy, who slept in red long johns and had not bothered to alter his costume for the interview. "The lady won't stop calling me Mr. Pix," he said. "I got so tired listening to her confessing everything she ever heard of, I locked her in the back room. The foreign guy, the Hungarian, with the busted hands is with her. She feeds him. You didn't tell me what to do with him."

"Marek Hricsó," Fred told Bookrajian. The vestibule was so full of people it was hard to concentrate. "You recall the piano player? The nephew?"

"Yeah. Who is not a friend of yours. Before we meet the sister, just for the hell of it, soldier, what has she been confessing?"

Teddy told him. "Devil worship, and dropping her father off a bridge, and in a past life she is Nicholae Ceauşescu, and someone is stealing a painting from her, and she's been framed, and what time is the train for Concord, and she yells for more gin, and don't believe anything her sister tells you, she got most of the stuff, she should be set up for life, and the devil is after her again—this lady has one shitload of shit on her mind."

Fred spread his hands, remarking, "The denouement coming down off this thing is going to take some time." He sat on the desk while Bookrajian and a mixed pair of officers followed Teddy to the back room. In a few minutes Bookrajian came back and told Fred, "You are excused. Pick up your car on Green Street. The stuff in it we keep. They'll give you a receipt. I want to see you tomorrow; no, later this morning. Call at ten. Can you do that? So I don't have to find a place for you to stay?" He rubbed his hands in the gesture that says, Come on, buddy. Give me an excuse. Just try me.

"I wouldn't mind seeing how my friend is making out," Fred said.

Fred drove to Arlington entertaining dread and misgivings. He had never seen Molly so threatened and had no idea how the aftermath would read in her. It was after three when he brought his car into her street. A darkly unobtrusive sedan sat at the far end of Molly's block. It stood out because of Arlington's no-overnight-parking regulation. Bookrajian was a cautious man. Fred flashed his lights in greeting to the watcher as he turned into Molly's driveway.

Molly met him at the kitchen door. She smelled not of gasoline, but of hamburgers and onions, shampoo and soap. She was wearing the red terry-cloth robe. She was excited.

"Come look!" she said.

"You got back all right."

"I got home, and I got *it* home also. I couldn't help it getting rumpled, and I thought they were going to frisk me—but I'm here and it's here. Come look." Molly dragged him into the kitchen, where she had her library's *World of Copley* lying open next to the last two fragments, one on top of the other, of the painting—still, Fred thought, slightly fragrant of gasoline, whose scent would always, from now on, make him think, with a twinge of anxious tenderness, of Molly's skin, against which they had been smuggled out of the building on Richdale Avenue.

"It's the same head in *Watson and the Shark*," Molly insisted. "It's just he's younger in yours. You got my note?"

"It's you I want to look at. Honey, I didn't . . ."

"Never mind. I'm going to shake and cry and bitch at you a lot, but first look at this, and then we should make love because we are alive. No. Not yet. First look at *Watson and the Shark* with me. It's the first thing I did after I hugged the kids and cried. I thought I recognized that face. I've seen it a hundred times at the MFA."

The reproduction of Copley's heroic-rescue painting lay next to the painted head. A naked swimmer, blond and male and young, splashed in Havana harbor in imminent danger of death at the jaws of a sea beast fifteen times his size curled around the lower right corner of the painting: one of three versions Copley

254

had done, spurred by the commission from Brooke Watson, the one-legged victim-hero of the encounter.

Molly pointed to the apex of a group of sailors racing their longboat through green braided water to Watson's rescue—some reaching to gather him aboard; some at the oars; one threatening the aquatic monster with a gaff. The figure standing tallest among the sailors, Fred could accept in theory—older by a dozen years, and worn with care and voyaging—could be the father, or older brother, or cousin of—or even Mr. Pix himself.

"The boy in trouble's Brooke Watson," Molly announced. "You're going to think I'm being dramatic when I say that the gesture on the part of the African sailor—he's not helping. It's a gesture almost of mortal ambivalence, as if he's saying to himself, 'If I save that man's life, how will he punish me later?'

"Brooke Watson, minus one leg, grew up to be a great success in England after the Revolution: a big merchant, Lord Mayor of London, and a member of Parliament; where, incidentally, he campaigned to preserve the institution of slavery in what remained of the British colonies."

"Could be," Fred said. "We'll check and see if that sailor has been identified. Meanwhile, the other plan you had . . ."

"I retain my red robe, symbol of my new virginity, until you explain this Mr. Pixie business." Molly pointed at the signature, in black letters, not far from the left cheek of the portrait's subject. "There's no way I can read anything other than I. S. C. Pix."

"You got a half-hour to spare, or do you want the miniversion?"

"The kids are going to wake up. Give me the mini."

"Speaking of the kids—Molly, what you said, about appointing me their guardian, I'm . . ."

"It was a moment of mental aberration on my part. Don't mention it, all right?"

"It's just, I'm touched. . . ."

"Pix," Molly said firmly. "That is all I care about."

"By 1765 Copley's excited, thinks he's going to be a real artist.

He gets the Latin bug. He often signs himself with his initials in monogram, J.S.C. But sometimes, since the Latin has no *J*, he goes with *I* for the first initial. Then the Latin *pinxit* means "painted," which he occasionally shortened to *Pix*. I. S. C. Pix means John Singleton Copley painted this. That's the short version. That's all."

"Unexciting but essential. If I don't make love with you now, I'm going into post-traumatic stress disorder syndrome in a big way," Molly said, "and maybe try the multiple personality route instead. We'll do it therapeutically, like role-playing—one of the techniques they use to dredge up hidden, secret, repressed whathaveyous. You be Watson, and I'll be the shark. To quote another famous American dead person, 'Watson, come here; I want you.' "

The morning brought heavy rain that seemed to rise out of the ground. Fred heard it as the background to Molly's scolding at the kids. He'd slept an hour but suspected she hadn't closed her eyes.

"But it's his birthday," Terry's voice wailed from across the hall. "What do you mean let him sleep? He'll miss it!"

Molly's voice mumbled something incoherent. The bedroom door opened and Fred cracked one eye to see Sam standing in the doorway. "I didn't know if you are awake," Sam said.

"Be down in two minutes. You got the time?"

"Seven. Make it five minutes, OK?"

Fred pushed himself through the new shower. It fell at the same rate of inches-per-hour as the rain on the bathroom window; but it was warm. Fred, under the sting of it, counted the players who were, at least for the moment, out of action: Manny, Ann Clarke, Sandy Blake, Eunice Cover-Hoover—the rat's nest of guilts and responsibilities for two deaths and how much else— that was someone else's problem. Martin Clarke was dead: an old man who may or may not have been some kind of grievous son of a bitch also. Oona Imry was dead. As he'd learned from Ann

Clarke, Oona had given Sandy Clarke a ride back to the safe house after Sandy sold her the second fragment and some silver, whereupon the antique dealer had to be eliminated by Sandy's mouse-infested protective-hero former-victim lover, Boardman Templeton. And Marek had been unkindly plucked from one profession and dropped into another, at which he would be either excellent or a fast failure. You can't be a sort-of-good dealer in antiques for long.

Who else? Molly was fine. Fred was unscathed. Clayton was at the Ritz. And the painting was almost complete. He'd drive the last parts to New Bedford first thing, before Bookrajian started getting cute with search warrants. As far as making it right with the owner or owners of the fragments—the one Marek had given Fred, and the last two smuggled out by Molly—Fred and Clay would worry about that later. The first thing was to get the painting back together. Something was owed to Copley, and to the memory of Martin Clarke.

Fred clothed himself and went down to the kitchen, which was inhabited by three persons surrounding warmed-up platters of egg foo young and thrice-cooked shrimp. "You remembered my birthday!" Fred exclaimed.

"We have a present for you," Molly said, after they all sat around the table and Fred had served everyone. Terry pulled the package from under the table. The hands of the kitchen clock reached seven-eleven. Fred tasted his egg foo young. "How on earth did you manage this?"

Sam turned crimson with pride. "We made Ophelia buy it for us last night, and Terry and I kept it all night under our beds. We remembered. Chinese for your birthday."

"It's delicious. Perfect. Is the package for me? A present?"

"Open the goddamned package," Molly said. "You don't know how hard three people worked to get it here."

Fred tore paper. "It's a glove! It's a beauty!"

"Let's try it!" said Terry.

Fred ate a shrimp and looked at his companions. Terry and

Sam were dressed and fed and fit. They had their gloves. Sam had a baseball ready. The rain poured down.

"Honey, it's raining," Molly protested toward them all.

"Jesus, Mom," Sam said, heading for the door, followed by Fred and Terry. "What do you want, snow?"